The Knight, The Wizard & The Lady Pig

BY PATRICIA LADD

First printing, July 2004

Copyright © Patricia Ladd, 2004
All rights reserved

ISBN 0-9663335-1-9

Pulished by Snow in Sarasota Publishing, Inc.
Printed in the United States of America
by Serbin Printing, Inc. – Sarasota, Florida

For Mr. Mike
The Master Storyteller

And also

For Jessica and Michelle
Truly admirable cohorts

About the Author

Patricia Ladd is a pathological liar and a dangerous megalomaniac who shouldn't be allowed to attend the IB programme at St. Petersburg High as it only seems to be adding to her intense paranoia.  Being only seventeen has never stopped her from acting like someone's eclectic, tea-guzzling granny and when she isn't locked in her room fighting with her imaginary friends and writing era-spanning epics of astounding historical accuracy, she can almost certainly be found amassing the largest personal library known to Floridian suburbia and presiding over Monty Python Club meetings with an iron fist.

Address questions, comments, and snide remarks to: ralph87@tampabay.rr.com or www.snowinsarasota.com

About the Illustrator

Natalie Gallagher will one day sue Patricia Ladd for convincing her that a few postcards are sufficient payment for her illustrations. She currently lives a few feet south of the Arctic Circle, subsisting entirely on cheese and caribou. The harsh demands of her primitive hunter-gatherer society are undoubtedly why she had to let the magnanimous Patricia Ladd write this bio, forcing the author to rely on her long-standing stereotypes about what life is really like in Wisconsin.

Misadventures

Misadventures in the Classified Ads

E theos grumbled something inaudible to himself, but ate the muffin anyway. It wasn't too terribly bad, truth be told, but it was the principle of the thing. Still, Sir Humphrey didn't seem to have a problem with it and Lady Orville would eat anything, so Etheos kept his comments to himself.

Yet sometimes he thought it just wasn't right for a knight to cook. Especially not blackberry pies.

But that was Sir Humphrey's specialty, and he actually did it quite well. And so it was that Etheos the Wizard sat in the kitchen eating muffins, watching the great big knight wander around in oven mitts.

"Don't we have any more nutmeg?" Sir Humphrey demanded exasperatedly.

Etheos shrugged. "I have some ground beetles if you want them."

"No," Sir Humphrey said with a sigh. "That just won't do. I need nutmeg."

"Suit yourself," Etheos replied, reaching for the paper. "It's really for wart potions anyway."

Sir Humphrey continued to bustle about, quite the sight being that he was six foot six and could lift an ox above his head, and Etheos began to read *The Frog Prince Post* unperturbed.

"Oh look, the Mayor's been kidnapped by trolls again," Etheos said blandly a moment later.

"Serves him right too," Sir Humphrey grumbled from where he was searching the pantry to no avail. "I heard that he has an uncle whose best friend's cousin's son is in league with the Black Guild."

"Just a rumor," Etheos yawned. "The Black Magic Guild has been banished for years."

"Yes, but—"

"Don't you think *I* would know about it, Humphrey?" Etheos demanded, glancing at the knight over the top of his paper.

"Well—yes, I suppose," Sir Humphrey conceded. "But you're just an apprentice wizard at the Academy—"

"Thaumaturge," Etheos corrected. "And a senior one at that. But we know what's going on at the Academy, probably more so than you do over at Galahad's Hall."

Sir Humphrey mumbled something to himself but then cried out, "Aha! Nutmeg!" and went about cooking his pie again.

Etheos shook his head and went back to the paper. Sir Humphrey really wasn't a bad sort for a knight, but you couldn't expect him to understand the delicacies and formalities of the Merlyn Academy. Still, Etheos liked him despite what some of his colleagues at the Academy thought. True, the knight was huge, rather dense at times, and a little too handy with his axe when angered, which wasn't very often anyway, but he was a true friend, a good roommate, and could make the best blackberry pie in the whole city. His insistence upon housing the Lady Orville in their modest flat, however, was another matter, and one that the two had never agreed upon.

And it was the Lady Orville who came trotting into the kitchen at that moment.

There were many stories about the Lady Orville circulating in different parts of the city. The Alchemists of the North Side all firmly believed that she had been involved in an unfortunate potions accident, the Bards of King Fiddle's square were all assured that she had been cursed at birth by a wicked stepmother, and there was even a rumor going around amongst the goblins in the sewers that she was an exotic princess in hiding. The Wizard's of Merlyn Academy, at which Etheos had been a student for some years, publicly denounced the court magician, who they blamed responsible, even publishing an article in *The Frog Prince Post* naming him a hedge wizard and no more, and refused to have anything more to do with her. So it had been left to the Knights of Galahad's Hall to look after poor Lady Orville. And the responsibility of doing so had fallen to Sir Humphrey.

The case went like this: the Lady Orville, a distant relation of the King, had turned into a pig. No one knew quite why or quite how. Of course the Black Magic Guild had been blamed and the Knights had spent a month turning the city upside down looking for a black magic plot, but when none could be found, the people lost interest and Lady Orville was left a pig. One of the Knights, who had just earned his shield, had tentatively suggested that someone go on a quest to turn her back, but the others had laughed at him and told him to go ahead if he really wanted to, for *they* would certainly have nothing to do with it. The fact was, Lady Orville made a much better pig than she did a lady. She had always possessed rather disturbing table manners and her looks were nothing to write home about. The fact that none of the Knights felt overly inclined to rescue her from her current state was understandable, since custom dictated that he who did must marry her. And so the Lady Orville stayed a pig. And she didn't seem to mind in the least.

She trotted good-naturedly into the kitchen on the morning in question, having grown rather plump in the year or so during which she had fed on Sir Humphrey's cooking, and snorted derisively at the wizard who was, he admitted later, in her chair.

Etheos blinked down at her.

Lady Orville snorted again.

"No," Etheos said, going back to his paper.

"Etheos, just get out of her chair!" Sir Humphrey said.

"No," Etheos said. "A *wizard* does not move for a pig."

"Well, you're only an apprentice wizard and she's not a real pig," Sir Humphrey said. "She's a lady of court; show some respect."

"Thaumaturge," Etheos corrected sullenly as he moved to a different seat.

The pig happily climbed into her chair and snorted impatiently to Sir Humphrey.

"Yes, my lady," Sir Humphrey replied, putting the pie in the oven. "It should only be forty minutes."

Etheos grumbled something and reached for another muffin.

Lady Orville glared at him.

"Etheos—" Sir Humphrey started to admonish him, but was never given the chance for Etheos leapt to his feet, eyes wide, staring at the section of *The Frog Prince Post* he had in front of him.

"By Mercury!" he swore. "It can't be!"

"What?" Sir Humphrey asked, startled.

"It's right here!" Etheos continued. "In the Classified Ads. But—how—why—they're just too rare!"

Sir Humphrey snatched the paper from Etheos and scanned it quickly. It contained the usual ads. *Experienced, Well-known Necromancer seeks Beautiful, Young Virgin for Sacrifice* and *Enchanted Looking Glass for Sale–Talks, has an attitude* and at first glance the big red-bearded knight saw nothing out of the ordinary. "What?" he asked Etheos again.

Etheos pointed excitedly to the tiny notice just below the ad for Genuine Black Cats. It simply said *Dragon for Sale. 113 Warlock's Way.*

"A dragon!" Etheos cried excitedly. "A real dragon! Not even the Academy menagerie has had one to study in—in hundreds of years! We thought they were all in hiding up in the mountains but—a dragon!"

Sir Humphrey raised a skeptical bushy eyebrow. "How could someone in the city keep a dragon?" he asked. "I think it's a joke."

Etheos waved away the objection. "Warlock's Way. Only the most experienced, retired wizards live there. He must be very powerful and wise indeed to keep a dragon." Etheos clapped his hands excitedly. "I must go see—right now. Otherwise someone else will get there first." And with that, he rushed off to fetch his cloak.

"But Etheos!" Sir Humphrey protested. "I just put the pie in and—"

"Well, you don't have to come," Etheos said, struggling with the clasp hurriedly. "Besides, you have duty at Galahad's Hall this morning."

"And *you* are going to get into trouble," Sir Humphrey added.

"Trouble?" Etheos demanded. "Why would I—I'm a senior thaumaturge at the Merlyn Academy! What sort of *trouble* do you suggest I can't handle by myself?"

Sir Humphrey, grinning under his beard, reached over and clasped Etheos' cloak for him. "Nothing specific, my lord thaumaturge," he said with mock respect. "You just never know what you're going to encounter in the city. T'would be helpful to have a knight with you, don't you think?"

Etheos scowled at him. "Fine. You can come. But let *me* do the talking. We're dealing with a refined, experienced enchanter. It would *not* be in our best interest for you to lop off his head."

"Agreed," Sir Humphrey said with a nod. "I'll just get Lady Orville's sunbonnet."

"No!" Etheos cried. "The pig is *not* coming!"

"You can't expect me to leave royalty in the house all by herself!" Sir Humphrey argued.

The pig snorted contemptuously at Etheos.

"But—but—fine!" Etheos grumbled. "But hurry up!"

Perhaps they looked a bit odd, the three of them walking down the street together, but not so odd as other things one might see in the big capital city. Still, strangers might give them a second glance and wonder about the oddity until some pleasant resident of the neighborhood explained who they were.

The big knight had a light mail shirt and long red beard with a pair of oven mitts stuffed into his belt near his dagger, a hefty battleaxe in his left hand. Etheos, though not a small man, walked along in his big friend's shadow, his black cloak and blue wizard's robes snapping behind him in the breeze. His face was not unpleasant, the only blemish being the two marks on his nose from where he was accustomed to wearing spectacles whenever he was studying the musty old tomes and spell books in the Academy's great library. But his appearance was often a disappointment to Etheos. His oak brown hair was depressingly ordinary, and, despite his efforts, he'd never been able to grow a beard. Hardly fitting for a wizard. Still, his green eyes were mysterious enough, and the hedge witch in the flat below his swore that she had seen them flash with untold power on occasion.

And then there was the plump little pig, Lady Orville, trotting along contentedly beside them, a ruffled sunbonnet tied under her chin. The first week or so that the good Lady had lived with them

Sir Humphrey had insisted that the street vendors and neighbors they passed bow to her to show their respect for the lady. But now things were different and the costermonger sometimes went so far as to throw her an extra apple core or fish head—any tidbit would do for a pig—that she gobbled up appreciatively.

Etheos was in a particularly grumpy mood this morning; he didn't like being accompanied by the boisterous knight, and especially not the pig, on this particular outing. So he stalked along the street with a deep scowl on his face. It frightened the little maid selling golden goose eggs so much that she nearly dropped her entire basket of goods from fright. When her mother admonished her, she exclaimed, "But mother! It's the wizard! He's angry!" and her mother took a deep breath and soon the rumor had spread down the street ahead of Etheos and Sir Humphrey. The wizard was angry.

It was understandable. Even though Etheos was just a thaumaturge, an apprentice wizard, though a senior one, he was probably the most powerful one the neighborhood had ever seen. Most student wizards chose to room on the Merlyn Academy campus or near it. Very few, if any, chose the somewhat modest community of Ghost Corner or, as some of the urchins had taken to calling it, Rat's Square. In fact, it was neither a corner nor a square, but a rather octagonal shaped collection of winding streets filled with miscreants and low lives as well as a few would-be noblemen down on their luck. There were quite a few rats out at all times of the day, scuttling along in the gutters and sewers with the goblins, eating whatever they could get. Some of them were reputed to be enchanted, but those tales were only believed by children and one or two rather crazed government officials. Whatever its faults, though, Ghost Corners offered cheap housing rates, which the budding wizard intended to take full advantage of until he was famous enough to build his own tower. And so his reputation, partly true and partly due to his habit of self-congratulation, as the grand enchanter of Rat's Square had spread.

Gradually the leaning, ramshackle apartments were replaced by solid stone townhouses and the streets widened into grand boulevards filled, not with lowly street venders, pickpockets, and, those

ever-contemptible drudges, gnomes, but with brightly dressed mer-
chants going about their business next to wealthy citizens, aldermen
and burghers. Fine ladies could be seen inside carriage windows
pulled by unicorns, and even the goblins that occasionally peered
out from the sewers seemed more respectable than the ones in Ghost
Corners, some even politely doffing their floppy hats to passersby.

Sir Humphrey met a few fellow knights in the streets as well, but
not as many as would be supposed. Those who were conscientious
would already have been at the Hall, and those who were not were
undoubtedly still abed, sleeping off a night on the town.

And before they knew it, they were standing on the biggest and
grandest boulevard of them all—Warlock's Way. It was a very
respected community. Not noblemen, they preferred to build houses closer to the palace. No, here were the notable, occasionally
eccentric, and always wise retired wizards. Many were professors at
the Academy; many had been to foreign lands and seen giants and
gryphons. Even Etheos began to walk a little more carefully in the
presence of such greatness.

Of course, there wasn't much by way of greatness on the streets
that morning. All was silent on Warlock's Way.

Etheos tried to peer into some of the walled gardens to no avail.
"Where's number one hundred and thirteen?"

"Over there," Sir Humphrey said, trying to hide his grin. "There's
your grand, respectable enchanter's house."

Lady Orville snorted.

Etheos stared. "There's a mistake," he finally said. "That can't be
it."

It looked like a common cottage, to be found in the middle of
the country, perhaps next to a modest farm, not next to the grandest and most elite wizards' mansions in the world. The shutters were
falling off the darkened windows and weeds were growing in between
the cracks of the front steps, which were falling apart. The chimney
had apparently done so long ago, as a great pile of bricks stood to
mark its resting place beside the house. A breeze could have knocked
the whole thing over. There was a skeletal, dead tree in the front
yard in which was perched a murder of crows.

"That's number one hundred and thirteen," Sir Humphrey clarified. "See? Look."

Perhaps the only substantial looking things on the house were the three brass numbers: 113.

Etheos groaned. "Let's go. There's no dragon."

Lady Orville snorted again.

"Exactly," Sir Humphrey agreed with her. "We didn't come all this way just to look at your grand enchanter's house, did we? Perhaps there is a dragon. Appearances can be deceiving, you know. Just look at Lady Orville!" And with that he pulled his friend up the walk and to the front porch before the wizard could even protest that Lady Orville had been a pig all her life, now she was simply looking it, and knocked on the door.

There came an inhuman screech from inside.

"You see?" Sir Humphrey said triumphantly. "That could've been the dragon."

"But it sounded like a—"

The door creaked open.

Even Sir Humphrey took an involuntary step back. Etheos' face was a picture of horror. Lady Orville snorted.

The woman on the other side of the door was old and bent. She was wrapped in numerous shawls and her black eyes had a very wild look to them. Her gray hair was stringy and she was missing most of her teeth. There was a black cat perched atop her shoulders. There were three more black cats at her feet. Each was giving the strangers a cold, hard glare.

"What do you want?" the old woman finally demanded. Her voice was high-pitched and unnatural.

Sir Humphrey gave Etheos a shove forward. "You wanted to do all the talking," he whispered.

"We—we—I think we've come to the wrong address," Etheos said. "So we'll just be—"

"If you're another one of those health inspectors from the palace you can take your condemned notice and shove it! I'm staying in my husband's house and that's final!"

The door slammed in his face.

Etheos and Sir Humphrey looked at each other.

Sir Humphrey burst out laughing.

Etheos glared at him. "I hate you. Come on, let's go back—"

"If you two are here about the dragon," a voice said from somewhere above them. "You'd best go around back."

Etheos stepped off the porch and looked around for whom had spoken. There was no one about.

"Did you hear—?" he started to ask Sir Humphrey.

"And quickly too," the voice said again.

Etheos looked up sharply into the branches of the dead tree. But there was no one there but the crows.

"Who said that?" Etheos demanded of them.

They stared at him, one of them cocking its head curiously. The one that cocked its head was strange. It was smaller than the others, and yet they all seemed to defer to him. Most remarkable was the silver streak that went from its head down to its tail feathers, staining all their tips the curious color.

Etheos frowned at it. "There's something off about that raven."

"Now don't—" Sir Humphrey started, but Etheos had already begun.

He threw his hand up dramatically—perhaps a little too dramatically—into the air and began to mutter, his voice growing steadily louder as he went. "*Zfeldu, E Ceoj Xyvz ek Lydfr! Zfeldu re Ieov Rvou Cevk! Y Zekkely Ieo! Eq Etheos Kequr Metuvkoj Ek Ejj Tywevyq!*" Etheos finished his towering crescendo and took a hasty step back, staring closely at the bird as if he expected it to turn into a six-headed water demon.

The raven just blinked at him.

Sir Humphrey burst out laughing again and Lady Orville snorted derisively.

Etheos wrapped his cloak tighter about him, scowling darkly. "Let's just go!" he said irritably. "We've wasted enough—"

"No!" Sir Humphrey said. "Come on! I really want to see this dragon now! Let's just take a peek 'round back."

And, without waiting for Etheos to say anything more, the big knight hopped off the porch and strolled past the rubble that had once been a chimney, leaping the wandering fence that attempted to enclose the back garden. Lady Orville, who followed along behind him, let out a tremendous squeal and began to dig into the ground, trying to get through as well.

Etheos rolled his eyes and followed the knight into the back garden, ignoring the laboring lady pig.

It looked to have once been a very nice place. The remains of a nice cobblestone walk could still be seen beneath the knee high grass and a crumbling fountain still stood in the center, though it was filled with snakes. There were vines growing from every gnarled tree and briars carpeting the ground. Two black cats were peering at them from the back window and one, a particularly large fellow, was perched on the roof, watching them closely.

Sir Humphrey whistled at the cat genially.

The cat hissed at him.

Sir Humphrey shrugged. "Odd," he said. "That cat has white eyes."

"What?" Etheos asked, trying to free his cloak from the brambles.

"It must be blind," Sir Humphrey said. "I don't see any dragon, do you?"

Etheos looked about at the twisted old garden. "No, Humphrey. There's no dragon. Which is what I—"

There came a loud roar, like the sound unwary victims hear just before a tidal wave swallows them whole. It came from the shed.

Like the house, the shed looked as if it was falling apart. It was painted an absurd color teal and, as the roar echoed about the garden, the heavy lock on its door clunked.

"How could a dragon possibly—" Sir Humphrey began.

Etheos' eyes were wide. "It must be a mighty spell indeed! One that can warp the restrictions of space entirely! A spell that can make a container's inside larger than its outside through the use of alternate dimensions! Brilliant!"

"Daft," Sir Humphrey added. "Well, let's go break the little bugger out of there. I bet he's cramped." He started forward, briars crunching beneath his boots, hefting his huge axe.

"No!" Etheos stopped him, grabbing his arm. "If you disrupt

the spell, it could blow us all to shreds! This must be done very carefully…”

Etheos frowned, staring at the shed.

“If it’s that difficult, perhaps you shouldn’t—” Sir Humphrey began.

Etheos had already raised his hand towards the shed and begun the spell. *“Ryku Ely Qmezu Fesu Le Kuelyld Kev Etheos rfu—”* A radish smacked Etheos on the side of the head.

He promptly fell to the ground with a cry, his hands flying into the air. There was a rippling effect in the air as his spell was released unfinished. There were no drastic consequences, however, besides Sir Humphrey’s beard turning purple for a moment and Etheos going out cold.

The thrower of the radish, the old woman who had answered the door, was standing at her open window aiming another at Sir Humphrey’s head.

“I told you before! I’m staying in my husband’s house and no King’s Eviction Notice is going to stop me!”

She threw the radish. It bounced harmlessly off Sir Humphrey. She screamed with rage and disappeared into the house, no doubt to get something bigger to throw, like a washbasin or a land mine.

Sir Humphrey, deciding it was prudent not to be caught trespassing in a psychotic old lady’s backyard, scooped up his unconscious friend and retreated back over the fence.

“Come, my lady,” he said to the pig who was still digging a hole. “We’ve got to get out of here.”

Lady Orville snorted irritably and followed along behind the burly knight, admonishing him with a series of grunts.

Sir Humphrey, the wizard thrown over his shoulder like a sack of potatoes, was going to run off down the street back to Ghost Corners without another thought to the dragon or the insane old woman, yet something stood in his path.

He blinked down at the strange raven sitting in the grass in his path. The raven looked up at him and then, of a sudden, took flight. It didn’t go very far, however, alighting on Sir Humphrey’s shoulder.

"By King Pellinore's Spectacles!" Sir Humphrey cried in surprise. "What—"

But then he saw the business card in the bird's beak.

He held out his hand curiously, and the bird promptly dropped the card into it, before flying away in the direction of Thieves' Den.

Sir Humphrey squinted at the card. Printed on it in a spidery black script was this:

Wyona Wyncliff E.P.
Adventurer, Smuggler, Spy, Magician, and Ballroom dancing
Champion
Over the Sign of the Crow, Thieves' Den

"Curious," Sir Humphrey said. "I wonder what that's supposed to mean."

He walked back down Warlock's Way, past the grand mansions with their carefully walled-in gardens. There were a few inhabitants about now. He passed an elderly chap in a conical hat walking an iguana. He gave the large knight—wandering down the sophisticated street with a man dressed in the robes of an apprentice thrown over his shoulder and a pig with a sunbonnet at his side—an odd look, but Sir Humphrey lumbered by without noticing.

When he came to the end of Warlock's Way, he stopped and considered his next course of action. True, he could go right, back to Ghost Corners. He could take Etheos home and mix up some honey and milk, for the wizard would surely have a headache when he awoke. He could go home to his pie, which was surely nearly burned by now.

Or…

He could turn left, wander through the twisted streets of the city until he came to Thieves' Den and find this Wyona Wyncliff and ask for help with this dragon. There was obviously a dragon in the shed, and, truth be told, he himself was curious about it. Whether or not Etheos still wanted to bother with it was a mystery, and probably would remain one until the wizard woke up. And so Sir Humphrey, who was always ready for adventure when it came to call, turned left, for better or worse, and set his feet in the direction of the most ill-reputed part of town and a most interesting adventure besides.

If Ghost Corners was where one looked to find squalor and poverty, Thieves' Den was where one went to be robbed and sometimes murdered in the streets. It was no secret that the entire network of thieves, pickpockets, and other criminals was based here. And it was here, somewhere, that their very leaders met to discuss matters of business. The Knights occasionally made raids into the shady houses or darkened alleys, only to find that one of the numerous spies and informants had already spread the warning and all illegal activity had been moved to some other hideaway. And since there was no shortage of disreputable hideaways in Thieves' Den, attempts at cleaning up the area were soon abandoned, almost before they had even begun. It was a haven of sorts, for any who thought they could survive there.

So it was an odd sight indeed for the inhabitants to see the big knight striding openly through their dank, gloomy streets. They knew him by sight, of course. Anyone who knew anything about the Knights would. Sir Humphrey was hard to miss with his thick red beard and legendary axe. Whilst many other knights, even most of his superiors, would have taken any other course of action before treading into Thieves' Den, and even then treading very softly, Sir Humphrey strode through purposefully, keeping an eye on his purse and the Lady Orville. Etheos was still slung over his shoulder.

He was watched through half-open shutters all the way down the twisted street, and about five young pickpockets took it upon themselves to follow him, seeing where he went in case it came in use later. Once Lady Orville tried to turn off into an alley that smelled a great deal like old cheese, but Sir Humphrey nudged her onward.

And then they came to the Sign of the Raven. It was a tavern, with grimy windows and a wooden sign on a creaky hinge bearing a crude picture of the black bird that gave it its name. Without pausing or hesitating in the least, Sir Humphrey pushed open the door and strode into the dimly lit room beyond.

There were few about in the rather seedy tavern this early in the day. The tavern keeper, who had been employed in mopping the floor, looked up and squinted at the strange sight, silhouetted against the light filtering through the door. The tavern keeper was a short, pudgy man with a bulbous red nose that quite resembled a plum.

"Can I 'elp yer, guv'ner?" he asked after a moment.

"I'm looking for a Wyona Wyncliff," Sir Humphrey answered gruffly.

"Upstairs," the tavern keeper replied, pointing to a set of stairs in the back. "May I ask yor business?"

"No," Sir Humphrey replied shortly, already making his way towards the stairs. He stomped his way up the narrow staircase, nearly dropping Etheos twice, and banging his head against the wall once, whilst the Lady Orville clambered up behind him as best she could. At the top of the stairs was a dark, narrow hallway lined with doors. Sir Humphrey stopped to consider, and then the slightly tarnished nameplate on the nearest door to the right caught his eye. *Wyona Wyncliff E.P.*

He knocked on the door and at the word "Enter" spoken in a light voice, he opened it and stepped inside.

It was a rather small office, but there was a fine carpet upon the floor and a large open window across the far wall. There were a few chairs scattered about, a full bookcase, and a rather large desk, at which sat a most curious young woman indeed. She stood as he entered, giving him the full effect of the strange way in which she was built. The thought crossed his mind that perhaps she wasn't human, but if she wasn't, then he couldn't quite say what she was.

She was unbelievably tall, and just as unbelievably slender. Although he was considered by most men to be a giant, this woman could look him straight in the eye, and he was positive her waist was only as big around as his arm. She had a long, somewhat ovular face, which was very pale indeed, with long straight black hair, which slightly-more-pointed-than-normal ears poked through. Her nose was aquiline and her eyes a lucid grey. But the strangeness did not cease there.

She stepped out from behind the desk, watching him; her gaze was unreadable. She moved with impossible elegance for one so tall and thin, gliding like a dancer almost. Her mode of dress was strange as well, he now saw. It reminded him of something, some picture perhaps, that he had seen before but he couldn't think of what.

"Please, sit down," she said quietly.

Sir Humphrey dropped Etheos in a chair.

The wizard snorted, tried to roll over, and fell off onto the floor. His eyes flew open and he leapt to his feet. "*Merlyn Mveruzr ku,*" he muttered the basic charm against evil as he looked about wildly. "Sir Humphrey! Where are we? What are we—" He blinked at Wyona Wyncliff, who was looking at him complacently. He had to look up at her, and it seemed to annoy him. "Who are you?" he demanded.

"I am Wyona Wyncliff," Wyona said quietly—Sir Humphrey got the impression that she always spoke in the same quiet tone—holding out her pale hand with its long tapered fingers for him to shake.

He stared at it, suspiciously. "Sir Humphrey, what are we doing here?" he demanded.

"Well, I was—Here." He handed Etheos the business card the bird had dropped into his hands.

Etheos read it, looked up at Wyona Wyncliff, and then read it again.

"I thought mayhap she could help us with the dragon," Sir Humphrey explained.

"Dragon?" Wyona said, her brow furrowing. "In the city?"

"Never mind that," Etheos said irritably. "Explain yourself."

Wyona stared at him with those calm grey eyes. "You are standing in my office, Sir Thaumaturge."

"How did you know that I was—" Etheos was about to demand.

"The lining of your robes is silver," Wyona reminded him.

Etheos blinked down at them, as if to ascertain that they really were. "So you know some of the Academy's ways?"

Wyona inclined her head politely.

Etheos, still frowning, took a seat. Sir Humphrey shrugged and did as well, Lady Orville lounging at his feet.

"You are dressed as one of the Sky Riders from the North," Etheos observed after a moment. "But you cannot be one of them."

Sir Humphrey remembered now. The Sky Riders, of course. The daring people who rode across the glaciers and great ice plains atop winged lizard-birds. Some believed these creatures were related to the dragons, but they were, in fact, much smaller and feathered. Stories, mostly purely romantic concoctions bearing no real relevance to fact, had drifted back to the city about these daring aerial acrobats. And their costume was the one thing the stories and illustrations got right.

Wyona wore soft leather boots, black trousers, and a loose white shirt. Over this was the signature tunic of the sky riders. Though in the pictures they were always brightly colored and decorated with jewels and medals, Wyona's was a serviceable black, made from a durable, warm material. It was sleeveless with a folded down collar stretching nearly to her slim shoulders and had small black buttons down the front to her waist. There were large slits in the front and back to make riding astride anything—a horse or a giant winged creature—simple and slits down both the sides as well so that a rider could reach a sword or dagger hanging from their belts. It was practical, form-fitting, and rarely seen at all in the city. The riders stayed up in the North.

"No," Wyona agreed. "I am not. But I have lived among them for a time."

"Indeed?" Etheos asked skeptically. "And what do you do now?"

Wyona spread her hands. "What I can."

"What's that supposed to mean?" Etheos demanded with narrowed eyes.

"You, Sir Thaumaturge," she said, sitting down with a slight smile. "Are altogether too suspicious. It's a wonder you have any friends at all." She smiled warmly at Sir Humphrey. The big knight smiled back. Though she was indeed quite odd looking, she was still rather pretty in an alien way, and Etheos didn't fluster her. Etheos glared at his companion.

When neither of them said anything for a moment, Wyona continued. "You say there is a dragon in the city?"

"No!" Etheos said quickly.

"We think so," Sir Humphrey said at the same time.

"We don't need *her* help," Etheos hissed at him. "I can go to the Academy and inform the Masters about that psychotic old woman with all her cats and they'll send in people *qualified* for the job to take care of it. Not some dressed-up highwayman."

Wyona smiled wider. "I assure you, Sir Thaumaturge, that I am not a highwayman, though I have been many other things in the past. And if you think the Masters of your Academy are going to do anything about Nimue and her cats—dragon or no dragon—then you are vastly mistaken."

Etheos blinked. "Who?"

"The psychotic old woman you mentioned. Her name is Nimue."

Etheos stared at her. "But that's the wife of Merlyn!"

"And that's why they won't do anything about her. Her husband did far too much. They promised that she could live in his old house on Warlock's Way if she wanted—even through the hidden treasure controversy—except no one knew she was going to live so long—or have so many cats."

"But Merlyn lived hundreds upon hundreds of years ago!" Etheos scoffed.

"Yes," Wyona agreed. "For hundreds and hundreds of years."

"How *do* you know all this?" Etheos demanded.

"I've been about," Wyona said. "If you'd like to see my full resumé—"

"That won't be necessary," Etheos said, standing. "Because we're leaving. Come on, Humphrey."

Wyona stood as well. "Since you don't care about the dragon, I don't suppose you'd care to hear about the secret way into her back shed then either?"

Etheos stopped in the doorway.

Wyona smiled.

"Alright," Etheos said resignedly, turning around. "Maybe you should tell us what you know."

Before Wyona could say anything further, there was a loud caw and a big, black crow swooped in through the window, landing on Wyona's hastily outstretched hand. The bird cawed a few more times and Wyona's serene face deepened into a frown.

The bird took flight and flew from the window once more.

"There is little time," Wyona said. "We must leave now before

St—before it's too late."

"Where are we going?" Sir Humphrey asked, as they followed Wyona's slim form into the hall.

"To find your dragon," she replied. "Before someone else does."

They followed her down the steep, narrow staircase, out of the tavern and into the street. Wyona's gait was quick due to her long legs, and Sir Humphrey was forced to carry Lady Orville while Etheos struggled to keep up. The usual shady inhabitants of Thieves' Den all made way for the tall woman in Sky Riders' garb, receding into dark alleys or doorways. Wyona paid them no heed in the least.

"You must understand that this is not the first complaint about the Lady Nimue," Wyona explained to them as they went.

"I wouldn't suppose so," Etheos panted. "The woman is psychotic!"

Wyona nodded. "But in the past there have been…" she hesitated. "Controversies against Nimue for other reasons entirely."

"Which were?" Etheos demanded.

Wyona hesitated again. "Rumor has it that her husband amassed a great fortune."

"Well, why shouldn't he? He was the greatest enchanter that ever lived!" Etheos said defensively.

"Indeed," Wyona agreed. "But he was said to have placed a spell over this fortune so that no one could find it, not even his wife. They say the marriage wasn't exactly a happy one."

"Well, look at her!" Etheos said.

"Wouldn't that make her a bit upset?" Sir Humphrey asked. "Being denied her husband's fortune and that sort of thing?"

"Yes," Wyona nodded. "Some people think that's why she's…"

"Psychotic," Etheos supplied. "What's the use of having a huge fortune lying about under a spell? The least he could've done was leave it to the Academy!"

Wyona smiled. "That's what the Academy thinks too. They've been waiting raptly for some time for Nimue to die so they can get inside that house and see about it." Her smile widened. "Not that it'll do them any good."

"Why not?" Etheos demanded. "The Masters of the Academy–"

"Don't know the specifications of the spell," Wyona interrupted.

"But you do I suppose?" Etheos said, rolling his eyes.

"It was easy enough to bribe the little hedge wizard who walked into the bar one day. He used to be the cook, you see. The spell stated that the vast fortune would only appear when someone worthy of heart, worthy of power, and worthy of cause appeared to claim it and put it to use."

"I don't think drunkards are a very reliable source," Etheos sniffed.

"You'd be surprised," Wyona said. "But then the entire thing is only a rumor—an urban legend, if you will. I don't hold much truth in it."

"Why not?" Sir Humphrey asked. "It sounds delightful to me."

"Of course it does," Wyona agreed. "But it's entirely too noble and fairy tale-esque to be the truth."

"You're just as cynical as Etheos!" Sir Humphrey laughed.

"What does this have to do with our dragon?" Etheos asked irritably, not taking kindly to being compared to the mysterious woman he didn't trust.

"Because everyone is always bothering her, after this treasure, Nimue is very…"

"Psychotic," Etheos said again.

"About people poking around her house," Wyona continued. "So we have to take a little … shortcut." And suddenly she turned into an alley to their right. It smelled strangely of burnt cabbage, and the Lady Orville squealed irritably.

Wyona was standing over a covered manhole, studying it speculatively.

"Sir Humphrey would you mind—"

"Of course," Sir Humphrey said immediately. "Here, Etheos." He dropped the Lady Orville into the disgruntled wizard's hands, bent down, and picked up the manhole cover as if it were a down pillow. He threw it nonchalantly to the side where it landed with an ear-splitting clatter.

"No!" Etheos said suddenly, trying to fight the struggling Lady Orville. "I am *not* going down in the sewers with the goblins and—"

"Come now, Sir Thaumaturge," Wyona said with a faint smile.

"Surely someone as powerful and learned as you is not afraid of a mere goblin."

"Of course not!" Etheos said indignantly, letting Lady Orville drop to the ground rather than fight her struggling, whereupon she immediately began to root about in the rubbish heaps. "It's the principle of the thing! Why, if I'm to be elected to the Masters' Council someday, I can't have it known that I once crawled around in the sewers like a rat!"

"Well," Wyona said, exchanging a wry smile with Sir Humphrey. "I'm sure I won't tell anyone."

"And neither will I," Sir Humphrey volunteered. "And Lady Orville can't tell anyone anyway, so you see you've nothing to worry about Etheos."

"But—" Etheos started to protest again, staring with a bit of trepidation down the dark hole.

"Don't worry," Wyona said, taking a lantern from somewhere on her belt. "If you're frightened, I'll go first." And before he could protest that he wasn't frightened in the least, she leapt into the manhole as if she were jumping into a pool of water and disappeared into the darkness below. There was a squishy sort of echo a moment later and a tiny light appeared down in the darkness.

Etheos followed suit soon after, leaving Sir Humphrey to scoop up the protesting Lady Orville.

"I'm not frightened!" Etheos was busy saying hotly to Wyona when he arrived.

"Of course not," Wyona agreed, starting along the narrow ledge at the edge of the round tunnel.

Etheos followed behind her, disgruntled, and Sir Humphrey's lumbering form took up the rear.

It was rather eerie in the sewer and, despite his claims of protest, Etheos would have had good reason to be afraid. The tunnel they were currently walking through was higher than Sir Humphrey's head in the center, where a mysterious stream of water flowed in the darkness, but where they were, teetering on the precarious ledge spanning either side, both Sir Humphrey and Wyona had to duck their heads. Although they saw no goblins or rats as they went, the faint scuttling noise and a strange bubbling in the water said that something was about. How Wyona knew where they were going was anyone's guess, but she seemed strangely confident in her choice of path. Their footsteps echoed loudly off the tunnel walls and the lantern provided relatively little light. They traveled for what seemed like hours to Etheos, who was holding a handkerchief over his nose and muttering minor spells under his breath.

"Your wizard," Wyona finally remarked quietly to Sir Humphrey over Etheos' head. "Seems awfully grumpy."

Sir Humphrey shrugged. "He has an ego problem."

"I do not!" Etheos shouted indignantly. He shouted it so loud that it echoed down the long tunnel for some time directly followed by a deep rumbling that shook the sides of the large pipe they were walking through, nearly sending the four of them toppling into the stream of murky water.

"*What is that?*" Sir Humphrey yelled over the roar, trying to keep his footing and a close hold on Lady Orville at the same time.

Wyona's face was, if possible, even whiter than before. "I believe it is the Goblyns," she replied.

"Goblins?" Sir Humphrey asked. "But they're harm–."

"No," Wyona said. "Not goblins. *Goblyns.* They live deep in these tunnels, in the dark, and feed upon the goblins—although I don't suppose a nice bit of human meat would offend them either."

"A fight then?" Sir Humphrey asked, setting Lady Orville down carefully. "Step back then, lads—and lady—" he added hurriedly. "I've got this one covered."

Sir Humphrey stepped down from the ledge and into the murky stream of rushing water in the center of the tunnel that covered up a good part of his big boots. He drew his axe back and executed a few practice swings as the rumbling got louder and louder. Before Wyona had time to offer any warning—though whether she would have remains under scrutiny—the Goblyns were upon them.

Actually, there was only one, and at first Sir Humphrey had trouble believing that this was the cause of the roaring noise, the Goblyns of which Wyona had spoken. It looked like a common goblin child, with skin the color of faded leather and stringy hair, a snub of a nose and large, round eyes. It was sitting on a little piece of wood that drifted down the rushing stream straight towards Sir Humphrey, and it was gazing up at him with the most imploring look.

Most people didn't like goblins, as a rule, though there was really not much against them besides the fact that they lived in the sewers. They looked a little strange, and they spoke a strange hissing language to each other at times, but their lives so closely mirrored the lives of the City's citizens above that one sociologist at the Academy had once protested that they deserved the same rights. He was immediately silenced of course, but what he said had more truth than most people were willing to admit. The stereotypical goblin slunk out of the sewers at night to steal from the homes above. There were many goblins who did this, yes, in Thieves' Den and Ghost Corners perhaps, but in the nicer neighborhoods of town, the goblins were more respectable, wearing real street clothes and fluent in the language of humans. Some even held menial jobs as errand runners in the city, but that was a rarity.

Still, the Knights of Galahad's Hall had been taught to treat goblins almost as they would regular people when going about the course of their duties. That was why when Sir Humphrey saw the goblin child, he lowered his axe and stared at it, his first thoughts being that he'd better try to find its parents before taking it down to the Hall, filing the appropriate paperwork, and sending it off to an orphanage. It seemed like a knight's job was nothing but paperwork sometimes.

"Humphrey, what are you doing?" Etheos demanded. The Academy's views on goblins were not as humanitarian. "Why aren't you killing it?"

"It's just a child, Etheos," Sir Humphrey said as the piece of wood floated next to his leg. "How can you—"

And then the small, rather plump figure hissed, baring rows of small, sharp teeth and leapt onto Sir Humphrey. It sprang higher than anyone could have expected, gripping his chest with little claws and then clinging to him, like a rock climber to a mountainside, while snapping and clawing at his face.

Sir Humphrey cried out, dropped his axe, and tried to pry the small creature off of him, but it was too tightly lodged and he ended up losing his footing and falling into the water with a great splash. He continued to thrash about in the water, screaming bloody murder, trying to rip the Goblyn from his chest.

Etheos blinked down at the strange sight before him, Sir Humphrey, the largest knight in the city, thrashing about in the sewers trying to dislodge what looked like a goblin child before it ate his face. Wyona watched impassively, her face unreadable. Lady Orville looked up at both of them, snorted derisively, and then leapt off the ledge with a squeal of war.

She was atop Sir Humphrey herself in a moment, squealing madly and head-butting the Goblyn. It served to free the Goblyn, which rolled off Sir Humphrey into the water. It leapt to its feet a moment later with a hiss and jumped for the lady pig. Lady Orville squealed, this time in fear, and tried to run away, but the Goblyn could leap far and was soon attached to her back.

That's when Sir Humphrey climbed to his feet, kicked the Goblyn from the noble pig's back, and hacked at it with his axe before it could rise and leap once more. All was silent again, except for the rush of water and Lady Orville's quiet whimpers.

"Well," Sir Humphrey finally said. "That wasn't so bad, was it? I don't know why such a little fellow made so much noise in getting here."

"Oh, that wasn't him," Wyona said, peering up the passage once more. "And although your defense was very admirable, *they* might have something to say about it."

Sir Humphrey blinked.

A multitude of large round eyes blinked back at him.

The tunnel ahead of them was lined with eyes and teeth, all staring towards the four intruders. A great hiss rose up among them and, before anything more could be said, they all leapt forward at once. There must have been ten thousand of them.

Sir Humphrey bellowed an order to retreat and Wyona finally drew a slim saber from her belt, but there were too many of them, a great cloud of flesh-eating teeth and hungry eyes.

And then Etheos stepped into the center of the tunnel. He raised his hand out towards the oncoming beasts and cried out "*Qurem!*" with such passionate force that it shook the walls of the tunnel and all the creatures, wide-eyed, stopped in mid-air. "*Zyu, ceoj xuequrq!*"

There was a great flash of light, and with a resounding boom the beasts all disappeared, leaving behind only a faint sulfuric smell.

Etheos looked over at Sir Humphrey and Wyona who were both—even Wyona—looking rather awed.

"Your wizard," Wyona finally said to Sir Humphrey, swallowing hard. "Perhaps he has his uses."

"I'll say," Sir Humphrey murmured.

Lady Orville whimpered.

"Shall we—shall we continue then?" Sir Humphrey asked.

And then the lightning began.

A great flash of lightning crashed above them near the roof of the tunnel, followed by a loud clap of thunder. A gale-force wind blew down the tunnel, fighting them, trying to push them back the way they had come. More lightning crashed overhead and it became darker as if they were standing in their own private thunderstorm.

"Wyona!" Sir Humphrey tried to call over the gale. "What is it?"

But he looked over at her, and abruptly stopped.

She looked scared, surprised, and determined all in the same instant. As she clung to the side of the tunnel for fear of being blown away, her lucid grey eyes no longer seemed passive, but alight with a fire, a hatred, that seemed misplaced in her elegant, composed nature. Sir Humphrey hardly noticed in his wonder at the strength of this emotion that as the lightning flashes illuminated her long black hair, whipping behind her in the wind, it seemed to have streaks of white in it.

Etheos was just about to shout a spell; though it is well he did not, for such a thing would have only made things worse, when everything abruptly stopped.

And a cat appeared on the ledge before them.

It was not just any cat, Sir Humphrey realized, but the one he had seen on the roof of Nimue's house, the black one with white eyes he'd taken for blind. It was sitting there, complacently, its tail twitching slightly.

Wyona let out a shriek when she saw it and raised her sword above her as if it were a battleaxe, bringing it down hard upon the feline. The cat was smarter than that, though, and leapt out of the way at the last moment, into the stream of water that had lessened considerably after the gale. Wyona shrieked again and lunged, but the cat once again leapt out of the way, leaving her to fall, surprisingly ungracefully into the questionable water.

And then the cat was no longer a cat, but a man with a wide smirk across his face.

The man was dressed in the costume of a fencer—black leggings, a loose black shirt, and a highwayman's coat in a bright, ostentatious purple. He had shiny black hair that was tied back in a horsetail and a wide, feline smile. He was tall and wiry and his eyes were the strangest part about him. They were a rather cynical black and at the moment they were dancing back and forth at the sight of Wyona, who stood livid, covered in muck, but every so often he would blink and they would appear as white as those of the cat that he had once been. He had his hands clasped behind his back formally, rather absurd since he was standing in the middle of a sewer.

Wyona was the first to speak. "You *wretch*." She was gripping her sword so hard her normally pale knuckles were red.

"Indeed," the man said through his grin. "Did I startle you?"

Wyona gritted her teeth.

"Didn't expect to see me here, did you?" he continued. "Thought I was still stuck in that collapsed mine you trapped me in, didn't you? Exceedingly foolish of you."

"Why don't you just *die?*" Wyona cried through her gritted teeth, lunging forward with her sword, but the man just laughed, and parried her with his own that came from behind his back. The two swords rang loudly as they hit each other with an echo that stayed in everyone's ears long after both had lowered their weapons.

Etheos watched the pair closely, with narrowed eyes, sniffing the air uncertainly. "If we weren't in these blasted sewers—" he muttered to himself.

"Get out," Wyona said, regaining some of her calm, but her eyes still aflame with anger. "Leave. This is not your place."

"Oh, I think it is," the man said. "Tell me, little bird, how much of it have you told these—" He looked over at Etheos and Sir Humphrey as if searching for a word and then gave up entirely. "Your newest peons, I take it? Come, introduce us, don't be rude, girl." His smirk widened as he saw the confusion on Sir Humphrey's face. "Never mind then," he said. "I know this one. A knight of Sir Galahad's Hall if I ever saw one. Large and brainless as they always were."

Sir Humphrey hefted his axe speculatively. "You know, Etheos," he said conversationally to his companion. "This fellow just reeks of the Black Magic Guild. I think it would be my duty as a citizen to—"

"No," Etheos said. "He's not a wizard."

The man's grin widened. "Indeed, and neither are you, little apprentice, though you made a pretty show of those Goblyns."

"*Mol*—" Etheos started to mutter a spell, but the man raised a hand in a strange clawing motion and Etheos fell back, three red scratches across his face.

"If I were you, little bird, I'd turn back now," he advised. "Things beyond here are likely to get rather sticky."

"If you think I'm going to run and cower from you after all you've—"

"I was giving you a chance, little bird, though you never gave me one." His cat-like grin slipped just a bit, but he recovered it admirably. "My card," he said, handing a business card formally to Sir Humphrey. And then he turned back into a cat, and slipped back up the tunnel before anyone could blink.

Sir Humphrey looked down at the card. The first name had been blacked out so all it said was:

Stryver E.P.
Fencer, Hunter, Translator, and Qualified Mountaineer

There was no address.

"Old boyfriend?" Sir Humphrey guessed.

Wyona sheathed her sword. "If you ever say such a thing again, Sir Knight, I shall be forced to slit your throat," she replied in her quiet, reserved voice. "He is an enemy I know of old."

"And he can turn into a cat," Sir Humphrey pointed out. "Can you do that?" he asked Etheos, who was fingering the marks on his cheek.

"No," Etheos said absently.

"He must be a powerful wizard then."

"No," Etheos said again. "He's not a wizard and I meant 'No, he can't turn into a cat'."

"But you just saw—" Sir Humphrey tried to point out.

"He is a cat who can turn into a human," Etheos said. "At least that's the Academy's view on the Changelings. They usually stay in the Changeling Forest to the north though. We almost never see them. What's he doing here?" he demanded of Wyona. "I'd bet Merlyn's beard that he isn't registered with the Academy like law requires the Changelings and—"

"Stryver's here for the same reason we are," Wyona said, starting up the tunnel, tracing the cat's path.

"The dragon," Etheos said.

"Wh—yes," Wyona said. "The dragon."

"And did you spend time with the Changelings too?" Sir Humphrey asked her as they walked along, Lady Orville in his arms. "Just like the Sky Riders?"

"Yes," Wyona said, though there was a very bitter tone in her voice. "Yes, I have spent much time with the Changelings. They're a cruel, hard people. And Stryver is the worst."

"But what would a feline Changeling want with a dragon?" Etheos mused to himself from behind them. "Why would he leave home just—"

"It's money," Wyona said. "He undoubtedly wants to sell it to the highest bidder on the black market–Stryver's no stranger to the black market–and as far as I know he lives in the City when he isn't off pillaging the countryside."

"But the Changelings don't—"

"They don't want him. He's been banished."

Etheos blinked. "Oh. Why?"

Wyona shook her head and didn't answer.

They continued slogging up the tunnel in silence for five more minutes listening to the drip of water and the scurry of rats before Sir Humphrey said, "I saw him at Nimue's house today. I just thought he was another one of her cats though. Why hasn't he taken the dragon before now?"

Wyona didn't answer.

"There are some powerful spells indeed on that shed," Etheos said after a moment. "They're very subtle; you can hardly tell they're there at all. But they must be, to keep a dragon in a shed. He wouldn't be able to undo them without knocking himself into oblivion."

"And I suppose you will?" Sir Humphrey asked with a raised eyebrow.

"Of course," Etheos said. "I am a wizard—"

"Thaumaturge," Sir Humphrey and Wyona reminded him at the same time.

Etheos scowled at both of them. "It doesn't matter! I'll be able to get to that dragon. You'll see! And *then* the Academy will give me my wizard's robes anyway."

"Don't count your nymphs before they hatch," Wyona cautioned.

"What?" Etheos asked, confused.

Wyona shrugged. "It's a saying in the East Swamps."

They continued on for another fifteen minutes or so until Wyona stopped suddenly and looked up at the ceiling of the tunnel on the left. "There," she said, pointing.

A few rusted rungs of the ladder were still intact, clinging to the sides of the tunnel just below the manhole cover. They were covered in a slimy substance that had Etheos making all sorts of faces as he climbed, but soon all four of them were standing in the very far corner of the overgrown garden behind Nimue's house between a great tree and the old fence.

"We've got to be quiet," Wyona whispered. "Not only are Nimue's cats everywhere, but—"

"There's another sort of cat prowling about as well," Etheos finished for her.

"Right," Wyona said. "Try to stay down and—it's this way." She carefully slipped around the edge of the tree and was about to continue through the undergrowth towards the shed when a foot slid out of nowhere to trip her. She fell, the tails of her tunic flying, and rolled quickly, a good thing too, because she soon found a sword point sticking in the ground next to her nose. She kicked with her long legs, tripping Stryver, before jumping to her feet, drawing her slim saber and bringing it down upon his own raised sword. Stryver, mud spotting his purple coat, struggled to his feet while blocking her saber and soon, throwing the caution she had advised to the winds, Wyona and the Changeling were engaged in a heated sword duel. It was hard to tell who looked more angry.

"You got those pirates to kidnap me," Wyona said through gritted teeth as she swung at his head and hit a tall bamboo plant instead.

"You got me lost in the Wawakill Desert for a year," Stryver countered, kicking a dead branch towards his opponent to trip her.

"You spiked the punch and then left me with those cannibals!" Wyona cried, as their swords locked, each bearing down upon the other.

"You told the Knights that I was the West Road Highwayman!" Stryver replied, pushing her sword away.

"You *are* the West Road Highwayman!" Wyona protested as the two stared at each other without attacking for a moment.

"I know," Stryver replied calmly. "But you didn't have to tell them that, did you, scatter brain?"

And then the two leapt into battle again, shouting accusations at each other, each one more ridiculous than the last.

Etheos, Sir Humphrey, and the Lady Orville watched, fascinated. Wyona moved with the impossible elegance and grace of one so strangely proportioned and the man in the purple coat, Stryver, had the agility of the cat that he was. By all accounts, they were evenly matched.

Etheos shook his head. "Come on," he said to Sir Humphrey. "Let's go get our dragon."

"But what about—" Sir Humphrey started to protest.

"Don't you see?" Etheos hissed. "This is perfect. Not only will *we* get to the dragon before he does, but if the psychotic old lady comes out, she'll see them and not us. Let's go."

The three made their way through the vines and thorns to the shed, from which was coming loud roars and various bangs. Etheos frowned, inspecting it for a moment, holding out his hand towards it.

"Impossible," he said. "The spells are almost invisible."

"Maybe that's why they call him the greatest Enchanter in the world," Sir Humphrey suggested.

"Just stand back," Etheos muttered.

Sir Humphrey, the bored-looking Lady Orville still in hand, took a step back.

"Farther," Etheos said.

Sir Humphrey took another step.

"Far—just go stand by that stupid old fountain," Etheos ordered.

Sir Humphrey went and stood beside the moldy old fountain, which at one point had been a lovely statue of the great Enchanter himself, while Etheos stood beside the shed, muttering and wiggling his fingers mystically.

After a moment he came to stand beside Sir Humphrey. "Just to be safe," he said. "I'm not sure I want to be near it when the dragon comes out." And then he waved his hand and said "Y *Vujuequ Ieo!*" with a passionate cry that raised a great wind up to howl through the garden, which was just loud enough to cover the snapping the fountain behind them started to make.

The lock exploded from the shed and the entire thing collapsed like a house of cards.

"*What?*" Etheos fumed. "It wasn't supposed—"

Something was moving amongst the rubble.

Etheos and Sir Humphrey both started forward. Shaking bits of plaster and wood from itself and blinking confusedly, there stood the dragon. It had green-blue scales, a long tail, and intelligent purple eyes. It was also the size of Lady Orville.

"It's just a lap dragon!" Etheos cried in horror. "No! No, this—" He turned around.

Where the fountain had been there was a fist-sized emerald, floating in mid-air, surrounded by a yellow light.

Sir Humphrey gasped. "That must be worth millions!"

"The treasure of Merlyn," Etheos whispered, taking a reverent step forward.

Meanwhile, the duel had abruptly ceased when the wind first came up, but neither Wyona nor Stryver had given the shed a glance. They had both been staring at the fountain.

"It's mine!" Stryver suddenly said, changing abruptly into a cat and making a dash at it.

But Wyona was faster.

Where the precariously tall woman had been, a jet raven, its back stained with white stripes, appeared. Before the cat could leap for the emerald, the bird had snatched it from the air with a triumphant caw. She circled the garden once, giving Stryver a particularly hateful look before flying off, a black speck against the sky.

There was silence in the garden as Sir Humphrey and Etheos stared after her. Stryver sullenly became human again. Lady Orville was sniffing the lap dragon uncertainly.

"She was a Changeling," Etheos finally said incredulously.

"Well, *obviously*," Stryver muttered, kicking a piece of the rubble dejectedly. "Didn't you see it on her card? Wyona Wyncliff E.P."

"And what does that stand for?" Etheos asked.

"Expatriated of course," Stryver said. "The Changelings banished us both. Some years ago now. We've been cheating each other with schemes ever since—like this one for instance. We both found out about the real secret to Merlyn's spell at around the same time. And she, being the resourceful little feather brain that she is, goes off and finds the worthy of heart, worthy of power, and worthy of cause, luring you all here with some story about a dragon, I take it. I, on the other hand, not being too fond of work myself, follow along, waiting for my chance to dart in and take the prize. That's the way it's always been. She does the work and I take the credit."

"Except she just flew away with your emerald," Sir Humphrey pointed out.

Stryver shrugged. "A minor detail. I'm the West Road Highwayman remember. That emerald might see its way into my hands by tonight."

The lap dragon, intimidated by Lady Orville's bulk, began to cry, a low whining moan.

Sir Humphrey looked at it pityingly. "I think, Etheos, the reason those spells seemed so subtle is that they only existed in your mind."

Etheos scowled. "Let's just go before the psychotic old woman comes out again."

"Too late," Stryver replied before changing back into a cat.

Nimue, the gnarled old woman, was at the window, a bowling ball in her hands, screaming something about government inspectors.

Etheos made a run for the fence, the Lady Orville right behind. Sir Humphrey hesitated, scooped up the whining dragon, and then followed suit. The dragon immediately quieted, wrapping its scaly tail around the knight's arm and almost purring contentedly.

Sir Humphrey caught up with Etheos and Lady Orville at the end of Warlock's Way. Etheos stared at the dragon. "Why'd you bring that thing?" he demanded.

The dragon hissed at him, sending a little puff of smoke into his face. Etheos coughed.

"He was crying…" Sir Humphrey said. "Besides, he'll make a lovely friend for Lady Orville. I think we'll have to call him George."

"That is possibly the stupidest—"

The dragon hissed again, this time sending tiny sparks into the air.

"George is a lovely name," Etheos amended. "I can't think of a better one."

"Let's go home then," Sir Humphrey said as the sun set over the City. "I know where we can get some burnt pie … "

The Demonic Misadventure

The officiating wizard, wearing the ceremonial gold robes, banged his staff for silence. "Spectacular display of power indeed," he said when the roar of the crowd had died down. "Congratulations, Conjurer Collins," he said to the victor, who was grinning smugly. "And best of luck to you, Conjurer Cecil, in finding your other ear." This was met with laughter from the crowd.

"Now then," the officiating wizard said. "Next we have…" He checked the names on his scroll. "Ah yes. A most interesting combination. Thaumaturge Etheos against Diviner Dara."

Those in the crowd, most of the Academy personnel, some dignitaries from the city, and a smattering of common folk, looked at each other, confused. It was impossible, wasn't it? For a mere thaumaturge to battle with a diviner?

"Isn't your Etheos pushing his luck a bit?" the hedge witch who lived in the flat below him whispered to Sir Humphrey, who had a pig in a sunbonnet sitting in his lap.

"Not at all," Sir Humphrey said. "Etheos tells me that he's gauged Dara's power a few times and finds it nothing to boast over. He isn't entirely sure how she made Diviner, actually. He's sure to win, so he says, and then they'll have to up his status to wizard."

The hedge witch nodded sagely. "Ah yes. That Etheos has a sharp head on his shoulders."

"Let's just hope he doesn't lose it," Sir Humphrey muttered to the Lady Orville.

The pig snorted, hopped off his lap, and began rooting around for peanuts on the floor of the outdoor amphitheater.

The two challengers entered from opposite sides of the field. Etheos walked confidently out into the sun, his blue robes blowing in the light breeze. From the other side came Dara the Diviner.

33

The crowd gasped.

Dara the Diviner looked like a six-year-old. She was wearing a green robe with sleeves slightly too long, which she used to wipe her nose. She tripped over the hem often. Her light hair was done up in braided pigtails by her ears and she wore a large pair of spectacles.

"Isn't she precious?" the hedge witch next to Sir Humphrey whispered.

Sir Humphrey scratched his head. "I don't rightly know. How can *that* be a diviner who ranks higher than Etheos?" But since he seemed to be surrounded by the hedge witch's friends, who all thought Etheos' challenger was adorable, and the Lady Orville had discovered an abandoned frog tart some rows down, he received no answer.

Etheos looked determined, ignoring the crowd completely.

"Challengers, salute!" the officiating wizard cried.

Etheos inclined his head rigidly.

Dara attempted to bow and tripped over her robe. This was greeted by a gentle laughter from the crowd.

"She's just the most darling thing!" the hedge witch beside Sir Humphrey exclaimed, dropping a stitch in her knitting by accident. "I do hope she wins. It hardly seems fair to put her up against big, strong Etheos, doesn't it?"

Sir Humphrey frowned. There was something more to this than met the eye.

"And let the battle of wits and wizardry commence!" the officiating wizard said in his grandest voice, banging his staff.

Etheos immediately spread his hands dramatically and began to mutter spells under his breath. A great wind rose up behind him, pushing Dara's little braids behind her, and the sun seemed to go behind a cloud. Thunder rumbled in the distance as Etheos' voice grew louder and louder.

"I do hope he doesn't hurt the poor dear!" the hedge witch cried, gripping Sir Humphrey's arm in fright. "Oh, was that a rain drop?"

And then it began to pour.

There were assorted screams from the stands as those in the crowd attempted to shield themselves from the sudden downpour. Most of the Academy personnel muttered dry spells of differing difficulty depending on their level of learning while those not gifted in magical abilities simply opened umbrellas.

Etheos remained firm on the field, his robes whipping about him in the torrent, completely drenched, his hair hanging in his eyes, which glowed with an intense, almost vengeful power. The little girl stared across at him, completely drenched, with one finger in her mouth, apparently not understanding what was going on.

Etheos raised a hand and roared in a voice so loud that even Sir Humphrey heard it from the stands, "*E Jydfrlyld, zeku zetl cvek rfu quhi re qurvyhu ki ceu!*"

A lightning bolt rocketed down from the dark clouds above, straight towards Dara. Dara calmly took her finger out of her mouth and pointed it at the lightning bolt. It seemed to stop in mid air as if frozen, yet still buzzing with its electric force, and then it changed its course and went directly at Etheos. Etheos struggled with a shielding spell but it was too late.

The weather immediately cleared back into the bright sunny day it had been before the battle had begun. Everything was the same except for Etheos lying on the ground, a faint steam coming off him.

"Well," said the officiating wizard after a moment. "I suppose that's what you get, Etheos old sport. Next time pick on someone your own size."

This brought laughter from the crowd and the officiating wizard went on to announce the next combatants.

Sir Humphrey didn't hear who it was, however. He'd already gone, clumping down the stairs of the amphitheater and leaping over the side, onto the green. No one tried to stop the big knight. Perhaps it was the oven mitts stuffed into his belt or the fiery red beard, but more than likely, it was the battle-axe in his hand. He strode purposely across the field and looked down at the fallen Etheos.

"I think this is the first time you've been struck by lightning," he remarked conversationally. "But the sixth time you've been electrocuted."

Etheos blinked awake, squinting in the sun. "Humphrey? Did I win?"

"Well… " Sir Humphrey offered his hand to help Etheos to his feet. "No."

"But—"

"I don't know why you wanted to fight a little thing like me."

Etheos turned swiftly. There was Dara, pushing up her large spectacles and wiping her nose on her long sleeve.

"It's hardly fair," she murmured.

"You little snake!" Etheos hissed. "Don't think you can get away with it! I know you cheated!"

"How?" she asked, looking up at him with big, wide eyes. "Everyone was there. Everyone saw what happened. I'm just better than you, that's all."

Sir Humphrey put a hand on Etheos' shoulder to hold him back.

"So I suggest," the little girl continued, a dark look coming into her eyes. "That you *don't* interrupt my studies again." With that she turned and strode away, across the Academy complex to one of the numerous towers.

Sir Humphrey and Etheos both stared after her open-mouthed. It was only visible for a second, but each would have sworn they saw, clear as day, a dark pointed tail, like that of a rat, poking out from beneath her robes.

Sir Humphrey and Etheos looked at each other.

"What was that?" the knight asked, as the girl slammed the door to the tower.

Etheos shook his head. "I don't know. But I know that wasn't a fair fight. And I'm going to find out how." He turned his head towards the top window in the tower. "Sir Humphrey, do you have a grappling hook?"

"Etheos … "

"Shhh!"

"But, Etheos!"

"*What?*"

"I don't think this is such a good—"

"What? You aren't scared are you?"

"No. I don't get scared. Except of squirrels. But that doesn't matter. I just don't really think we're supposed to be here."

"Sometimes, Sir Humphrey, my friend," Etheos said, swinging the grappling hook over his head. "One must take difficult measures to make things right."

"Do those include breaking about twelve city laws and about fifty Academy rules?"

Etheos shrugged, pulling tight on the rope.

"In case you'd forgotten, Etheos, my friend," Sir Humphrey said. "I'm a Knight of Galahad's Hall. We take our oaths rather seriously. I'm afraid I can't—"

"Sir Humphrey!" Etheos said, exasperatedly taking off the dark mask he had pulled over his face before they had begun the clandestine outing onto the Academy's property. "Why didn't you say something *before* we left?"

Sir Humphrey shrugged. "That would've given you the chance to knock one of those sleepy spells on me. This way, I can just say you were using mind control. Can I go up first?"

Etheos rolled his eyes.

It was a long, sweaty climb up the rope for both knight and magician. Finally, painstakingly, they reached the top. But a heavy curtain was drawn over the window.

"Perfect. Just perfect!" Etheos fumed. "We're going to have to think of some other way to—perhaps a spell—"

"Etheos I don't think that's such a good—"

There was a loud crash from inside the room and an even louder roar. The curtain was pulled aside, giving Etheos and Sir Humphrey just enough time to fall back into the shadow, clinging madly to the rope, before the window shattered. Out flew a black figure, with wings on its back and horns on its head. It turned once to look back at the window, cackled, and then flew off towards the city making an inhuman shrieking noise.

"Come back here you stupid brute!" came a shout—distinctly Dara's—from the window. "Oh, I'll never get it right!" She sighed and shook her head—in the process looking downwards and spying our two precariously hanging heroes.

"What's *that* about?" She snapped her fingers and a light appeared there. "Etheos!" she shrieked. "What do you think you're doing?"

"I was just—run!"

And so Etheos and Sir Humphrey scrambled over each other, falling most of the way down, until they somehow both made it to the bottom, running across the lawn and away into the night, leaving Dara screaming at her window.

They only stopped for breath when they were many blocks away, panting and leaning against the side of a house.

"We've got to—to find out what that—that thing was," Etheos said, trying to catch his breath. "It looked like—like a—"

"Demon?"

Etheos looked up at Sir Humphrey. "Yes."

"And those are dangerous?"

"Very."

"That little girl had better be careful then…"

"She—Yes. We've got to get a better look at what's going on in that room, though. We've got to get some proof. Otherwise, very soon, the both of us are going to be arrested. They'll drag us away and lock us in the dungeon."

"And we don't want that," Sir Humphrey replied, nodding vigorously. "Believe me, I know."

"Then we have to find some way to get into that room!"

"Well, what do you suggest we do?" Sir Humphrey demanded. "Fly?"

"Why—" Etheos stopped. "Yes. Yes, that's exactly what we'll do."

Etheos knocked sharply on the door.

"Face it, Etheos. It's too late at night for anyone—"

"Come in," came the voice. "But this better be good," it added irritably.

Etheos gave Sir Humphrey a smug smile as he pushed open the door.

Sir Humphrey rolled his eyes. "This is *such* a rotten idea. Do you learn nothing from your mistakes?"

They stepped into the rather dimly lit study of Wyona Wyncliff, whose impossible yet graceful form was bent over her desk, writing furiously with a quill pen.

"Evidently not," she replied in her quiet voice without looking up at them. "I didn't think I'd be seeing you two again. What do you want?" She frowned, looking up at them with those lucid grey eyes. "Where's the lady pig?"

"At home, asleep," Sir Humphrey replied. "This outing was a little too dangerous for her."

"Well, I admit, wandering about in Thieves' Den at this hour of the night is rather dangerous but—"

"We came from the Academy," Etheos began.

"A dangerous place indeed," Wyona said with a nod, going back to whatever she had been writing. "Demons."

Etheos blinked and stared at her. "You—you know about them?"

Wyona shrugged. "I had word about some growing demonic activity."

"And it doesn't worry you?"

"Why should it?" she asked, looking up again. "It's nothing to do with me."

"But the practitioner raising these demons," Etheos said. "Is little more than a girl. Dara—"

"Who out-ranks you, I believe," Wyona added.

Etheos' cheeks flared. "Yes, but she's been *cheating*. We were there just now, at her tower and we saw—"

"Did she invite you?"

"Well … not … exactly."

"I see."

"But we saw a demon—it must have been a third or fourth degree imp at least—fly out into the night from her window, towards the city. She can't control them!"

"And yet somehow she's using them to show you up?" Wyona asked, raising an eyebrow. "Your logic is a bit shaky, Sir Thaumaturge."

"Damn logic! I know what I saw, and I want her stopped!"

"And so you've come to me? I'm flattered by your vote of confidence in my skills—and also slightly startled at your willingness to forget being most ill-used by me in the past—but I'm afraid I've far more important things to do, good evening."

And she continued to scribble on the paper, ignoring them entirely.

"Wyona, we aren't leaving," Etheos said, sitting down into a chair. "You know you owe us—"

Wyona looked up at him coolly. "I owe you?"

"You made off with that huge emerald—"

"Which quite coincidentally disappeared the *very next day*," Wyona interrupted.

Etheos stopped. "Stryver?"

Wyona rolled her eyes and said, "As much as I'd simply adore helping you win a petty grudge match against a six-year-old prodigy diviner—the pet of the Academy no less!—my current business means life or death for any number of important people so if you please—"

"But it's life or death for us too," Sir Humphrey rumbled. "The Knights are probably already after us."

Wyona stared at him. "Whatever did *you* do, Sir Knight?" There was a loud *caw* and a raven flew in through the large open window to land on Wyona's shoulder. She opened the note that was tied to its leg.

"Followed this tar-head, here," Sir Humphrey replied, waving at Etheos. "We were caught in a rather precarious position—"

"Hanging out of Dara the Diviner's window by grappling hook," Wyona finished for him, reading off the note. "Yes, I've just received the notice for your arrest."

Sir Humphrey and Etheos looked at each other. "But why would they send *you* a notice for our arrest?" Sir Humphrey asked.

"Because they think, very rightly so, that it may have some import in the case I'm currently working on," she explained.

"And what is that?" Etheos demanded. "The army of demons that's probably even now loose in the city?"

"No," Wyona said. "The plot to assassinate the king."

Sir Humphrey swore. "There's a plot to assassinate the king? But—no—who could possibly—"

"I'd very much like to know myself," Wyona replied. "Being that if I don't find out in a few days they'll chop my head off."

Etheos stared at her. "But—but how—"

"With an axe, I'd imagine," Wyona replied, going back to whatever she was writing. "And, congratulations, you two now seem to be suspects."

"*What?*" Etheos raged as Sir Humphrey's face went white and then red in quick succession. "How can that be? We weren't even at the palace! Is it so much of a crime to hang outside the windows of innocent looking little girl-wizards on grappling hooks in the blackest hours of the night?"

Wyona gave him a withering look. "If you aren't going to say anything useful, shut up. Some of us—" She looked at the both of them. "All of us now have our lives to worry about."

"But why are we suspects?" Sir Humphrey asked. "You don't believe—"

"No, I don't believe you're behind the plot," Wyona said. "For one thing, it's too complex for the both of you to handle without mucking up. But I can see why some people think so."

"*Why?*" Etheos demanded.

Wyona blinked. "You didn't know that Dara wrote all the protection spells placed upon the castle and the king?"

Etheos stared at her.

Sir Humphrey cursed. "We're in deep trouble."

"Yes," Wyona agreed. "You are."

"But—but you've got to help us!" Etheos said. "It's Dara! I know it is! She's the one plotting against the king with her—with her *demon armies!*"

"We only saw one demon, Etheos…" Sir Humphrey reminded him. "And I don't think little Dara could be—"

"She's not *little* Dara!" Etheos fumed. "She's not *precious* Dara and she's not *sweet, innocent, perfect little* Dara! She *struck* me with *lightning!*"

"Only because you tried to strike her first…" Sir Humphrey reminded him. "What should we do?" he asked Wyona. "We aren't trying to kill the king. We didn't know."

Wyona spread her hands. "It really isn't—"

A rock sailed through the open window and struck Wyona on

the back of the head. She bit her lip and rubbed her head irritably, stood swiftly and leaned out the window. "It was *open*, idiot!"

The stranger standing in the street below flashed her a cat-like grin. "Yes, I know. Have you got anything else yet, bird brain?"

"In a matter of speaking, tuna face. Have you?"

The cat-like grin smiled up at her again. "Perhaps I do, perhaps I don't. Would you care to share yours?"

"Not in the middle of the street, no," Wyona called down. "Come up—and *quietly* or you'll wake the bloody landlord."

Stryver—for indeed it was he, in his ridiculous purple coat and all—gave a mock gasp. "I've been invited into the holy sanctum. Such an honor has—"

"We don't have *time* for this, dog bait. Just get up here."

"You know, cats *eat* birds," Stryver muttered, disappearing into the shadows.

"You've said that before," Wyona muttered, stepping away from the window and sitting back down, staring forlornly at the mass of papers on her desk. It was strange to see her in such despair, with such lines under her eyes. It was not the graceful, serene Wyona they had known. And to be collaborating with Stryver …

"I thought you hated the cat?" Sir Humphrey said.

"I do," Wyona replied bitterly. "And he hates me."

"Then why—"

"Love of life, Sir Knight," she replied. "We're both in the same boat. And it's sinking."

The door opened, nearly hitting Sir Humphrey, for the room was not altogether large, and Stryver edged his way inside. He had the same cynical black eyes that occasionally turned white when he blinked, but, like Wyona, he had a new edge to his appearance, a sort of haggard desperation that made him look all the more dangerous.

"What are these two dunderheads doing here?" he demanded, looking from Etheos to Sir Humphrey.

"Adding to our troubles," Wyona replied. "Apparently those thick-headed knights—no offense, Sir Humphrey—have issued a warrant for their arrest after they were caught hanging under Dara the Diviner's window on a grappling hook."

"They're suspects, then?" Stryver asked, narrowing his eyes suspiciously at the two of them.

"According to the Knights, yes, but I think it's idiocy."

"Yes," Stryver replied after a moment with a nod. "Much too complex for these two." He pulled up a chair and sat down with his usual feline grace. "And so you're harboring suspected criminals because—"

"Let us help you!" Sir Humphrey suddenly said.

Stryver and Wyona both looked at him with raised eyebrows. "You?"

"We can be of some assistance," Sir Humphrey replied. "Etheos is pretty handy with spells and enchantments and I—I'm—I have an axe. Besides, it's the only way to clear our names."

Wyona shrugged. "Couldn't hurt I suppose."

"Actually—" Stryver started to protest.

"Did you get anything useful out of that nutcase clairvoyant or not?" Wyona demanded.

"Can I ask why?" Etheos asked.

"Why what?" Wyona asked irritably, still glaring at Stryver.

"Why are the two of you working in conjunction with the king—and each other? How do you know there's even a plot to—"

"The king," Wyona said. "Has no knowledge of the plot against his life, nor of the great measures any of us are taking to foil it. It's meant to stay that way."

"Then who—"

"The king's grandfather used to keep a clairvoyant in his entourage," Stryver said. "Except most people seem to believe that she wasn't there for her abilities to tell the future."

"What was she there for?" Sir Humphrey asked, as Stryver seemed unwilling to go on.

"The king's grandfather was…young and impulsive. And this clairvoyant was young and beautiful—or so they say. You get the picture. This clairvoyant, though—her name is Mag now—didn't take too kindly to—well, she didn't like that she wasn't being appreciated for her powers of clairvoyance. So, she did the usual thing for revenge."

"Killed him?" Sir Humphrey guessed.

"No!" Stryver said. "What is it with you knights? Always thinking about chopping things up. She cursed the descendants, obviously. She prophesized that the old king's son's son would be brutally and rather gorily slaughtered by the first full moon in his twenty-eighth year."

"Which happens to be tomorrow night," Wyona added.

"But how do you know the curse is even real?" Etheos said. "Without the proper spell working or summoning it could just be empty words."

"Well, that's why no one worried about it," Stryver said. "Until the Captain of the king's personal guard received a certain note."

"This note," Wyona added, holding up a sheet of parchment.

Etheos took it from her and read it aloud. " 'It's too late for you to protect him. The Curse has already arrived. Your king shall be no more'."

"That does sound a little threatening," Sir Humphrey agreed. "How did you two get involved?"

"The Captain of the king's guard is a very persuasive man," Wyona said with a shrug. "He has known for some time that Stryver and I were in the city as illegal Changelings—not registered, you know—but he never did anything because we weren't really hurting anyone and—"

"And *now*," Stryver interrupted. "When there's a threat, the dear Captain comes to us and says that he doesn't care how we do it, but we're to stop the plot before the king dies or he'll frame us both for the murder and have us executed. Who cares if another couple of Changelings die anyway? And it would be just like our kind to plot against the king, wouldn't it?" he added bitterly.

"Why you two?"

"Because we're the best obviously," Stryver said. "Or *I* am, at any rate. Personally I think *she's* along because—"

"Did you get anything out of the clairvoyant or not?" Wyona interrupted.

"Yes," Stryver replied. "Though not much. As far as she can remember, the curse is entirely real."

"And what form will it take?" Wyona demanded. "Please tell me you got that much."

Stryver frowned. "Just before I had to whack her over the head, she said something about summonings. If she used a summoning to cast it all those years ago it would have to be—"

"Demons," Etheos finished. "You see? It's *Dara*! Dara's trying to kill the king! That demon's probably already on its way to the castle!"

"Is that all you got?" Wyona asked, ignoring Etheos completely.

"It was difficult!" Stryver protested. "You have no idea how—"

"There's lipstick on your collar," Wyona pointed out.

Stryver jumped and tugged at his collar, trying to see it. He tried to wipe it off without much success.

"So very difficult," Wyona muttered.

"She's over one hundred years old!" Stryver shouted. "I'm never going to be the same again," he added, putting a hand to his forehead.

"Just as well," Wyona replied with a shrug. "Didn't like you very much before anyway."

"Do *you* have anything new?" Stryver demanded.

"I analyzed the handwriting on the note," Wyona replied. "And whoever it is doesn't live anywhere near the palace—"

"It's *Dara*!" Etheos said again.

"Or in the City at all for that matter," Wyona finished. "It's a stranger."

"Or someone disguising their handwriting," Stryver pointed out.

Wyona threw up her hands. "It's impossible. The king is going to die tomorrow night, if not before, and we've no idea who's behind it—much less how to stop it. Besides that, they'll probably use demons. Have you ever been up against a demon?"

Stryver shook his head. "I've seen a few conjurers eaten by them though. Not a very pretty sight."

Wyona sighed. "They're going to chop our heads off."

"Sort of like that time back in the Forest, isn't it?"

"No, *they* wanted to hang us."

"Well, the solution's the same…"

PATRICIA LADD

Wyona blinked at him. "What?"

"Seems logical enough to me."

"May I ask what—" Etheos began, but both were ignoring him now.

"He'd never let it slide," Wyona replied with a shake of the head. "He'd go after us."

"That doesn't mean he'd catch us."

"You've said that before."

"And I was right, wasn't I?"

"You weren't the one who nearly got his tail feathers plucked out!"

"Well, I wasn't the one poking around where I shouldn't, either, was I?"

Wyona glared at him. "I'm not running."

"Then I wish you a very pleasant beheading," Stryver replied, standing and straightening his coat. "As for me—"

There was a very loud, strangled *caw* and another raven flew in through the window, crash-landing sprawled upon Wyona's desk. Wyona stared at it, wide-eyed. It gave another strangled *caw*, quietly this time, and then closed its eyes.

Wyona's eyes flashed. "They'll *pay* for this!"

"Who will?" Stryver asked. His eyes were dancing and a smirk was painted on his face.

"Well—" Wyona snatched the parchment tied about the dead raven's leg and read it hurriedly. What little color there was drained from her pale face and she looked up with wide eyes. "Stryver—"

Stryver snatched the note from her hands and read it over. "Same, I suppose?"

Wyona nodded.

"Brilliant."

Sir Humphrey, rather tired of being ignored, grabbed the note from Stryver, who didn't seem to notice, and read it, with Etheos at his side.

Tonight is the night. We're ready. Are you?

"The same handwriting," Sir Humphrey muttered. "They're going to kill him tonight, aren't they?"

46

"That's what it says," Stryver agreed, though he didn't take his eyes off Wyona. "It's suicide," he said to her. "You'll never prevent it on your own, and then you'll be there, right where they want you. You'll be dead tomorrow at first light with the common criminals."

"I've got to try."

"You're a madwoman."

"You're a coward."

It seemed to sting Stryver. He glared at her. "We'll see who's a coward. I'll be there. You open the door."

Wyona nodded, and in a moment she was no longer there. Instead, the small raven with white streaks circled the room once and then flew out the window in the direction of the palace.

Stryver muttered something under his breath and then turned to the door. "What do you think you're doing?" he demanded of Sir Humphrey as the knight made to follow.

"Coming, of course," Sir Humphrey replied. "It has as much to do with our lives as yours."

Stryver must have thought the better of fighting about it, because he said nothing more the entire way to the palace.

"We're going the wrong way," Sir Humphrey rumbled in the darkness. "The entrance is over there!"

"Only if you want to go through all the nonsense of being searched and questioned and poked and prodded," Stryver said, seeming to blend with the shadows like a ghost. "It's much easier 'round back."

"I didn't know there was a back gate," Sir Humphrey said, slightly put out, as it was the sort of thing that any good Knight of Galahad's Hall should know.

Stryver grinned. "It's not a gate. Hardly even a door. Just something I've found awfully useful on a number of occasions. Here."

He stopped suddenly, looked both ways, and then leapt across the street and into the thick shadows of the palace walls. Etheos, with a little bit of mage light in his hand, and Sir Humphrey followed.

They waited there for several minutes before there was a sort of creaking noise, and a narrow part of the wall swung aside. Wyona's head poked out of the niche. "Took you long enough."

"Some of us can't fly," Stryver said, following her inside the narrow crevice.

It was indeed narrow; Sir Humphrey had quite the time scraping through.

They found themselves standing in one of the back gardens, the shapes of clipped hedges and flower arrangements looking particularly eerie in the night.

"Where to?" Sir Humphrey asked, hefting his axe and looking into the shadows warily.

"The King's Chambers of course," Stryver said. "Through the kitchens?" he asked Wyona.

"Most likely," Wyona replied with a nod.

Stryver's form abruptly blurred into a black cat with white eyes that stalked off through the gardens.

Wyona looked as if she were about to change form as well when Etheos said, "We're coming too."

"Not like that, you aren't," Wyona replied. "They'll see you and then you'll *really* be suspects."

Etheos scowled at her. "I *think* I can manage a simple invisibility spell."

"As you like," Wyona replied before becoming the white striped raven again and flying in the direction Stryver had gone.

Etheos muttered something, put a hand on Sir Humphrey's broad shoulder and intoned a few short phrases in the language used for such spells. Then he suddenly vanished.

"Etheos! Where are you?" Sir Humphrey called hoarsely.

"Right here, dolt!" Etheos hissed from somewhere next to him. "That's why it's called *invisibility*!"

Sir Humphrey looked down at his feet, but found he could not see them.

"Which way are the kitchens then?" Etheos' voice asked.

"This way," Sir Humphrey said, walking towards the soft light of a lantern.

"*Which* way?" Etheos replied. "I can't see you!"

"Here," Sir Humphrey said. "Hold on to my belt." He waved his hand about in the air, searching for Etheos.

"Ouch!" Etheos cried as Sir Humphrey's hand hit something solid. "I think you've broken my nose!"

"Sorry," Sir Humphrey said. "Just hold my belt. Watch the oven mitts. I know the way."

They started off in that direction, where one of the doors was kept open by the lazy boy who stayed up to keep the fire going. They walked through the kitchens without any mishap, except Sir Humphrey turning too sharply once and knocking Etheos into a wall. Then it was up into the main castle, down some dimly lit hallways lined with portraits of old nobility—all with exceedingly large noses—and up another flight of stairs that twisted annoyingly so that one was never sure how far they had to go. They reached a landing that was somehow quieter than the rest. It seemed like someone in the castle was always moving. There was always a bustle somewhere, someone up working, some guard keeping watch. But here on this landing, the floor devoted entirely to the king, all seemed quiet. Deathly quiet.

"I don't like this," Etheos said. "Where are those two? And what's that noise?"

Sir Humphrey strained his ears to hear. All seemed calm to him. But there it was! A faint lazy buzzing noise that rippled through the still air at regular intervals. "What is it?" he asked Etheos. "It doesn't feel natural."

"Keep going," Etheos said. "But carefully. And if we meet a demon, for the love of Merlyn, don't look in its eyes."

Sir Humphrey slowly made his way across the long purple rug on the floor of the hallway. It seemed like his footsteps made a painful amount of noise. The farther they went, the louder the buzzing, and the more frequent.

Etheos inhaled sharply and stopped dead. "Sir Humphrey! Do you feel that?" he whispered.

"Can't say I—" But then he did. It was like a crackling, a ripping within his head. And then it subsided to a soft moan that he felt rather than heard. It was altogether eerie.

"What is it?" he asked.

"It's the sound of broken spells," Etheos said after a moment. "Strong ones, and a lot of them. They must be—"

"The protection spells on the king," Sir Humphrey finished.

"Hurry!" Etheos said.

Sir Humphrey began to run, lumbering down the hall and making the paintings jump on their hooks. Etheos struggled to keep up, tripping a few times, but maintaining his grip on the big knight's belt just the same. Sir Humphrey stopped at the end of the hall in front of a pair of gilt double doors. One was ajar and there was someone whimpering inside.

Sir Humphrey banged open the door, his battleaxe at the ready.

The scene that he met was an interesting one. The room was large, the walls covered in rich tapestries in gold thread, a platform bed in the center with long, thick hangings. A huge fireplace stood on one wall, the fire flaring dangerously at regular intervals. Etheos later explained that it was the presence of the demons.

There were six of them. Five were the size of children, but with dark wings, horns, claws, and nasty-looking teeth. Their eyes burned red and they each had long pointed tails. Two of these were holding the king in mid air, grinning with a sort of playful evil at him. The king was the one whimpering. There was a slash through the chest of his long white nightgown and, by the looks of the bedclothes, there had been quite a scuffle; he was now dangling his feet in the air, his eyes tightly shut. There was a very good reason why.

The larger demon—the one Etheos was positive he'd seen flying out of Dara's window—was about the size of a man. He and the other three smaller ones had Wyona backed against a wall. It was not just Wyona, Sir Humphrey saw as he started forward. Stryver was there too, but he was lying on the ground, his arm still sticking out in a strange position as if he'd been turned to stone and simply fallen over, his unblinking, cloudy eyes staring at the ceiling. Wyona was standing in front of him, holding her slim, cruel saber out before her, with her head turned away from the four demons in front of her, her arm covering her eyes. She stood no chance to fight them, not being able to see them. But what had become of Stryver?

"He must have looked one of them in the eyes," Etheos said from behind Sir Humphrey.

At the sound of the door and voices, the demons all turned to see who it was. They stared harder when it appeared to be no one. Sir Humphrey felt a pop, and suddenly he could see Etheos, hand still tucked in his belt, staring resolutely at the floor. "Don't look in their eyes, Humphrey," he said again.

Sir Humphrey stared at the floor too, but not without some misgiving. "Stop!" he yelled in his most authoritative voice. "You are hereby under arrest for breaking and entering, attempted regicide, and—and being unregistered aliens from a nether realm of untold pain and horror come to plague mankind," he added, his voice shaking just a bit. "Surrender now and—and—"

"And what?" The voice was so deep that Sir Humphrey could feel it in his bones.

"And maybe we'll just send you back where you came from," Sir Humphrey said.

The demon, what must have been the large one, though Sir Humphrey couldn't see, threw back his head and laughed. The small demons floating in the air about him cackled.

"You think, little human, that *you* can tell *us* what to do? We, who have come to complete an obligation left us by one of your own kind years ago? I do not think so, little human! Get them!"

Wyona, however, had not been idle. While the demons' eyes had been turned away from her, she had swept Stryver's fallen sword off the floor and skewered two demons through the heart at the same time. Their dark carcasses fell to the floor, liquefying into a small dark pool, before slowly disappearing altogether.

The remaining imp leapt to obey his demon master, flying over to the knight and magician while the larger demon turned with a roar of frustration on Wyona. Wyona shielded her eyes once more, keeping her sword in front of her, while kicking Stryver viciously with one foot. He didn't stir.

The imp that came for Sir Humphrey and Etheos would have been quite frightening in a group, but did not, it seemed, work well by itself. It snarled, rather pitifully, and flew at Sir Humphrey.

Etheos, without looking at it, intoned three harsh words and it froze in mid-air, flapping its little wings helplessly. It began screeching.

"Sir Humphrey, if you would," Etheos said.

Sir Humphrey raised his axe in the direction of the screeching, and it was abruptly cut short.

Both knight and wizard looked up. The larger demon was advancing with a very wicked grin towards Wyona, who was now not only kicking Stryver but shouting curses at him as well.

Sir Humphrey raised his axe and started towards the demon.

"Don't be stupid," Etheos said, grabbing him. "That thing will kill you."

"Yes, and it'll kill her in a minute," Sir Humphrey replied. "It's not like a dead man—"

"He's not dead," Etheos said. "Just stunned. He must have only looked one of the small ones in the eye."

"How does that—" But Sir Humphrey's objections were cut short as the demon kicked his foot out to one side. Wyona, sensing the movement out of the corner of her eye, lunged towards it with both swords.

The demon laughed and reached out a clawed fist towards her unguarded chest, claws sinking deep into her skin. Wyona let out a choking gasp, dropping both swords and hanging off the beast's claws as the demon inspected the blood beginning to flow past his hands with the critical eye of a professional.

Etheos threw his hand forward and said *"Evyqu ely zeku re eov eyz!"*

Stryver blinked, his eyes going milky white for a full five seconds before leaping to his feet with the agility of a cat and grabbing his sword from the floor.

The demon was too preoccupied with blood, the universal obsession of his race, and did not notice.

Stryver took in the situation in a moment as Wyona, eyes rolling back in her head, fell off his fist and onto the floor. He stared at her for a moment, a vein throbbing in his neck, and then he said "You thieving, careless bastard" and ducked the demon's clawing reach by crouching beside Wyona and searching her pockets.

Sir Humphrey was about to step forward with his axe to behead the demon, reminding himself later to give Stryver a thorough lecture about looting the corpses of the dead while there were still demons trying to kill them all, but Stryver said "Knew it!" at this point and drew something out of Wyona's pocket, stood, and held it out firmly in front of the demon.

It was a mirror.

The demon hovered quite still for a moment in the air and then it let out an inhuman roar before trying to turn and fly out the window. It never made it. It began to glow in a strange white light that soon engulfed him. Then the ball of white light compressed, becoming smaller and smaller until it was about the size of a fist before it zoomed into the mirror in Stryver's hand. The mirror glowed white for a moment and then turned back to normal, except it no longer reflected the room but a series of moving shadows.

The two demons holding the king in the air both made a noise akin to "eep" and disappeared with a pop. Well, one of them disappeared with a pop. The other turned into a six-year-old girl wearing green robes and pigtails. Both she and the king fell to the floor.

"Dara!" Etheos gasped. "I *knew* it!"

Dara the Diviner looked about her. She saw the king and her eyes went very wide. She saw Sir Humphrey and Etheos and they went wider. She saw Wyona surrounded by blood and began to cry.

"I—I want my mommy!" She wiped her nose and face with her sleeve, but continued to sob on the floor.

The king gave her a funny look before standing and adjusting his white night cap, which was embroidered with gold thread to look like a crown. "I'd like someone to explain to me what's going on!" he said gruffly, looking at Sir Humphrey, as he was the only reliable looking figure in the room. "What's happening, Sir Knight? Is the city under attack? Why have those monsters come to murder me in my bed?"

"It was a curse, your majesty," Sir Humphrey said. "Set by a jealous clairvoyant upon your grandfather. Those demons—"

"Were controlled by her!" Etheos said, pointing at Dara. "*She* summoned them, your majesty! It's her fault!"

The king looked down at the wailing little girl at his feet. "This child? Summoned demons?"

"I'm not a child!" Dara sniffed, rubbing her nose. "I'm a diviner! Second class! I wrote—I wrote all the spells protecting you right now!"

"Or not protecting him!" Etheos raged. "If you can't tell, Miss *diviner*, they're all broken!"

"Well, that's not my fault!" Dara wailed. "How was I supposed to know that a horde of *demons* was coming to call?"

"Because you summoned them, that's how! You summoned them to kill the king by the first full moon of his twenty-eighth year!"

"I'm twenty-five!" the King yelled. "I am!" he insisted to Sir Humphrey's raised eyebrow.

"That's stupid!" Dara yelled back at Etheos, looking like she was going to have a tantrum. "You're stupid! The full moon isn't for another *week* and the king's birthday is in three months!"

"Actually, it's tomorrow," the King corrected her. "And this is a pretty lousy birthday present if I do say so."

"No it isn't!" Dara yelled at him, folding her arms across her chest. "It's in three months!"

"Oh, isn't it obvious?" Stryver yelled at all four of them from where he was kneeling beside Wyona. His face was very red and he looked exceedingly angry. "You've been inhabited by a demon for three months because you were the only one who knew precisely what spells were on the castle and the king, and therefore the only one who could break them effectively thus making you the best candidate for demon possession. The threatening notes you wrote to the guards as well as your out-of-character behavior are all part of your possession, explaining the gross differences in handwriting and magical skill. Now that the demon lord is trapped in the mirror, the imps under his command have no choice but to abandon all possessions, duties, and side projects in this realm and return to the one from whence they came." He said all of this in one breath and took a moment to inhale sharply while everyone else stared at him. "Now will you *please* be quiet?" He didn't let any of them answer, but turned back to Wyona, who wasn't breathing, bowing his head and mur-

muring to himself under his breath.

The king gave him a strange look and whispered to Sir Humphrey, "Who's he?"

"Stryver, your majesty," Sir Humphrey replied. "And Wyona Wyncliff. Changelings, your majesty, who—"

"Oh, Changelings?" the king said with a sigh of relief. "Is that all? I thought for a moment it was someone important. Wouldn't do to have someone important dying in a bloody mess on my imported rug. I'd get nasty letters from foreign embassies and it'd probably start a war and all that mess." He frowned. "Come to think of it, I don't think I much care to have someone unimportant dying in a bloody mess on my imported rug either. You there!" he called. "Can't you do that somewhere else?"

"There is very little *time*, old man," Stryver said in a hiss, without looking up. "Please don't interrupt again."

"What? Is it some sort of primitive Changeling funeral—Old man!" the king exploded. "Old man! I'll have you know, impudent boy, that I am twenty-five years old tomor—today! That's hardly *old* is it? I don't think I care for your tone and your friends insistence upon bleeding all over my—"

"Look!" Dara said. "She's breathing again. I don't think dead people usually do that."

Indeed she was. Stryver, who was completely ignoring the king's blustering, had gone on muttering under his breath over Wyona. And she was breathing. Raggedly, faintly, but it became stronger as he went on.

The king didn't seem to be impressed. "And what are a pair of Changelings doing in my bed chamber at this hour of the night? Are you registered? You were behind that demon attack, weren't you? You can't—"

"With all due respect, your majesty," Sir Humphrey said, watching Wyona's chest rise and fall. "Shut up."

The King stared at him. "How can you—"

"*Quyjulzu!*" Dara said, waving her hand.

The King's mouth kept moving, but no words came out.

"Well, it was awfully annoying," Dara said defensively when

Etheos gave her a disapproving look. "Besides, how would you like to do a resurrection spell with a great hot head yelling things at you?"

"A resurrection spell?" Etheos said, watching as Wyona's breath grew stronger. "But those never work! Besides, he isn't even a wiz—"

"Well, it's something like it then," Dara said with a shrug. "Maybe I'll write a thesis paper on it and they'll promote me to Grand Wizard."

"Not before I do," Etheos muttered under his breath.

Wyona's eyes suddenly snapped open. She took a deep, gasping breath and sat up. Though her Sky Rider's garb was still covered in blood, there was no wound to speak of. She looked around the room, apparently not surprised at seeing Dara or the king trying without success to shout. Then she turned to Stryver and slapped him across the face. "You interrupted my nap," she said, sounding rather miffed.

"Such thanks I get for saving your life," Stryver muttered, picking up his sword.

"Well, I got even less thanks from you after I saved yours," Wyona retorted.

"Oh!" Dara said, laughing and clapping her hands. "So that's it. I'd nearly forgotten about that."

"What?" Sir Humphrey asked.

"Would *you* like to explain it, Etheos?" Dara asked. "Since you're the powerful, wise thaumaturge?"

Etheos glared at her. "No, go ahead," he muttered, having no idea what she was talking about.

"It's a very old magic, going along with one of those primitive but strong principles that old magic always does," Dara said. "A life for a life. Some time ago Miss Wyona must have saved his life and so he had the power to recall her back to hers. Of course, it only works if one has a strong concentration, powerful force of mind and—" Dara broke off, staring hard at Stryver, and then burst out laughing.

"And what?" Sir Humphrey demanded.

Dara continued to giggle. "He probably wouldn't like me to say," she said. "Though I'm sure knowledgeable old Etheos can tell you."

Sir Humphrey looked inquiringly at Etheos but Etheos muttered, "I'll tell you later" through gritted teeth by which he meant as soon as he could look it up in the library.

The king was hopping up and down now, in a righteous rage.

"I suppose I'd best release him," Dara said. "Else he'll hurt himself."

"Give me—us a head start at least," Stryver said. "He probably can't wait to behead us for attempted regicide."

"They won't want to admit that demons can find their way into the Academy," Wyona agreed with a nod.

And the one became a cat and the other a raven. Both went to the window, one soaring out into the night and the other leaping, presumably towards a tree.

Dara waved her hand and the king could once more be heard. At full volume. " … And who let those Changelings in here in the first place? What sort of idiot guardsmen would let those shady characters—where'd they go?"

"They got away, your majesty," Dara said, rising to her feet. "And—" She yawned. "I'm sleepy. I haven't had my nap today."

She disappeared in a snap and puff of smoke.

"Can you do that?" Sir Humphrey asked Etheos.

"Shut up!" Etheos said irritably.

"You two!" the king said. "I suppose, since you haven't fled like dirty rats—or Changelings—you must be responsible for saving my life from whatever the hell happened here. For that, I think I'll award you both Magenta Medals of Merit at my birthday celebration tomorrow. Because my life—hey! What happened to my solid gold wash basin?"

"Probably Stryver, your majesty," Sir Humphrey said. "Valuable things have a habit of finding their way into his coat. May we go now, your majesty? There's a pig waiting for me who's probably already very grumpy with me for not being home."

"Tyrannical wife, eh?" the king said with a nod. "Yes, I know what that's about. Get on home to her, then."

"Actually, your majes—" But Etheos pulled him out the door before he could correct the king again.

The Ghostly Misadventure

S ir Humphrey waded up the street, ignoring completely the muck floating by his boots or the heavy downpour all around him. The small woman in his arms—Mrs. Merrill Malone who lived in the flat below he and Etheos—was holding a battered umbrella over their heads, but water was dripping from it, pinging onto his helmet, and running down into his hair. It had been raining for two weeks straight. More than half the city was flooded. People were holed up in the upper floors of their homes, too frightened to risk going out in it. The streets had become rivers, navigated by urchins atop ramshackle rafts and idle bits of sewage and refuse.

Sir Humphrey had laughed in his usual jovial spirits when it had begun to be a problem. "The city was due for a good cleaning anyway, Etheos. Now all that trash will float down to the merchant district." He chuckled. "I hear tell that the Lord Chamberlain has taken up residence in his house maid's room in the attic to avoid the waters." Now, however, it really was no laughing matter. Everything was in complete and utter chaos.

Who knew how many the rushing waters had killed? How many villains had been left to prowl the streets unchecked? The knights were doing all they could, but they were foot soldiers, not sailors. People were panicking, and that didn't help matters. There was little food to be had, even if one did have the courage to venture out, and some said that the Goblyns and other terrifying things had crawled up from the sewers. Sir Humphrey himself had been patrolling the merchant district the previous night—being the only member of the force capable of withstanding the torrent there which would surely have swept other knights away to drown—and he could've sworn he'd seen a great, slimy tail as big as a horse sliding beneath the surface. He had convinced himself it was a trick of the light and went on with his duties.

And there were plenty of duties to be had. Even on his days off he found it necessary to help out, like today for instance, escorting Merrill Malone to see her sister, who had been hiccupping up minnows of increasing size since the flood began, and wanted to consult Etheos before they turned into trout. Etheos, however, was in no mood to be consulted about hiccups. He was still very upset because he hadn't been to the Academy in a week and was sure his peers who were lucky enough to be caught there were using the time to get ahead of him.

"It's not fair," Etheos muttered, sitting at the table with his arms folded sullenly across his chest, watching Sir Humphrey cook the scrawny chicken they were set to have for supper. "I could be locked in the library right now."

"Cheer up, Etheos," Sir Humphrey chided him, still in a rather gloomy mood from trekking with Merrill Malone through the desperate city. "It doesn't matter so much. Why, you were just telling me last month how the Academy library is grossly inefficient."

Etheos shook his head.

"How they didn't have the third edition of the sixth volume of *Murderous Mint Patties and Other Deceptive Treats*," Sir Humphrey continued.

"No, they didn't have the second edition of volumes four, eight, and nineteen," Etheos corrected. "And it's really aggravating too, because you know they're selling them just down the road at Lark the Bard's—" He stopped and broke into his scowl again. "Not that it matters anyway. Since I'm stuck here."

George the Dragon, who had been excitedly exploring the contents of the third pantry, poked his head around the door, his face covered in flour. He coughed once or twice, shooting tiny sparks.

Sir Humphrey frowned at him. "Get out of there!" he said irritably. "That's no place for you. And don't you go bothering the Lady Orville!" Sir Humphrey ordered as he saw George's eyes twitch towards the coat closet that was her room. "You know she's been feeling very under the weather!"

"I think we're all feeling under the weather," Etheos said, scratching George's scaly head as the dragon leapt up onto the table. "It's because there's so much of it."

Sir Humphrey shook his head. "The Lady Orville's worse off. Even since before the rain. It's because of the Astur House, you know."

Etheos frowned. "That old wreck? On the edge of Ghosts Corners? What's that got to do with anything?"

"Didn't you read it in the paper?" Sir Humphrey asked sharply.

"No, of course not. There hasn't been any paper for a week and a half!" Etheos protested.

"Before that," Sir Humphrey said. "Someone's bought the Astur House."

"Can't imagine who," Etheos said. "Moldy and rotting is what it is. It'll fall apart right over their heads."

"That's what they're hoping," Sir Humphrey said. "They're tearing it down. The article didn't say who they were or what they were planning to build on the site. I saved it. It's over there in *The Pirate's Cook Book*."

Etheos reached over and took the cookbook from where it was lying with a few others on the opposite side of the table. Sir Humphrey was accustomed to clipping out articles of interest and sticking them in between the pages of his cookbooks. Etheos was forced to flip through a report on dairy farms from three years ago (which had a lovely picture of the farm just next to Sir Humphrey's sister Elda's, as was noted in the margin), three status reports from the commander of the Knights of Galahad's Hall in which Sir Humphrey was alluded to, though not named, and even a small, battered clipping noting Etheos' rise to the rank of Thaumaturge from Prestidigitator, his name underlined in a list of five or six. At last he came to the one in question, between a recipe for tuna soufflé and one for raspberry cordial, easily the newest article, though much of the ink was blurred together from the inescapable wet. Etheos was still able to make out the picture, though, of the towering, dark mansion that stood on the border between Ghost Corners and Thieves' Den, its large front windows gaping and its rusty gate untended.

"Good riddance," Etheos said. "That old place has been deserted for years. Finally, all those silly rumors of it being haunted will stop."

"I shouldn't think so," Sir Humphrey said. "If anything, it's stirred things up. Especially the stories of the lost buried fortune of Lord Astur. Some people say the anonymous new owners are searching for it. And that his ghost is guarding it."

Etheos closed the book with a resounding snap. "How many times do I have to tell you, Humphrey? There's no such thing as ghosts. At least not unless it's a very special, disastrous circumstance."

"I think Lord Astur is a special, disastrous circumstance," Sir Humphrey said, carrying the plate of chicken to the table. "All his family died so tragically. His wife of the plague, his son in that accident at the Academy library—"

Etheos shuddered. "It's everyone's nightmare to be crushed under a stack of encyclopedias. Knowledge is deadly."

"—And then, his son-in-law, his only heir after that, died in that freak unicorn mauling incident. Tragic, really. Poor Lord Astur. Had no one to leave his fortune to."

"What about his daughter?" Etheos asked, frowning. "Whatever happened to—"

Sir Humphrey stared at him. "But Etheos—don't you remember?"

Etheos blinked. "No. Should I?"

"Well she—she happened to be on the wrong end of a curse at the king's annual wine guzzling."

Etheos' eyes widened. "So—"

"Etheos, have you *ever* paid attention to the Lady Orville?"

"She's a *pig*!" Etheos protested.

"She's a lady of court!" Sir Humphrey argued. "Daughter of Lord Astur, widow of the late Lord Orville, and rightful owner of Astur House and the lost fortune. That is, if it weren't lost."

"And if pigs could rightfully inherit," Etheos pointed out.

"That too," Sir Humphrey agreed, shaking his head. "Sad bit of business anyway. Why if I—"

He was never able to finish for a loud crack of lightning sounded outside and the window blew open.

"Drat this confounded weather!" Sir Humphrey stormed, rising to close it as the various papers lying strewn about the room took flight in a flurry of white, ink-stained flakes and the candles all blew out.

George was faster, however, pouncing in the dark.

There was a loud screech and hiss, a few sparks flew, and by the time Etheos could shout a light spell, there was George sitting with confused disappointment in the lap of Stryver, who was sitting on the floor of their kitchen, soaked through, the collar of his purple coat singed.

Stryver scowled at George and shoved him away, standing and trying to adjust his coat, which was dripping onto the floor. "It's exceedingly rude to try to eat visitors," he chided George, wringing out his hair into a little puddle of water on the floor. He looked up at Sir Humphrey and said, "Well, it's raining cats and dogs out there," by way of apology.

"Cats, anyway," Etheos said. "What do you want, coming barging in here like this? We were just in the middle of supper."

"So I see," Stryver replied, casually taking a piece of chicken off the nearest plate. "Although it tastes a bit dry to me. Could do with more pepper."

"You can make your chicken any way you please," Sir Humphrey said. "This is how I make mine and since you weren't invited—"

"Quite right," Stryver said, placing his hands behind his back. "I've actually come on business."

"Really?" Etheos asked. "Where's Wyona?"

"How the devil should I know?" Stryver asked. "Probably holed up somewhere bemoaning her wet feathers. Can't fly like that, you know. Not that I particularly like being this wet myself," he added, looking down at his drenched clothing and then imploringly at Etheos, who completely ignored him. He shook his head after a moment and then continued. "But it is urgent. I must borrow your dragon."

"George?" Etheos cried. "What do you want with him?"

"To borrow him," Stryver repeated.

"Why?" Etheos demanded. "What're you going to do to him?"

"Nothing!" Stryver insisted. "I wouldn't dream of hurting—"

"Why do you need to borrow my dragon?" Etheos asked. George, who was sitting at his feet, looked just as curious and suspicious as his master. "You'd better explain the whole thing or I won't even consider it. I know you, Stryver, you're always up to no good."

"That's an unfair stereotype," Stryver said with a sniff. "Not *always* up to no good." He looked as if he were about to continue, perhaps with an example, but did not, sitting down instead, perhaps because he could not think of one. "You're a knight," he said to Sir Humphrey. "Have you ever heard of the Order of the Dragon?"

"No," Sir Humphrey said. "But it sounds like Black Magic to me."

"Yes," Stryver agreed. "Their members do have a habit of being arrested under that charge. It's a cult of sorts, a Masonic group that worships the image of the dragon."

"Seems like something we at the Hall would know about," Sir Humphrey rumbled with a frown.

"They aren't very large," Stryver replied with a shrug. "Only take in a select group, many of them high-class city officials too. They don't do anything harmful really. A few strange rituals and chants, animal sacrifice, the occasional black magic spell...but nothing really disastrous like burning down stables or kidnapping virgins in the night. They just have a dragon obsession and like wearing funny-looking robes. Sort of like yours," he added to Etheos. "Except with bejeweled little masks."

"If they aren't doing anything particularly dastardly, then how are you involved with them?" Sir Humphrey asked.

"Well, the thing is, they happen to have, in their possession, the papers of some past members—some exceedingly rich past members—and among them, so I've heard, is a treasure map."

"And you want to get at this map?" Etheos asked. "Where does George come in?"

Stryver shrugged. "A mere distraction. It will only take ten minutes or so. Their headquarters is not far, and being that, without this rain, it would be a full moon tonight, they're sure to be meeting now. I'll just take your dragon, pop down there, and come right back. Promise."

"I wouldn't trust him, Etheos," Sir Humphrey said with narrowed eyes.

"Of course I don't trust him," Etheos said.

"Oh, come on, please?" Stryver said, somehow perfecting a sad puppy look. "You're the only one I know who's got a dragon, and it seems an awful waste to steal one just for ten minutes."

"Why don't you just find Wyona, follow her, and take the map when she gets it?" Etheos asked. "You know she probably has a better plan than you anyway."

"For the last time, bird brain is not here, does not know about the Order and the map, and does *not* have a better plan than me!" Stryver exploded. "Who ended up with the treasure of Merlyn?"

"Only after you stole it from her," Etheos said.

"Are you going to lend me your dragon or not?" Stryver asked.

Etheos was still frowning.

"Aren't you just the least bit interested in the treasure?" Stryver asked. "I'd be willing to give you…some of it."

"What do you think, George?" Etheos asked, looking down at the lap dragon.

George remained still for a moment, as if considering. And then leapt forward onto Stryver, knocking him to the ground once more. Stryver looked as if he were about to curse and shove the dragon away again, but then thought the better of it, picking him up and standing instead.

"Thanks a million. Won't be but a minute." And he headed for the door.

"No you don't," Etheos said. "I'm coming with you."

"What?" Stryver demanded.

"I don't trust you," Etheos said, tugging on a heavy pair of rain boots.

"But—but—"

Sir Humphrey sighed. "I suppose I'd best come as well. There's no telling what sort of trouble you three are liable to get into."

Before Stryver could protest anything, Sir Humphrey shouted a goodbye to Lady Orville, still in the closet, and shoved the Changeling and Etheos out the door, down the hall, and into the torrential weather.

It was slow going indeed outside. Etheos was nearly sucked under twice, and Stryver had an uncanny ability to blend in with the shadows so that, were it not for his continuous stream of curses regarding the wet, they would have had no idea where to go. As it was, Stryver led them down the street, turning left, and then doubling back up another one, stopping in front of a darkened, narrow house that looked just the same as the others. The journey, on a normal night, would have taken seven minutes. In those conditions, it took them thirty. Sir Humphrey nearly tripped on what had once been a flight of stairs leading up to the front door, and the three paused on the landing where the water was only a small puddle.

"They used to meet in the basement," Stryver said, wringing out his hair once more. "But I daresay that's changed."

"Are you sure they're in there?" Etheos asked skeptically. The windows were boarded up.

"Of course I'm sure!" Stryver hissed. "I've been planning this for—for some time."

"I'm sure," Etheos said. "We aren't going to just walk in the front door are we?"

"Why not?" Stryver said, having finished fussing over his hair, reaching for the knob.

"It just doesn't seem the proper way to sneak into the meeting of a secret Black Magic organization," Etheos said. "I mean, Wyona would have this brilliant plan involving secret passages and disguises and—"

"Well maybe that's why she always loses to me!" Stryver said hotly. "We're doing it *my* way." And with that, he opened the door.

He had to duck rather quickly because a glinting throwing star went sailing towards his head and out into the darkness beyond, thrown by the guard, who had obviously anticipated their arrival and had another throwing star and a jagged-edged dagger in his hands. He was dressed in a long, green robe and his head was entirely shaved except for a dark forelock. Over his face he wore a gold mask that bore a chilly, impassive expression. He screeched a strange battle cry and threw another star, which embedded itself in the doorframe, only narrowly missing Stryver, who had stepped nonchalantly into the house. Then he rushed forward, his dagger raised, shrieking.

Stryver calmly drew his own sword in one fluid motion, knocked the dagger from the man's hand, and ran him through, all so quickly that Etheos thought he might have missed it.

The man made a strange gurgling noise and fell onto the floor, a pool of dark blood forming beneath him.

"You see?" Stryver said. "That's the easy way. Bird brain always does things the hard way. My way's better."

"Actually, I think—" Etheos began.

"Well, no one asked you, did they?" Stryver retorted hotly. "Now follow me, be quiet, and don't touch anything!"

He sheathed his sword after meticulously wiping it with his handkerchief and continued up the stairs, his feet making no sounds against the old wood. They turned down a corridor at the top and, silent as the grave, crouched outside two large double doors, one ajar, through which flickering candlelight was pouring.

Sir Humphrey could tell that the room beyond had been originally furnished as a visiting parlor, but the members of the Order of the Dragon had done the best they could. Most of the heavy motheaten furniture had been pushed to one side and covered in dark cloth, giving an ominous presence to the shadows, for the room was lit only by an ornate chandelier filled with dripping candles and a brazier on the hearth. The room was filled with members—perhaps fifteen or twenty—all dressed in the same dark green robes as the guard downstairs, and all wearing the rather disconcerting gold masks, though some of theirs were decorated more ornately than others. Three figures stood near the brazier, before the barren hearth. One of them, in the center, was a man with an entirely shaved head and a large emerald in the center of the forehead of his golden mask. He was speaking when the three peered through the crack, chanting in a strange language that Sir Humphrey could not understand, but which Etheos whispered sounded very like a folk song about daisies in Ancient Scriptorian. To his right was a taller figure in the same green robe and gold mask who stood with his hands folded across his chest in an X as if he were a corpse in a coffin. His hair, unlike most of the others in the room, was not shaved, but mingled with the shadows in dark waves. To the central figure's left was a smaller man, seated and scribbling down something with a cheap quill on cheaper parchment. His golden mask was covered with ink-stained fingerprints and he had a terrible cough.

"Brothers!" the man in the center finally said, lapsing into common tongue after his chant had ended. "I do offer my most sincere and grieved apologies at this most unpleasant setting, but our usual secret lair is under the depths of a great sea, teeming with untold horrors sprung up from the vile refuse and sewers of this evil city."

There was some assorted grumbling from the members of the Order at this point.

"Fortunately and most happily, the Sacred Dragon smiles upon our endeavors once more for our dear and most beloved brother Smittus was able to rescue—not without peril of life and limb—our most sacred tapestry and effigy."

He gestured above his head where one could just make out a threadbare, rather second-rate tapestry hanging above the mantel along with a golden statuette of a long-bellied dragon.

"Our reverential thanks, most dear and beloved brother Smittus," the assorted party chanted together.

The man writing furiously—obviously Smittus—leapt to his feet at this loud chorus chanting his name, brandishing his quill pen and looking about nervously. When he saw there was nothing to fear, however, he took his seat once more, which Sir Humphrey saw was atop a stack of books, another such stack lying beside him.

"Dear brothers of the most sacred and ancient Order of the Dragon!" the leader continued. "Let us begin our most secret proceedings."

"Let us begin, O Reverential leader," came the responding chant, though Sir Humphrey thought some of the members in the back sounded rather bored.

"Let us begin with a prayer of thanksgiving to our most sacred and wise protector, the Sacred Dragon, for his deliverance to us of the means to gain a new, more glorious headquarters!"

"Let us give thanks to the Sacred Dragon," came the reply. Yes, they definitely sounded bored. It reminded Etheos distinctly of the time—back when he was just a boy—when his professor had forced the entire class to recite conjugations of wizardric verbs for an entire hour.

"Let us give thanks to the most Sacred Dragon and commend to him the soul of our dear, departed, and most beloved brother, Fleet Wings, and give thanks that in his death, at least, our Order can benefit all the more."

"Give thanks to Fleet Wings," replied the members. Sir Humphrey could hear one of the ones standing in the back humming softly to himself.

"We shall build ourselves a new lair, my brethren!" the leader intoned. "A new domain where we may all live in perfect harmony with the Sacred Dragon and grow and expand until this wretched city and all the surrounding lands have seen the light and come into our power!" He seemed to be very excited. His followers were less enthused.

"And on this sacred spot—"

They never got to hear the rest of this stirring and most assuredly moving speech, for Stryver, without warning, grabbed George from Etheos, pushed open the door, and walked easily into the room.

The members of the Order of the Dragon were so startled that they made way for him, aghast looks on their faces, until he was face to face with the leader himself, who looked properly scandalized.

"Good evening, gentlemen," Stryver said casually. "And my respects to the most Sacred Dragon, of course," he added as an afterthought, giving the statuette a military salute.

"What—what is the meaning of this?" the leader spluttered. "Who are you? How did you get in here? GUARD!"

"Now don't get so excited!" Stryver cried. "I was just in the neighborhood and thought I'd drop by with a little gift for my dear friends. Here you are." He lifted up George and plopped him into Smittus' lap. The little man yelped, throwing his quill into the air and trying to shove George away. George didn't seem very pleased, and hiccupped a few sparks of fire onto him.

"A *dragon?*" the leader cried, seizing George at once.

"That's right," Stryver said, and no one seemed to notice—except the man on the other side of the leader who still had not moved, but had very sharp eyes—that he had slipped one of Smittus' books into his coat pocket. "I thought to myself, who better to appreciate such a formidable, worthy specimen of the dragon than you lot?"

"A worthy gift, sir," the leader proclaimed, after examining George closely. "He's magnificent."

George took very well to being called magnificent, and allowed himself to be admired and stroked.

"Were you looking for admittance, sir?" the leader asked.

"Not just yet, no," Stryver said. "But I would think it a high compliment if your most esteemed order would look well upon me."

"Indeed," the leader replied. "Then you must stay for the celebration."

"Oh, celebration?" Stryver asked with polite curiosity.

"Yes," the leader said, motioning to Smittus, who produced a small golden bowl from somewhere in his pocket. "The celebration of your joyous gift."

"Sounds like a smashing good time," Stryver said, edging towards the door. "But I've really got to—"

"Oh, don't be so hasty," one of the members nearest him piped up. The Order of the Dragon was actually starting to look lively now, eager smiles appearing behind their masks. "This is the best part."

"Really?" Stryver asked. "Are you going to worship him or teach him how to do tricks or something?"

"Oh no," the member laughed. "No, we cut his throat and then drink his blood. It's great."

"What—"

But Stryver had no time to stop anything, and neither did Etheos, who burst through the door as well, though no one noticed. The leader had already taken hold of George's head in one hand, stretching his long snake-like neck out with the practiced air of one who had slaughtered animals in such a way many times before. Smittus held the bowl at the ready, and the tall man finally lowered his hands. There was a golden dagger in one of them.

The leader was chanting in another language again as the taller man readied the knife. Strangely, he did not seem as excited as the others.

"And now," the leader intoned, slightly disjointedly because of George's furious struggling. "Our high priestess shall cut his most sacred throat."

Before anyone could do anything more, the High Priestess raised the knife high in the air and, after hesitating only a moment, cut the cord on the wall nearest her, which held the gigantic chandelier. It fell to the floor with a crash. Everyone screamed, and the candles spilled onto the carpet, which burst into flame in an instant. In a moment, members of the Order of the Dragon were running about the room screaming, thrashing, and causing general havoc because their long robes were on fire and the blaze quickly spread to the dark drapes and walls.

The High Priestess cast off her mask and seized George from the leader's astonished hands.

"Wyona!" Sir Humphrey cried.

"Knew she had a better plan than you!" Etheos shouted to Stryver, but found that the feline Changeling was nowhere to be seen.

"Sorry, dear," Wyona said complacently to the leader, who was howling and batting at the hem of his robes. "But it isn't working out." And, George in hand, she walked calmly through the blaze, sidestepping bursts of flame and shrieking members of the cult, and reached Sir Humphrey and Etheos at the door.

"Well," she said, handing George to Etheos. "Perhaps we should go."

There was no time to argue with her then. The house was falling down around their ears. The fire had spread and it was a wonder they made it down the stairs, bits of ash and flaming pieces of wood crashing down about them like a deadly rain. They followed Wyona's long strides right out the front door, and didn't stop until they were into the street, wading through water easily chest high on Sir Humphrey and Wyona. Etheos, trying not to think about what the squishy thing he had just stepped on was, followed a little behind, battling the water, George seated precariously atop his head, tongue flicking out of his mouth speculatively. He didn't like swimming, as a rule.

They followed Wyona almost blindly down the street, and neither Sir Humphrey, carrying his axe above his head, nor Etheos, trying to recall the single swimming lesson he had received in youth, thought to say anything when she did not lead them back up the way towards their apartments, instead turning the other way, towards the outskirts of Ghost Corners. In fact, none of them said anything at all until they were standing before the gates of the foreboding mansion, a bulky mass in the darkness.

"What the—" Etheos began, but nearly slipped and went under in his astonishment.

Wyona shoved open the gate, which nearly disintegrated in her hands anyway, and led them up what used to be a very nice front walk, past once beautiful rose bushes long untended—and now drowned in any case—and up the crumbling front steps until they stood in the shadows, beneath a phrase in ancient script carved into the wall, which none of them could even see in the darkness. Sir Humphrey would later return in more favorable conditions and determine its meaning to be either "Forever Vigilant" or "Jump for the Weasel" depending on the dialect. Sir Humphrey, it should be noted, was never a very astute scholar in the first place, let alone where dead and decaying dialects were concerned.

"This is the Astur House," Wyona said without preamble. "Recently acquired by the Order of the Dragon. They want to make it their new headquarters. And possibly find some gold as well."

"You mean *that's* the treasure map Stryver wanted?" Sir Humphrey asked.

Wyona pursed her lips. "He very nearly ruined things for me. Luckily, I've already gotten the only thing of value they had. Here."

She grasped the large, rusting handle and gave a good tug. The door opened with a swift shriek of protest from the hinges. Wyona stepped inside calmly, the floodwaters still ankle deep in the room beyond. Sir Humphrey and Etheos hesitated on the threshold.

"It's supposed to be haunted," Sir Humphrey said warily.

"It probably is," Wyona replied calmly. "But I don't fear shadows."

Sir Humphrey walked in resolutely after her, though Etheos— who was about to give his lecture on ghosts being exceedingly rare— noted that he held his axe at the ready, though what use he thought it would be against spirits, the wizard had no idea.

"If you would be so kind, Sir Thaumaturge," Wyona's voice said from somewhere in the darkness.

Etheos reached up to the dim outline of a candle in an iron holder in the wall, said a word, and it flared to life. They were standing in an entrance hall with high ceilings and what must have once been impressive elaborate wood paneling. Now, however, it was worm-eaten and covered in thick cobwebs that shrouded the carvings beyond recognition. The floor they stood on, under the water, had once been a costly marble, and the entrance hall opened out into a magnificent front room with a grand staircase spiraling upwards and a fireplace on one wall, over which hung a faded coat of arms and a ceremonial sword. A large mirror, lined with spider web cracks, graced an entire wall near at hand. The flame from the candles, which Etheos was lighting as they went, flared back at them in it, bathing them in a strange half-light that did nothing to dissuade the eerie feeling weighing close on Sir Humphrey's heart.

"You see," Wyona said, drawing a folded parchment from her pocket (she had discarded the cumbersome green robe somewhere on the trek and was dressed once more in her Sky Rider's garb). Etheos took the parchment and, squinting in the dim light, saw that it was a letter discussing import taxes in a spidery, faded script.

"What—"

"Turn it over," Wyona suggested, frowning at her reflection in the gold-edged mirror.

Etheos flipped it over and saw these words, inscribed in a sprawling hand, which he read aloud, almost as if he were reciting a spell.

When full moons rise and dead men speak
When the clever prey upon the weak
And homes, long gone, are known once more,
Then one long past shall point the way
By the light of coming day
Behind the golden tower door

"What does it mean?" he asked.

"It was the only thing of value among Lord Astur's papers," Wyona said distractedly, stepping closer to the mirror and placing a tentative hand on its cool surface. "The Order of the Dragon won't miss it."

"I shouldn't wonder why," Etheos said. "It isn't a proper prophecy at all. Everyone knows such things can't be written in plain languages for everyone—"

There was a loud crash and clatter, like pans falling, which echoed through the door to their left. Etheos and Sir Humphrey whirled at the noise, but Wyona acted as if she didn't even hear, running her hand along one of the darkened cracks in the mirror.

"What was that?" Sir Humphrey asked, holding his axe in front of him.

"Probably ghosts," Wyona said complacently.

"There's no such—" Etheos turned to glare at her, but he was never able to finish what promised to be a very enraged rant, for at that moment Wyona screamed. Sir Humphrey later realized that she must have seen the misty figure in place of her own reflection. The hazy form of a young girl floated out of the mirror, went right through Wyona as if she weren't even there, and circled above their heads twice before alighting on the topmost stair of the grand staircase that was free of water. Sir Humphrey lifted Wyona to her feet as she had fallen with an ungraceful splash into the floodwaters, and took a few steps forward, his axe before him. She looked young, perhaps twelve years old, with a slightly pointed chin and thick curls that floated around her face as if she were underwater. Her dress seemed to fan about her as if gravity did not weigh her down, and she seemed to be entirely composed of a glowing mist that made her expression somewhat hazy and transparent. But it was not hazy enough to miss the marks on her neck, as if she had been strangled.

"What manner of unnatural—"

"Are you friends of Uncle's?" she asked, a perplexed look on her face.

Sir Humphrey stopped, just as confused, at this entirely normal sounding voice. "What—"

"You don't look like Uncle's friends," she continued. "And it's awfully late for visitors. I didn't even hear you knock."

"Well, we—" Sir Humphrey lowered his axe and her dark little eyes—indeed the only part about her that was not glowing—alighted on it. Her expression changed to one of horror and in the next moment she was shrieking.

"Guards! Wentworth! Amelia! Help! Help! They'll murder us all!" Her scream, so shrill and piercing, echoed about the entire empty house.

Well…nearly empty…

The door to their left burst open and five bulky men in full dress armor clanked out. Except that their feet weren't touching the ground. They seemed to be composed of the same glowing mist as the girl, and in their hands they bore spears and swords, bearing the crest of Sir Galahad's Hall. They stood at attention for a moment, and then rushed at the three, spears thrust forward and swords raised, their boots floating above the water.

Etheos shrieked out a spell in what sounded like a shrill, old woman voice, and a stone wall suddenly appeared in front of them, but the five guards rushed right through it in an instant as if it weren't even there. Wyona promptly became a raven and soared over their heads to land at the top of the stair with a shrill caw.

Sir Humphrey let out his battle cry and, in one mighty stroke, swung his axe towards the oncoming foe. It flew right out of his hands, missing the attack entirely—though nearly lopping off Etheos' head had he not the sense to duck—and crashing into the far wall, causing little bits of plaster to fall from the ceiling. Sir Humphrey turned and sprinted surprisingly lithely to the fireplace, wrenching the sword from its place on the wall. It was much smaller and lighter than anything Sir Humphrey had previously wielded—except once when he'd been sent on Safari and forced to use a machete—and it felt like a child's toy in his large hands.

Still, not to be daunted, he roared and leapt towards his assailants, swinging the flimsy sword wildly. They raised their spears threateningly, not letting off the charge. The two neared each other, each showing the fearless strength and matchless bravery that Sir Galahad's Hall has always been famous for, past and present. One of the knights thrust his spear forward, burying it deep in Sir Humphrey's chest, going right through his mail and out the other side—which would have been the most extraordinary of things, had not the knight himself done the same in another moment.

Sir Humphrey would remember feeling exceedingly cold and hearing strange, garbled voices in his head for a moment, as the knight—shadow of a long defeated warrior—passed through him. And when he next turned to face them, they were gone as was the girl on the steps. Wyona was standing in her place, her face once again unreadable.

"I told you there were ghosts," she said calmly.

Etheos was shaking. "That—that was—" He cleared his throat and squared his shoulders. "The Academy should be informed of this situation at once! The Masters are the only proper authorities to deal with a supernatural situation of this—this magnitude. We should go now and—"

Wyona smiled wryly. "Running away, Sir Thaumaturge?" She shook her head. "You saw them attack Sir Humphrey, didn't you? They can't hurt you."

"How do you know?" Etheos asked. "They could have all sorts of powers that we don't know about! That's why Sir Humphrey and I—Sir Humphrey! Sir Humphrey, what are you doing?" he demanded.

The knight was sloshing about, trying to peer through the murky water. "Looking for my axe!" he said, frowning. "I could've sworn it landed over here."

A sharp, inhuman screech echoed through the house, filling the still air about them.

"Sounds like a dragon," Wyona remarked.

"Yes, perhaps George—" Sir Humphrey began.

"George!" Etheos cried, looking about frantically. "Where's George? George!" he called. "George, where are you?" his voice sounded through the empty house unnoticed. "We have to look for him!" Etheos insisted, climbing past Wyona up the stairs. "Merlyn knows what sort of trouble he'll have found in a place like this."

"And what about the ghosts?" Wyona asked him, arching a dark eyebrow and looking up at him speculatively. "Shouldn't we wait for the proper authorities?"

"Of course not!" Etheos cried. "My dragon is somewhere up there, and we're going to find him! Come on!"

Wyona and Sir Humphrey exchanged a look, which Etheos would certainly have protested, had he not already been at the top of the stairs, looking one way and then the other. "George!" he called, but there was no answer. "I hope nothing's happened to him," he said as Wyona and Sir Humphrey joined him, Sir Humphrey still carrying the ceremonial sword for lack of a better weapon. "Without his advertisement sales, how am I supposed to pay for lab supplies? Why, phoenix teeth alone cost a fortune!"

"Phoenix don't have teeth," Wyona remarked, but so quietly that Etheos did not hear her over Sir Humphrey's rumbled response.

"But, Etheos," he protested. "You said yourself that George's advertising career was just a phase. You know the public is going to get tired of seeing his picture next to *Biped Bill's Bicycles*—"

"The astounding new invention! Fly through the streets faster than a dragon!" Etheos interrupted enthusiastically.

"Yes," Sir Humphrey said, rolling his eyes. "But you always said it was only temporary for George—Lancelot knows why it's lasted as long as it has! Bicycles! Humbug—surely you care about George for more than his public image?" Sir Humphrey, it should be noted, did not have much faith in so-called modern technology.

"Of course I care more about George than for just his advertising capabilities!" Etheos said hotly. "Do you know how much dragon's liver actually costs? And with the gizzard too—"

"Etheos!" Sir Humphrey cried. "You ought to be ashamed of yourself! Thinking of slaughtering George like that! I would never even consider slaughtering the Lady Orville!"

"Even if we had no sausage?" Etheos asked incredulously. "Why, you're going to have us eating chicken for the rest of forever! And Stryver's right, you know. It is terribly dry and could do with some—"

"Shhhh!" Sir Humphrey insisted, his face growing red. "You're going to upset Wyona, talking about eating birds like—Wyona?"

He realized that Wyona was not walking down the dark and narrow hallway just behind them, but had rather stopped to peer with a frown at one of the paintings that lined it.

"Wyona?" he asked again.

"I do assure you, Sir Knight, that I care nothing for the winged species, for I really am not a bird at all," she said, her eyes never leaving the painting. "Only half of one. Sort of… "

"What is it?" Etheos asked. The two walked back down the hall to join her, staring at the portrait. It was a lap dragon, which looked rather like George except with lighter, polished scales and clipped claws, preening complacently on the lap of a little girl. It was, without a doubt, the same little girl whom they had met downstairs, except very much alive, at least at the time the picture was painted.

"Are you noticing a pattern here?" Wyona said, turning and continuing down the hall.

"Every time you're around we meet certain doom?" Etheos suggested.

"All these paintings," Wyona said, ignoring him entirely. "Contain dragons."

It was true. After the little girl, there were a few more portraits on either side of different, nicely dressed nobles with the same lap dragon in their laps, but after that, things began to get more interesting. They were set in a multitude of different scenes, each containing a dragon-like creature and, if one looked carefully enough, a man with a large nose and an explorer's hat. There was a steamy jungle scene with a great lizard beast sitting in a tree, its mouth open in a full roar at the intruders to its domain who stood below it. There was a nautical scene featuring a noble galleon and a great sea serpent poking its head from beneath the waves. Right next to it were the high mountain peaks of the north covered with snow and ice, the gray sky before them filled with winged creatures bearing riders whose dress was remarkably akin to Wyona's.

"Sky Riders," Wyona whispered as they passed.

They came to the end of the hall then, and there was just one painting left and, unlike all the others, it did not bear a dragon at all, rather it was a portrait of a woman. She could not have been to middle age but she had the same large nose as the man in the explorer's hat that made her seem far older. She wore a typical court dress of pink with a lacey headpiece and her eyes looked rather smug and spoiled.

"Lady Orville!" Sir Humphrey cried.

"She's ugly enough," Etheos conceded.

"Etheos!" Sir Humphrey chided. "If you weren't my friend I—I'd challenge you for the lady's honor."

"You wouldn't be the first knight to fight for the honor of a swine," Wyona replied with a wry smile, turning right and continuing along another hallway lined with antiquated suits of armor.

"What's that supposed to mean?" Sir Humphrey demanded, narrowing his eyes.

Wyona shrugged, running her hand lightly over a dusty breastplate. "I do not put much stock in the nobles of court."

"Oh, if the Master heard you talking like that! He would have a right fit!"

Wyona stopped dead at the voice, which seemed to come from all around them, sending Etheos and then Sir Humphrey running into her.

"But who are you? The Master never sees visitors so late. Oh, and not ones so strange as you either!"

From beneath the very floorboards in front of Wyona came the wispy form of a rather plump older woman in an apron. Like the little girl they had met downstairs, she seemed to be glowing faintly and Wyona could make out a strange dark spot at her breast as if she had been stabbed through the heart. The woman took no notice; her face was set in a worried scowl of disapproval.

The woman seemed no less surprised than the three themselves. She looked Wyona up and down and said, "But aren't you a strange one! You look like you've come out of one of the Master's pictures, you do! In fact, I'm sure of it! Yes! You must be his guests, then. Oh, but it's not the hour to be wandering these halls, no."

"Please, ma'am—" Wyona tried to say.

The woman gave a startled little cry. "Oh, but you're a woman!" she said, as if she had not noticed that before. "Oh, but the Master won't like that, not at all. Oh no. You'd best leave. You'd best leave right now. Yes."

"Please, ma'am, we have no intention of doing so," Wyona replied, seeming only faintly annoyed. "We're looking for a dragon—"

"One of the Master's dragons!" the woman—who Sir Humphrey suspected to be a housekeeper—cried still louder. "Oh, but no one touches the Masters dragons! Oh no. You'd best leave. Yes. Else I'll have to summon Mr. Writkin, and he shall certainly deal with you!"

"Did you call me, Ms. Morris?" The form of a rather small, bald man with a decidedly hunched back wearing a rather worn suit charred with fire materialized right before their eyes. He had a long nose and his long fingers were pressed together, almost as if in prayer.

"Oh, yes, Mr. Writkin!" Ms. Morris exclaimed. "It's these intruders you see!"

Mr. Writkin turned his long eyes towards the three by now rather consternated intruders. "But are they not the Masters' guests?" he inquired. "This one seems to be from the North—"

"But it's a *woman*, Mr. Writkin!" Ms. Morris hissed in a scandalized tone.

Mr. Writkin turned back to Wyona, looking her up and down once more—his neck made a strange popping noise as he craned it up to see her face which Etheos found rather perplexing as ghosts have no bones—and turning to Ms. Morris once more. "Why so she is!" he replied. "Most peculiar."

"Just what I thought."

"The Master will not be pleased."

"Just what I said!"

"They should be dealt with accordingly."

"So very wise of you, Mr. Writkin!" Ms. Morris acclaimed.

Wyona, becoming bored of this, had frowned slightly, and then simply strode right through Ms. Morris as if she wasn't even there.

Ms. Morris gave a properly scandalized shriek, cried "Oh, I never!" and promptly disappeared, her despairing sobs echoing down the hall for some time.

Mr. Writkin cried, "Now don't fret, Ms. Morris!" and followed, leaving Sir Humphrey and Etheos to catch up to Wyona who was already disappearing into the darkness ahead of them.

"Where did all these ghosts come from?" Etheos said. "Ghosts aren't supposed to appear unless there's some great catastrophe like a shipwreck or a fire." He rolled his eyes. "We still have some very pig-headed, insufferable spirits left in the alchemy lab ever since that chemical explosion destroyed the east wing. They *insist* upon whistling constantly and I think one or two may even be helping Dara cheat on exams." He narrowed his eyes sharply and muttered something.

"It is a mystery indeed," Wyona replied, as if she didn't care one way or the other. "This stair, I think." She turned left sharply and began to climb a twisted, rickety staircase into the dusty darkness above.

"Do you know where you're going?" Sir Humphrey asked, holding the flimsy saber at the ready.

"I don't think you're really looking for George," Etheos muttered. "He could be anywhere in this drafty old—I bet he doesn't even realize the danger he's in. I hope he doesn't do anything to damage his organs."

Sir Humphrey kicked him.

"I'm sure George does realize the danger," Wyona replied, stepping out into a long corridor lined on either side with unique stone statues of fantastic, unreal creatures with many heads and beastly teeth. "He can take care of himself."

"And how would you know?" Etheos retorted, giving a three-headed cat to his left a glare.

"If you'll recall, Master Thaumaturge, where you acquired your dragon."

"We rescued him from that crazy old lady with the cats," Sir Humphrey said.

"Rescue," Wyona said with a smile, laying a hand on a large fish-like creature with clawed feet and a gaping mouth. "That's an interesting way of putting it. Did you ever wonder what the Lady Nimue was doing with a lap dragon?"

"We assumed—"

"Wrong," Wyona interrupted Etheos. "I bought him from Lord Astur many years ago, when he was still alive and breeding dragons, because he was the only one with any spirit."

"I was going to guess that!" Etheos lied.

"Lord Astur was going to have him killed because he was too unruly. I thought he was more useful myself."

"For what?" Etheos asked.

"Scaring the tavern keeper," Wyona shrugged. "I haven't paid rent in years."

Etheos was shaking his head.

"He responds to the name Copernicus. Try it if you don't believe me," Wyona sniffed, continuing down the hall. "And I have a feeling he knows where we're going better than we do."

She continued down the corridor, taking her hand from the hopelessly deformed fish statue without a second glance. If she'd bothered, she would have noticed that its eyes were glowing. The strange symptom soon spread to its fellows as well. But none of them noticed. Although another pair of eyes, misty white, staring from the branches of a dead tree outside the window, did.

They came to a set of large oak doors, or what had once been a set of large oak doors at any rate. One was gone entirely and—from the looks of the frame—had been ripped off its hinges while the other was lying nearby covered in a putrid-smelling green mold. Wyona stepped into the room beyond, ducking to avoid the thick cobwebs hanging from the frame, which caught Sir Humphrey by surprise a moment later. He cried out, struggling to dislodge the sticky substance from his beard and hair, eventually tripping and falling to the floor.

Wyona gave him a withering look.

"It's all right. I'm all right," Sir Humphrey assured her, standing once more and picking up the flimsy ceremonial sword that he had dropped. "This was the library, I take it?"

Indeed, what he had tripped on was a pile of old books, pages rotting in their binding, titles long past readable. The walls were two stories high and filled with built-in shelves, some near the top beginning to crumble, spilling their contents in great streams of decaying knowledge out onto the floor.

"A pity," Wyona said, stepping carefully over what had once been a complete set of *Encyclopedia Dragonica* before a family of mice had taken up residence. "Lord Astur's library once astounded even the Masters of the Academy for its expanse and thoroughness. He donated generously to your Academy library every year. Well, until his son was literarily wounded, of course."

There was a sad quality about the room, filled with decaying knowledge. Everything from the books to the heavy curtains was damp, for the windows were broken, allowing the torrential rain to find its way inside. Etheos, who treated his books with reverential care, often attempting to read them with the use of a small mirror so as not to crack the binding, was appalled beyond words at such literary destitution. He stared about him, horrified, kneeling to run a hand over a torn copy of *Terribly Tremendous Torture Chambers* as if it were a fallen comrade in battle.

Sir Humphrey had an entirely different approach. The mold was making his allergies act up and he trod right over the pile of books, tearing pages with his muddy boots and wiping his nose with one of his oven mitts as he went. Wyona was inspecting the ladder to the second tier critically, for it didn't look as if it could hold, and so she didn't look up, but Etheos cried, "Humphrey! Show some respect! How can you just—"

"Etheos, I just—ah—ah—ACHOO!" The sneeze was so great that it seemed to shake the room itself. It echoed uncannily throughout the old house.

"Wonderful," Etheos grumbled, standing. "Ghosts must have heard that."

There was a loud thump. Wyona whirled to see four or five books fall from their shelves to land around her, seemingly disintegrating in the air until she was surrounded in a flurry of pages.

"What was—" And then she saw the glowing eyes, staring at her from the shadows. There were four of them.

She drew her sword, moving slowly over to the ladder. "Humphrey," she hissed. "Behind you, in the shadows—"

Etheos shrieked as a stone fish with claws and sharp fangs leapt out of the shadows onto him. There was nothing for it after that.

"Run!" Wyona shouted as five or six more deformed creatures, all made of stone, leapt from the darkness.

Sir Humphrey swung at them, but the flimsy sword simply glanced off to one side. "Confound it! If I only had my axe!" he roared, kicking back a chipmunk with a spiked tail. Etheos was still battling with the fish statue. "*Xezh syju cyulz!*" he shouted, and it seemed to keep the beasts at bay, but it did nothing to stop them. The other spells he shouted proved useless against cold creatures made of stone. After deflecting a number of blows with her saber with relatively little result, a giant pig with a head on each end had Wyona backed against the pile of books, over which she tripped. Yet, rather than succumb to a nasty death at the hands of granite teeth, Wyona became the small raven and soared high above their heads, landing on the second tier and becoming human. "The ladder, wizard! The ladder!"

Etheos ceased his shouting and made a run for the old wooden ladder, but he hadn't gotten to the sixth rung before it broke in his hand and he fell all the way to the bottom to be swamped by three stone creatures, screaming unintelligible spells all the while with no discernible effect save creating a few tiny sparks in the air.

"Stupid, useless wizard!" Wyona raged, running to one of the long, heavy curtains and tugging it free from its rungs. "Here!" she cried, throwing the fabric down to him. "Grab hold!"

Etheos, still shouting like a maniac, grabbed hold of the curtain and, after much cursing from Wyona and struggling on his part, he reached the relative safety of the second tier.

Sir Humphrey was another matter. He was backed against the opposite wall, and when Etheos and Wyona had both escaped, the strange statues turned their attack on the poor knight, armed only with the practically useless ceremonial sword and his oven mitts.

"What are they?" Etheos cried. "Why aren't my spells working?"

"They're made of stone!" Wyona shouted back. "It isn't as if much can hurt stone!"

"Etheos!" Sir Humphrey cried. "Help!"

"Little help he'll be," Wyona muttered to herself, seizing a book from the shelf and throwing it at one of the stone creatures. It fell harmlessly off its back.

"Speak for yourself!" Etheos cried. "Why—"

But then, just as they had before the statues began to attack, an entire shelf of books fell to the ground. The statues immediately ceased their assault on Sir Humphrey, glowing eyes turned towards where the books had fallen. Then, almost as one, they scurried over to root about in the shadows, though what they were after was anyone's guess. Sir Humphrey didn't waste time wondering. He took a running leap of astounding power, grasping the bottom of the railing along the second tier. The railing, like the ladder, began to fall apart in his hands, but Etheos lunged forward and grasped his big friend's arm. Wyona took the other and, through a group effort by all three, the big knight was pulled out of harm's way, oven mitts and all.

"What—how—" Etheos stammered as he tried to catch his breath, looking down at the stone statues, which began to mill around on the floor below them, occasionally glaring up with their eerily glowing eyes at the three.

"People aren't the only ghosts that walk these halls," Wyona shrugged.

"Yes, but those were significantly more substantial than the others," Sir Humphrey said.

"Spells," Wyona replied, stopping before a large stone fireplace that interrupted the natural progression of the bookshelves. "Powerful ones to protect the fortune of Lord Astur." She frowned at the fireplace, running a hand along the mantel and tracing the outlines of the old bricks with her fingertips. "What an odd place for a hearth," she murmured.

"How are we going to get down?" Etheos asked. "With those things down there? I suppose we could make a run for the door, but after that? And where's George? We'll never find him now. This is entirely Stryver's fault. Why? Why did we listen to him, Sir Humphrey?"

"We?" Sir Humphrey protested. "It was you that—"

"We're trapped in here. Forever," Etheos continued hopelessly. "I'll never be a full wizard now!"

"Ha!" Wyona cried.

"Well at least someone's—" Then even Etheos stopped and stared, for a brick to the right of the fireplace had disappeared entirely, and then the entire fixture swung to one side, revealing a flight of twisting stairs.

"What did—how did—you knew that was there?" Etheos demanded.

Wyona shrugged, keeping her saber at the ready. "This way, Sir Thaumaturge." And she started up the dark staircase.

Sir Humphrey and Etheos looked at each other for a moment.

"There's really nowhere else to go," Sir Humphrey pointed out, squeezing through the opening. "Come on."

Etheos, giving the brooding statues one last glance, followed.

The stairway was exceedingly narrow and dark. It twisted disconcertingly so that each soon lost track of the others, feeling very alone and very lost in the dark. Finally, after what seemed like an eternity to Etheos but was really only a matter of minutes, he came to a landing. It was a sort of study, with a desk whose legs were elaborately carved in the shape of lap dragons, lit by soft, flickering candlelight. Sir Humphrey and Wyona had already arrived, staring wide-eyed at the man sitting at the desk, George resting complacently in his lap.

He was a ghost. He did not, however, have the same far-away expression as the other ghosts they had seen. He was looking at Wyona sternly, but with a very practical expression on his face. Obviously he was the large-nosed man from the paintings downstairs, none other than Lord Astur. He was patting George with one languid hand while inspecting his three visitors critically.

"So," he finally said. "Explain yourselves."

"If you please, my lord," Etheos said. "You have my dragon—"

"You mean *my* dragon," Lord Astur said. "Poor little Copernicus. He always did have too much fire in him—literally—and sometimes I regret very much selling him to this young lady here." He sniffed at Wyona. "You've no excuse, young miss. Women have no business gallivanting about in the noble garb of the Sky Riders."

"Even if she is equal to the task of riding with them?" Wyona countered, glaring right back at him.

"Women are not equal!" Lord Astur thundered. "They have too many emotions and—and no upper body strength!"

"Yes, and that might cost you dearly, my lord, if you weren't already dead," Wyona replied. "I've come to ask the whereabouts of your fortune."

He laughed coldly. "As if I would tell the likes of you! A woman masquerading as one of the noblest of mankind!"

"It doesn't matter if you tell me or not," Wyona replied, starting towards him. "Because I know perfectly well where the door behind you leads."

"Stop!" Lord Astur cried, standing swiftly and spilling George to the floor. "Stop! I will not let you!"

"You're only a ghost," Wyona replied, walking around the desk. "I've dealt with the likes of you already tonight and you've no pow—"

Lord Astur held up his hand and Wyona stopped in mid-stride. Then, in a flash, she was hurled violently backward towards the stair, rolling down into the darkness and out of sight.

"Bah!" Lord Astur said after her. "Witch! Thief!" He shook his head, sitting back down. "Well, my pets will deal with her."

"Those creepy statues?" Sir Humphrey asked.

Lord Astur's dark eyes swiveled towards the knight. "Well, and what have we here?"

"Sir Humphrey, Knight of Galahad's Hall!" Sir Humphrey replied, saluting smartly, thinking the good Lord Astur could find no fault in him.

"Very well, Sir Knight, and what's that you've got in your hand?"

Sir Humphrey looked down at the flimsy sword. "Well it's only—"

"You stole that from the wall downstairs, didn't you, rogue?" Lord Astur thundered. "So this is what the knights have become! Nothing more than a thieving band of villains who would rob a man in his own home with his own noble weaponry! Bah!"

Before he could raise his hand and give Sir Humphrey similar treatment, the knight dropped the sword on the desk. "I meant no disrespect, my lord. I simply needed it to defend myself."

It was well that he did not add "and little good it did me" for the Lord Astur nodded and said, "Tis a mighty weapon indeed," though in his eyes he still did not look convinced.

However, when next he turned to Etheos, his expression softened. "And what of you, lad? A wizard, I see. And how many years have you been at the Academy?"

"It seems like forever," Etheos grumbled.

Lord Astur laughed. "Yes, that's exactly what my boy would have said. Have you seen him?"

"No, my lord," Etheos replied. "Though I have seen the plaque in his memory in the back of the library. I have not heard anyone speak of his ghost."

"Ah, just as I supposed," Lord Astur replied with a shake of his head. "He was always a studious boy, Paul. He could have been a fine lord of court, attended the best parties, and lived an extravagant life second only to the king. But that boy, that boy chose a life of study and learning. It's expected that in death he would not waste his time with such silly, haunting affairs. I myself would not be here were it not for the matter of the inheritance. Thieves!" he suddenly cried. "No good scoundrels! They'll rob me of it yet. That's why I—that's why I've got to make sure that no one, no one gets to it."

"You're just going to keep it locked up in there forever?" Etheos asked.

"Seems an awful shame," Sir Humphrey agreed.

Lord Astur glared at him and then turned to Etheos, "Perhaps you're right. Gold is no good to the dead." He gave a short laugh. "Not that I know anyone living anymore. Save my little friend here," he added, patting George on the head.

"The Lady Orville," Sir Humphrey said. "Your daughter. She's still alive."

"Bah! She married that wretched Orville fellow. Never forgave her for bringing that sort into the family! He used to wipe his nose on the dinner napkins, you know, and always used his snail fork to eat his phoenix. No, not her." Lord Astur shook his head. "They are all disappointments, all of them." He sighed. "Except—except dear Paul."

"Your son is still remembered for his integrity and dedication," Etheos ventured tentatively. "When the Masters proposed adding a new wing to the library, it was supposed to be named after him."

"Really?" Lord Astur asked. "And what became of this proposal?"

Etheos shook his head. "It was never finished because of budget cuts. Pity too, because all that was left was a roof, and when the spring rains came all the books the librarian had put in there to take the weight off the Classical shelves in the Circes Hall got all soggy and whole classes of Classical Studies students failed their exams."

"A shame, a shame indeed," Lord Astur agreed distantly, his eyes darting back and forth in thought. "You remind me much of Paul, lad. Tell me, what do you want most in the world?"

"To become a full wizard, my lord!" Etheos replied without hesitation.

"Indeed," Lord Astur said, stoking his wispy beard in thought. "That settles it then. Because I have no worthy living heir—and hardly any worthy dead heir either—I shall leave the entirety of my fortune to—"

"Thank you, sir!" Etheos cried excitedly.

"The Academy Library," Lord Astur finished.

Etheos' face fell. "Oh."

"It's just behind that door, up the stairs," Lord Astur continued, pointing to the door behind him. "In the tower room. You, my lad. You go fetch it, and give it to the Academy Masters. Tell them to finish the Paul Astur Wing! You do that for me."

"Yes, my lord," Etheos replied, walking rather dejectedly through the noble ghost on his way to the door, something that the Lord Astur was willing to overlook in his excitement. "And if you see that dratted cat," Lord Astur added. "Turn him into a tea cozy."

"Cat?" Sir Humphrey asked, startled.

"There's been a bothersome black cat poking about of late," Lord Astur said. "I saw him earlier this evening and dispatched of him! He'll think twice before coming up here again!" He laughed genially. "Tell me, Sir Knight, what goes on in court since I have been away?"

Sir Humphrey sighed and launched into the story of the king's aunt holding a mandatory etiquette class for all the lords and then throwing the Lord High Chamberlain into the stocks in the West

Side Market when he did not attend, followed by the nasty affair of the Ambassador for the Desert Kingdom and the saucepan of gravy that nearly started a war.

Etheos opened the door and climbed the stairs, which twisted annoyingly in the fashion of the previous ones. He had not climbed very far when he came to the tower room. It had windows on all sides, looking surprisingly new compared to the rest of the house. The sun was just rising in the east, creating a sparkling glitter that could drive man wild. The entire room was filled with gold. It was not just the table, which held the wealth of kings, but the curtains, sewn of gold brocade, and the rug, the window frames with inlaid gold and the fresco on the ceiling of a great wingless dragon flying off into a great golden sunset. It took Etheos' breath away.

"Think of it, Lady Orville," he muttered. "This could have been yours if you hadn't married a stupid pig." He sighed, taking out a small silk bag. "Then again, he was your type." He turned the bag over and dumped out a pile of dust—which he always told people was from a pixie but had really been gathered from his own bookcase at home—before holding his hand over the bag and saying "*Xi rfu metuvqu, ieo quejj lusuv xu cyjjuz!*"

He inspected the table critically then and finally selected a shining golden diadem, dropping it into the bag. This was followed by a golden scepter and a handful of coins. Etheos emptied the entire treasure trove into the silk bag, and then pulled down the curtains for good measure, though strangely the bag never seemed to be full. In fact, when he was standing in a simple barren room—with an admittedly glorious ceiling he hadn't figured out how to dismantle—the bag still felt and looked quite empty. He took one last look around, peering in all the corners to be sure he hadn't missed one coin, and then put the bag in his pocket and walked dejectedly back down the stairs.

" … And then the queen insisted that we all come and have pink lemonade, even though none of us really wanted to, and the little squire—poor clumsy lad—ended up spilling the whole pitcher on her white dress. So she up and left, ran off with the Keeper of the Seal, who's still doing a fine job of keeping the seal—despite all our attempts—somewhere overseas."

The Lord Astur was laughing when Etheos stepped through the door. "Court politics. Where would the public be without such entertainment? Ah, there you are, my lad. All set?"

"Yes, my lord. I'm sure the Academy—the Academy will be very grateful. Everyone will be very grateful. Particularly the Classical Studies students who are still trying to survive in the half-completed wing, which is exceedingly difficult since they've also turned it into an indoor swimming pool."

"And are you grateful?"

"Yes, terribly, my lord. Can't become a full wizard without an accurate library, can you?"

"There's that Astur spirit!" Lord Astur said with a smile. "Very good! The best of luck to you, my lad! And to you as well, Sir Knight." He became stern in the next moment. "And don't you forget to put that sword back on your way out!"

"Yes, milord!" Sir Humphrey said, smartly saluting.

The Lord Astur, perhaps recalling his days of military training, saluted back, waved once to George and then disappeared, the candles blowing out at his departure.

"Come on, George," Etheos said, starting down the stairs. "We've had a time looking for you."

"What's the matter, Etheos?" Sir Humphrey asked, following George. "You were just telling me how the library was woefully incomplete yesterday! I should think you'd be happy!"

"I am happy!" Etheos insisted. "It's just…think of all we could've done with this money!"

"Like what?" Sir Humphrey asked. "Bought a solid gold life-sized statue of Merlyn? Come off it, Etheos, you know perfectly well when left to your own devices you just waste things anyway. Besides, everyone will benefit from a better library at the Academy—particularly those Classical Studies students…"

Etheos grumbled something. "You're right of course, as ever."

"Where do you suppose Wyona got off to?" Sir Humphrey asked as they came out of the fireplace on the second tier of the library. "Hope those stone buggers didn't give her any—"

Etheos waved him into silence and Sir Humphrey, frowning, came to stand beside the wizard at the railing looking down on the first tier. He didn't know what he expected to see. Perhaps Wyona being cornered by the viscous enchanted statues. They were nowhere to be seen, however, except for a few piles of rubble scattered here and there. It looked as though they had disintegrated into dust. Wyona was kneeling on the ground, her tunic ripped and her lip bleeding. Her slim saber was lying near the wall and she was cradling her sword arm against her chest, her head bowed.

Stryver was standing behind her, carefully closing his pocket watch, holding his own sword to the back of her neck.

"You've broken my arm," Wyona said quietly after a moment.

"You always break your arms," Stryver retorted. "It's from having hollow bird-bones."

"Well, it isn't as if it's anything I can help," Wyona said. "And if you're going to kill me, you'd best do it now before any of those infernal ghosts show up."

"I shouldn't think they would. The sun has risen."

Sir Humphrey had very carefully picked up a heavy volume lying near him, *A Complete History of the Merlyn Academy Volumes I-X*, and, with astounding stealth for one given to clumsiness, held it out over the railing, preparing to drop it on Stryver's head.

"Well, go ahead then!" Wyona finally cried, exasperated. "You know you've been waiting to slit my throat for years, and now I'm defenseless and there are no witnesses."

Stryver rubbed his moustache with his spare hand and ever so slightly raised his sword.

Sir Humphrey let the text fall.

At the same instant, Wyona and Stryver both leapt out of the way, Stryver transforming into the black cat even as he ran, leaping out the window, and Wyona rolling towards her fallen sword, grasping it with her good hand and brandishing it at her now fleeing foe. She stared after him, lowering her sword in disbelief.

"But why did he run?" she asked, evidently addressing the question to herself.

"Well, not many would care to face me," Sir Humphrey replied, leaping down from the second floor with such a crash that many of the books fell from their shelves. "Even if I am only armed with this useless thing," he added, swinging the ceremonial sword around once. "Lucky we dropped by, eh?"

"Yes," Wyona replied distantly, still staring after him. "Lucky." She jumped as George the Dragon came crashing into her, gliding down from the second tier. "Hello, Copernicus." He licked her nose with his snake-like forked tongue and hopped down, running over to Etheos who had descended with a yelp from the second tier as well. "How did things go with Lord Astur?" she asked. "Did you get the treasure?"

"Yes," Etheos replied, standing and dusting off his robes before lifting George onto his shoulder in his preferred position. "All for the Academy Library," he added somewhat bitterly.

"Think on it this way, Etheos," Sir Humphrey replied. "Maybe they'll promote you to full wizard after your generous contribution."

A light came into Etheos' eyes. "Maybe they will! And maybe they'll give me a full professorship! Wouldn't that be grand, George?"

George didn't look convinced.

"At least the rain has stopped," Wyona replied, patting George on the head. "Although I don't suppose I'll be doing much flying until my arm's healed."

Etheos gave her a speculative look and then took several paces back. "Oh, don't even think about it!" he cried. "You can't steal the money from me! Because I put a spell on it! Yes!" he cried excitedly as her face fell. "It can only be opened by the Master Librarian at the Academy for the purposes of a donation! So don't even try!"

"Etheos!" Sir Humphrey said. "Don't be so rude! I'm sure Wyona—"

"She was!" Etheos insisted. "She was going to pick my pocket! Well, no one—not even some sly Changeling—is going to rob me of this promotion!"

"You're just too smart for me, Etheos," Wyona replied, hiding her smile as she sheathed her sword. "I guess I'd best just go on home."

"Yes, that's right," Etheos said with a proud smile. "You just turn right around. Because this time Thaumaturge Etheos is too smart for you."

"Who's too smart for whom now, Etheos?" Sir Humphrey asked as the two left the Academy library.

"Shut up!" Etheos fumed. "This is typical! So bloody typical! Bah!" He spat at the sign before continuing down the steps. Sir Humphrey chuckled to himself and nodded genially to the plaque, which read in nice bold letters "The Wyona Wyncliff Wing."

Misadventures in Dancing

Sir Humphrey sighed. "I look like a butterfly," he groaned. "Believe me, Sir Humphrey," Etheos said, smoothing out the silver lining of his best set of robes. "You do not look like a butterfly."

"I do!" Sir Humphrey protested.

"A very large butterfly then," Etheos said. "Turn around."

Sir Humphrey sighed again and turned to face Etheos. He was dressed, not in his usual light mail, but a maroon doublet that looked rather tight, especially around the shoulders. His wild mass of copper hair was in a thick braid down his back, but his messy beard, which he had tried to comb without much success, still spilled over his collar. A light blue cape, which the hedge witch in the flat below had assured him would match perfectly with his eyes, was thrown over one shoulder and the largely ceremonial jewel-studded belt around his waist seemed about to pop.

"You don't look…so bad," Etheos said. "It'll be fine. Everyone will be too drunk to remember you by the end of the evening anyway."

"I'm not going," Sir Humphrey said, sitting down with his arms crossed. "It's stupid. You can't make me."

Lady Orville, wearing an exquisite diamond headpiece with a fine lacey veil, trotted into the room. She snorted angrily at both Etheos and Sir Humphrey, sitting down by the door expectantly.

"You'll disappoint the Lady Orville," Etheos reminded him, pinning on the Magenta Medal of Merit the king had awarded him. He was very proud of it and wore it whenever he could, admonishing Sir Humphrey when he threw his in a kitchen drawer next to the dishrags. "She's been looking forward to this since you promised to take her last Midwinter. You're always saying that just because she was unfortunate enough to end up on the bad end of a curse doesn't mean we should treat her like any less of a lady. You're her escort!"

The Lady Orville narrowed her eyes at Etheos, as if trying to decide if he was being sarcastic or not.

Sir Humphrey didn't budge.

"Well, you can stay home moping if you must," Etheos said with a shrug. "But I promised the Lord Overseer that I would introduce him to George. He's very curious about him, even if the Academy said he was—" Etheos shot a look towards his bedroom to make sure George wasn't nearby and then whispered, "—Too mangy a breed to be acceptable for admittance."

"I hope you and George have a lovely time," Sir Humphrey replied stubbornly. "I'm not going. I *hate* the Midwinter Ball. It's always too hot inside and too cold outside, the food is too delicate to eat, and *you* always go off fawning after the Masters or the city officials and leave *me* to talk with the stuffy old pepperpots who're too old to dance, all of whom claim to be the king's great aunt!"

"It's your own fault," Etheos shrugged. "You should mingle more. Make some new friends maybe."

"Not looking like this I won't," Sir Humphrey sighed.

"Well, if you're going to be this way, I don't want to go with you anyway." He whistled towards the door to his bedchamber. "Are you coming, George?" he called. "Wouldn't want to miss your big night!"

The door crashed open and out bounded George the dragon— lap dragon to be more precise—who ran at Lady Orville excitedly. Lady Orville turned up her nose at the dragon imperiously, but George had gathered too much momentum on his headlong race out of the room, his long tail twitching in the air behind him, and he ended up crashing into the lady pig, who gave a great squeal of rage, as this was not the first time it had happened.

George the lap dragon was still about the size of Lady Orville, but with an exceptionally long tail and some rather small wings on his back. He couldn't fly with them, but he could use them to glide and gain speed in an impossible display of aerodynamics. In this way, George was often to be found climbing with his thick claws atop bits of furniture and then leaping off to glide down, and more than like- ly, crash into something. It was a bit of a nuisance in the small flat.

Merrill Malone, the hedge witch in the flat below, often kindly asked them to try and keep it down, thinking it must be Etheos trying to magically summon the top five winners of the Miss Nymph beauty pageant into his room again, though that had only actually happened once, summoning, instead, an army of centipedes.

"George," Etheos said disapprovingly. "Come on." He lifted the dragon and set him in his preferred position—draped across the wizard's shoulders—with his snake-like tongue flicking out occasionally near Etheos' left ear and his long tail dancing in the air near his right.

Etheos picked up an enchanted umbrella from beside the door, one to keep out all weathers, extreme temperatures, and unpleasant odors, said "Good night then, Sir Humphrey. I'm sorry that you're too scared to come with us", winked at Lady Orville, and stepped out the door. He waited on the landing and counted to eight in Gnomish before the great form of Sir Humphrey lumbered out the door holding the white silk ribbon, the other end of which was tied around the Lady Orville's neck. He grumbled something at Etheos before clunking down the steps. Etheos and George grinned at each other and followed.

The two made their way quickly through the streets of the rather run-down district where they lived, Sir Humphrey edgy because he had had to leave his axe at home and he was only armed with a dagger in his boot and the oven mitts stuffed in his ceremonial belt. Etheos walked calmly down the center of the street, George hissing things into his ear. George was a bit of a curiosity at the Academy. Though there were one or two small dragons like him in the menagerie, lap dragons, the only breed of dragon that still existed in this part of the kingdom, were mostly the pets and ornaments of the rich. Not a few of the city officials had commissioned portraits painted with their own finely polished lap dragons—or if they hadn't the patience to purchase one, they rented the Academy's. These lap dragons had polished scales, some tinged with gold, as well as manicured claws and training to behave like most of the city commissioners wives: to be pretty and sit quietly. George was nothing like his contemporaries.

He ate anything in sight and had an insatiable curiosity, exploring new things and people with his snake-like tongue and tail. This had been the death of many of Merrill Malone's flower boxes. None of the properly trained lap dragons climbed on furniture or tried to fly. And Etheos was positive that none of them could spit fire if they wanted to. The Academy Masters would tolerate George, but Etheos' fellow students loved him, especially when he would play his own brand of catch, which involved teacups stolen from the Academy dining hall and small blasts of fire. George's fame had slowly crept about the city, until the Lord Overseer, the youngest on the city council and considered by many to be an adventurous, sporting sort, had asked Etheos personally if he might be introduced.

Etheos was proud, there was no question. True, he had not wanted to keep George at first, but everyone seemed to have forgotten that. When he found that George was popular and could be used to further his ambitious career, he took a new liking to the lap dragon, one that Sir Humphrey was assured had actually taken root in a true friendship. The Lady Orville was not so optimistic. But then, she was prejudiced against the dragon from the start due to his multiple attempts to eat her.

They soon left the dimly lit, run-down section of town and came upon the wide boulevards and walled-in gardens of the richer side. The streets were filled with carriages pulled by the finest horses and unicorns. Inside, one could catch glimpses of elegantly dressed ladies in fine, shimmering jewelry. Etheos and Sir Humphrey strolled casually along, trying to look at ease amongst the elite of society even though they were not.

The Midwinter Ball was held, as the name suggests, every midwinter at the mayor's grand house. The king and his court held balls and masquerades all throughout the year, but the midwinter was strictly for the city. Although some of the lords and ladies accepted invitations, few were given. The ball was attended instead by city and Academy officials, prominent businessmen, and the peculiar class of wealthy yet unlanded men that hung in a precarious limbo between the palace and the mayor's mansion year round. The officers of the Knights of Galahad's hall were city officials and were allowed to extend their invitation to a few of the normal, more modest ranking knights as a courtesy. Sir Humphrey, being rather well-known even outside the force for his boisterously kind heart, was always invited, and now that he had been granted a Magenta Medal of Merit, Etheos was as well, a convenience meaning that he would have to forgo the various extreme, complex, and more often than not disastrous methods he had used to slide his way inside in the past. Etheos, ever the social climber, knew the importance of the Midwinter Ball.

The Mayor's Mansion, with its many stories and large windows, was brilliantly lit that night. The glow of candlelight and the twinkle of firefly lamps sparkled off the elaborate dresses of the ladies. Etheos' eyes gained a slightly predatory look as he watched the assorted well-dressed city officials and their wives enter. The Masters of the Academy came in groups of two or three, their robes snapping and their heads held high with the air of knowledge and wisdom they liked to hold at such gatherings. Most everyone who passed them going into the Mayor's Mansion was too proud to stare at the dragon.

Etheos, Sir Humphrey grunting beside him, climbed the stairs to the front doors, which were thrown open as the stream of exquisitely dressed made their way into the marble halls of the mansion.

"I hate this," Sir Humphrey muttered.

The Lady Orville, who seemed to be trying to smile charmingly like a court lady, grunted disapprovingly at him.

"Should have stayed home," Sir Humphrey continued. "This belt is going to snap, I just know it."

"Then try not to move," Etheos suggested.

"What, you want me to stop breathing?" Sir Humphrey said irritably.

"It's a start," Etheos said, scanning the people before them like a lion scanning a herd of antelope.

"Ethe—" Sir Humphrey started to protest.

"Etheos!" an excited voice called.

Etheos turned swiftly.

The Lord Overseer had just emerged from a side door wearing a huge grin. He was tall and athletic with wide brown eyes and a laughing face. He came forward and shook Etheos' hand heartily. "So wonderful to see you! So glad you could come! Is this George?"

George's tongue flicked out of his mouth, tasting the air around the stranger speculatively.

"Yes, yes," Etheos agreed excitedly. "This is George. George, this is the Lord Overseer. He's been very anxious to meet you."

George, deciding he liked praise, leapt off of Etheos' shoulders and glided to the floor, surprisingly not crashing into anyone present. It made Sir Humphrey narrow his eyes, suspecting that the multiple crash landings he had witnessed the dragon perform in the past were entirely intentional.

"Isn't he wonderful!" the Lord Overseer exclaimed. "He's perfect!"

"Perfect for what, my lord?" Etheos asked.

"Etheos," the Lord Overseer said, turning to him in a serious voice, but with a happy smile on his face. "I've been looking for a mascot for our hang-gliding competition. It's the newest sport among the youth, you know, and our new Death Cliffs Hang Gliding Competition is exactly what we need to earn some money for charity."

"Which charity?" Sir Humphrey rumbled.

The Lord Overseer waved his hand. "Bathe the mermaids, shave the gnomes, something like that. It doesn't matter. What I'm interested in is getting competitors. Not everyone these days is willing to jump off Death Cliffs and plummet to the ground ten thousand feet below with only a flimsy piece of tarp in their hands. I know!" he cried, misinterpreting Etheos' look of disbelief. "Cowards. Anyway, if we could have a mascot like this fine dragon, George, I think we'd really earn the right amount of gold for those poor, hairy gnomes. What do you think?"

Before Etheos could agree whole-heartedly, there came a shrill cry of "MELVIN!" and the Lord Overseer's face suddenly went pale and his eyes went blank.

A woman in a very large, lime green headpiece stormed out of the side door through which the Lord Overseer had come. "Melvin!"

she cried. "What are you doing with that disgusting creature?"

She appeared to be glaring at Sir Humphrey.

"Me? But—" Sir Humphrey started to stammer.

"A flying lizard, especially one of such a dubious appearance, is *not* something you should be associating with! Come! The mayor is probably looking for you!" She seized the Lord Overseer's hand and dragged him away. He seemed to be incapable of saying anything besides "Yes, dear."

"I'll talk to you later, then!" Etheos called to him. "Can you imagine it?" he said excitedly to Sir Humphrey. "George, the mascot for the Death Cliffs Hang Gliding Competition to Shave the Gnomes."

"I'm thrilled," Sir Humphrey muttered. "I suppose there's no chance of you talking about something else for the next month is there?"

But Etheos wasn't listening. "Think of all the important people we'll get to meet! Think of the publicity! They might even make me a full wizard!"

"Now why would—" Sir Humphrey started to protest, and then he stopped, narrowing his eyes at someone who had just entered. "Etheos, isn't that someone we know?"

"It doesn't matter," Etheos said, not even bothering to turn around. "Don't you see what an opportunity—"

But now it was Sir Humphrey who wasn't listening. "But why would—" He stepped away from Etheos, following the trail of people from the entrance hall and into the ballroom, dragging Lady Orville along with him, as he still had the silk ribbon in his hand.

"Stop! Stop right there! You there!"

"What?" Sir Humphrey asked, turning.

A small man was standing behind him, a pair of spectacles in his hand, which he kept dropping by accident.

"Who are you?" the man asked. "What's your name and title?"

Sir Humphrey blinked.

"I must *announce* you, of course," the man said, rolling his eyes and dropping his spectacles once more.

"Oh," Sir Humphrey said. "I'm Sir Humphrey, Knight of Galahad's Hall. And this is the Lady Orville," he added.

The man blinked down at the pig. "Interesting," he commented. "All right then." He cleared his throat and then cried in a surprisingly loud voice over the din of the assembled. "Sir Humphrey, Knight of Galahad's Hall and the Lady Orville." He coughed a few times. "Thank you," he said. "You! You there!" and he went off to harass someone else.

Sir Humphrey shook his head. "Formalities are disturbing," he remarked to Lady Orville, who snorted derisively at him. "Oh. Right." He bent and untied the ribbon from around her neck. "Off you go. Don't get into too much trouble."

The Lady Orville, pretending she did not hear this, trotted happily off into the crowd, to earn a few stares from the assorted, chattering officials and their wives in particular. The music had not started yet, though it sounded as if the minstrels were warming up. Sir Humphrey scanned the faces of those near him, wondering where he had lost—

"Thaumaturge Etheos of the Academy and George the Dragon," came the voice of the jittery little man and, in a moment, Etheos was beside him.

"Why did you run off like that?" Etheos demanded. "I didn't know you were in such a rush to begin the dancing. In fact," he frowned. "I didn't know you danced at all."

"No," Sir Humphrey said. "I thought I saw Wyona Wyncliff."

Etheos burst out laughing. George leapt from his shoulders to glide to the ground once more before scurrying off unnoticed by either. "Wyona Wyncliff? That's silly, Sir Humphrey. How could she possibly be here?"

"She was on the arm of an old man with a very large nose," Sir Humphrey said, still looking about searchingly.

"Well, that describes about three fourths of the city council," Etheos replied. "Humphrey! Stop jumping about like that! You're making a spectacle! And it can't be her! She's an unregistered Changeling. Someone would spot her and arrest her in a second. Besides, how would *she* know anyone who has an invitation?"

"I *saw* her!" Sir Humphrey persisted.

"Humphrey—"

Etheos was cut off by a scream from somewhere to their right.

A group of people who had been standing near the long curtains were hurriedly taking steps back as George was climbing up them, hissing periodically.

Etheos cursed and slipped through the crowd. "George! George, get down here!" he yelled up to the dragon from the floor below the long curtain.

People were turning and laughing now. Sir Humphrey, frowning, moved through the crowd, looking at every face carefully. He knew what he had seen.

George was causing quite a spectacle, making faces at Etheos from high above the ballroom.

Sir Humphrey passed near the Lord Overseer who was still in the grasp of his rather shrew-like wife, who was loudly commentating on the incompetence of everyone else in the room. "This is a disgrace, Melvin! Look at those minstrels! I bet they're drunk! Though no better than last year when the mandolin player dropped his hat into the punch and said the most *indecent* things to the Chamberlain's daughter! Why does the Mayor allow such people to the ball? Surely such debauchery belongs at the King's masquerades, not here! We have all earned our positions through merit, Melvin! It's something to be proud of! And I *wish* someone would get that horrid dragon down!" she cried, exasperated by Etheos' persistent calls and the laughter of everyone else in the room.

Strangely, at that moment, the curtain burst into flame above George, and the dragon found himself clinging to nothing but air. Luckily, he spread his wings at the right moment, and glided down to the floor, landing on the Minister of Sewage's head. Everyone had a good laugh and then the minstrels struck up a song.

The floor was immediately cleared, and those willing to dance emerged from the crowd. Sir Humphrey, giving up his search, began to look around for a waiter carrying wine. It always did bother him that he could never get anything decent to drink at these gatherings.

He saw one across the dance floor, trying to escape from the Academy Master of Oinomancy before he could drink his entire tray.

Sir Humphrey was about to head over towards him when a voice nearby caught his ear. He was standing at the edge of the dance floor, and there was the Lord Overseer, grinning his wide grin, his eyes now alight as he had somehow broken free of his wife. He was talking animatedly to the girl he was dancing with, who was dressed in a very fine midnight blue dress cut off the shoulders in a way that was not quite conventional, but not quite foreign enough to attract attention. And then they turned to dance away, and Sir Humphrey saw it was Wyona.

Sir Humphrey was startled. There she was. He knew he had seen her. But how different she looked now, not in tough Sky Rider's garb, but in a dress, dancing, with a smile on her face. She almost looked normal. Almost. But it was impossible for her to blend in completely. She was too tall and slender, too impossibly graceful. Instead she moved with a sort of exotic beauty that made more than a few people stare twice at her. Most of them took her for some foreign ambassador's wife and sought no further explanation for her presence. None of them could possibly suspect that she was a Changeling, for in their view, a Changeling would come skulking in, slinking with the devious, underhanded cunning and malice of his race. Her disguise was brilliant, for it wasn't a disguise at all.

She was still pale as ever, but it contrasted rather nicely with the midnight dress that looked black at some angles but shone with a purple tint in others. Her dark hair was done up and set with pearls and there was a midnight scarf, of the same material as the dress around her neck, fluttering behind her as she moved. Sir Humphrey wondered if she had found a way to wear her sword underneath the dress.

She was here for a reason, and he wanted to know what it was.

When the pair swept past him again, Sir Humphrey stepped forward, halting their progression. The Lord Overseer blinked at him in confusion, and Wyona gave him a look that bespoke death quite plainly. Sir Humphrey ignored her.

"May I cut in?"

The Lord Overseer, looking perhaps a little too surprised to argue, took a step back, and in a moment Sir Humphrey had taken Wyona's hand and swept away across the floor. Considering that he could hardly breathe in the doublet, and that he had been trained to run across the city and hack people's heads off, Sir Humphrey was not a bad dancer at all. Wyona did not look in the mood to notice.

"Just what do you think you're doing?" she demanded, staring him straight in the eye. She still looked calm and collected, just slightly perturbed. "You're going to ruin everything."

"What?" Sir Humphrey asked. "What are you up to? Why are you here? What happened to the man with the big nose?"

"He's sitting in there," Wyona replied, with a nod towards the room where tables of tiny snack foods were set up. "He's too old to dance. He thinks I'm his cousin."

"And why would he bring you?" Sir Humphrey asked, perplexed.

"Because I'm prettier than his wife, I'd imagine," Wyona replied evenly. "Besides, she was unavailable."

"Why?" Sir Humphrey asked suspiciously.

"Well, if you have to be so nosy, I locked her in a closet."

"And what are you doing here?"

"Dancing, if you hadn't noticed."

"Tell me the truth."

"No," Wyona replied. "It's none of your business at all."

"It's entirely my business," Sir Humphrey said. "As a knight of Sir Galahad's hall."

"Oh, you think I'm up to no good?"

"I think," Sir Humphrey replied, just as carelessly. "That I might have to have you arrested for being an unregistered Changeling."

"Surely you wouldn't arrest me?" Wyona asked.

"Not if you tell me what's about here."

Wyona glanced in the direction of the Lord Overseer who had once again been captured by his wife, his eyes glazing over. "There's a genie about, Sir Humphrey."

"A genie?" Sir Humphrey asked. "You mean the three wishes kind?"

"What other sort of genie is there?" Wyona asked. "Of course, the three wishes kind. Someone in this room has found a genie and I think I know who."

"The Lord Overseer?"

"Yes. Two days ago, a pear tree bearing solid gold fruit appeared in his back garden."

"Probably just a rumor."

Wyona gave him a long look. "No, Sir Humphrey, it's very real. I perched in it myself."

"Well, couldn't a wizard—"

"Sir Humphrey, I assure you, it had 'genie' written all over it."

"But I thought genies were really rare," Sir Humphrey said.

"They are," Wyona replied, giving the Lord Overseer a look again. "But they have great power. Greater than any wizard. This is a magnificent chance."

"And what are you planning on wishing for?" Sir Humphrey asked curiously as the dance ended.

"That is none of your concern," Wyona replied. "Keep yourself and the arrogant wizard out of my way." And she turned on her heel and swept away.

A few moments later found Sir Humphrey, laden with a plate of the "delicate looking" food he hated so much—including stewed griffin egg and nymph wafers—standing out in the cold air on the balcony. He was all alone, in this rather dark overlook of the garden, staring thoughtfully in at the brilliantly lit interior. A genie? Such a thing was hard to imagine. There were legends about them of course, imprisoned in lamps or shoes, but the thought of a real one was staggering.

"Are you going to eat all of that?"

Sir Humphrey turned to see Etheos standing beside him, George sitting across his shoulders once more. "No," Sir Humphrey replied, shoving the plate at Etheos. "It's too—"

"Delicate, yeah," Etheos said, shoving a cracker piled with griffin egg into his mouth as if he hadn't eaten in a week.

"Why aren't you following the Lord Overseer around like a lost puppy?" Sir Humphrey suddenly asked.

Etheos scowled. "He's busy talking to some lady in one of those…dresses. You remember what happened last time."

Sir Humphrey tried to mask his laughter by coughs but eventually gave up.

Etheos glared at his laughing companion sourly. "It isn't that funny! Lots of people at the Academy are much worse than I am. And I'm completely over that now."

It was not as uncommon as one might suppose for Academy scholars, long devoted fully to their studies, to grow a little skittish around members of the fairer sex. Although there were a number of female scholars, the number was a relatively small one. In Etheos' more youthful days he had been so squeamish around women—particularly ones dressed in ball gowns cut low off the shoulder—that he had once stumbled, tripped, and knocked an entire bowl of Burrowing Slugs onto the Enchantment Committee Chairman's daughter. She had been released from the medical ward after a few months, about the same time that Etheos emerged from hiding in his closet. The story still brought tears to Sir Humphrey's eyes.

"And then the way you tried to pick them off her—one by one—and just dropped more onto her!" he laughed, as he did each time the event was mentioned.

Even George the Dragon appeared to be grinning.

"You're blowing it completely out of proportion!" Etheos said. "I tripped. It could've happened to anybody! What was a bowl of Borrowing Slugs doing there in the first place?" He was yelling so loudly that some of the people inside were beginning to stare out at them. "Besides, it happened a long time ago! I was young and stupid!" It was surprising that despite the number of people looking out at the furious Etheos and the laughing Sir Humphrey, no one noticed the blind cat that had leapt from a tree and was sitting on the balcony watching them with mild interest.

"As opposed to being old and stupid now?" Sir Humphrey asked.

Etheos glared malevolently at him, too enraged for words.

"All right, I'm sorry, Etheos," Sir Humphrey said. "I didn't mean anything by it."

Etheos continued to glare.

"It was pretty funny though … "

Etheos looked as if he were going to start shouting again when a voice next to him said, "Please don't do that. You'll blow my cover."

Etheos yelped, and whirled around.

Stryver, his purple coat spruced up for the occasion, was sitting cat-like on the balcony next to him. He stood and removed a silver-topped cane from his sleeve like a magician.

"How did you get here?" Etheos demanded.

"Snuck up the tree, of course," he replied. "What? Did you expect me to come walking right through the door?"

"That's what Wyona did," Sir Humphrey remarked. "And no one tried to arrest her."

"*What?*" Stryver cried. "Bird brain is here?"

"No," Etheos said, rolling his eyes. "Sir Humphrey just thinks she is. She can't be."

"Funny, because I was just dancing with her," Sir Humphrey remarked.

Etheos blinked. "You can dance?"

"Better than you, my lad," Sir Humphrey replied loftily.

"No one spotted her for a Changeling?" Stryver asked with a frown.

"Well, her eyes don't exactly change color every ten minutes," Sir Humphrey replied. "But no. No one seems the least suspicious. It's—it's the way she's dressed, I think."

"Damn," Stryver cursed. "She's beaten me. How much has she gotten out of pear-boy?"

"The Lord Overseer? They were dancing before, but he's got a rather tyrannical wife which I imagine is making things more difficult."

"Good, good," Stryver said. "I want that genie."

"*What* genie?" Etheos demanded. "What's going on? What are we talking about?"

"What are you going to wish for?" Sir Humphrey asked.

"None of your business!" Stryver snapped. "I'm going to go find Wyona and have a *talk.*"

"How are you going to explain that neat trick with your eyes?" Sir Humphrey called after him.

Stryver shrugged. "I was cursed at birth by a vindictive warlock.

It gets sympathy as well."

Sir Humphrey chuckled and was about to follow, fully curious as to what sort of talk the two Changelings were going to have. But Etheos caught his arm.

"*What* genie?" he repeated. "Humphrey! You're going to explain what's going on to me right now!"

By the time Sir Humphrey had explained the whole story to Etheos—a task made more difficult by his persistent cries of "A *real* genie?"—much time had passed and the older members of the party were already starting to leave the ball. Sir Humphrey and Etheos wandered back into the ballroom to note that there were a few people still dancing, and probably more than a few raiding the food tables in the next room. Sir Humphrey scanned the room for Stryver or Wyona.

"They aren't here," he said. "Must have gone some place private where their attempts to kill each other would go unnoticed."

"Well," Etheos said. "If we can just find the Lord Overseer—" He stopped, his mouth dropping open. "Humphrey—is that—"

Sir Humphrey turned to see where Etheos was staring, and realized his mistake. In his search for Stryver and Wyona he had peered behind the crowds lining the dance floor, into the darker corners and other likely places where heated arguments could take place, not at the dance floor itself. Yet there were Stryver and Wyona, dancing.

It was not the fact that they loathed each other entirely that made the scene so odd. It was that, bearing in mind their hatred, they danced beautifully. Stryver's cat-like agility and Wyona's inherent grace seemed to compliment each other seamlessly—and the way it was done, with such easy, careless, elegance was almost breathtaking. They did not look particularly angry; Etheos thought they were arguing quietly under their breath, though what evidence he supported such a conclusion with, besides knowledge of their characters, remains to be said.

Sir Humphrey flipped a business card from his pocket. "It does say 'ballroom dancing champion' right here on her card," he said with a nod.

"Yes, and his says 'Fully qualified mountaineer' if I remember correctly. Those are completely fake, Sir Humphrey."

"Well—"

"This is pointless. Let's go find the Lord Overseer and—"

The dance ended, Sir Humphrey watched Wyona and Stryver closely. They stood still after the others had moved away, staring at each other, though if it was in anger or something else, Sir Humphrey could never be sure. As he had noticed when speaking to Wyona on a number of occasions, she usually remained calm and collected towards anything. Stryver, it appeared, was a master of the same art.

Stryver said something. Wyona said something back. The cat-like grin played across Stryver's face momentarily as he replied. Wyona looked as if she were about to give him a black eye, but thought the better of it, looking around at all the finely dressed people. Instead she turned on her heel, giving Stryver's foot a good stomp with it as she did so and glided quickly from the room.

Stryver, whose foot hurt quite a bit more than he was willing to admit, stepped away from the dance floor as well. Etheos and Sir Humphrey accosted him there.

"What was that about?" Etheos demanded.

"Are you really a fully qualified mountaineer?" Sir Humphrey asked. "Because Etheos says—"

"Why are you two always poking your nose in things?" Stryver asked them, his hands placed casually in his pockets.

"We have two noses," Etheos corrected.

"Oh, sorry," Stryver replied. "I was confused because there's only one brain between you, and that obviously belongs to the pig. Because she's noticeably *absent*." He nodded at George as he brushed past them.

"Wait!" Etheos said, as he and Sir Humphrey followed, matching Stryver's pace. "You have to tell us! Why were you—"

"Look," Stryver said, stopping abruptly. "This may be some big game, some fun adventure to you two, but you've got no idea what this means to—to me." It sounded as if he were about to say something different and then stopped himself. "You've got no idea at all."

"What about Wyona?" Sir Humphrey asked.

"I'd imagine it means a great deal to her as well," Stryver replied with a shrug. "Enough to put her hair up. She hates doing that, you know. You've no idea how annoying—"

He was cut off as a single scream, long and piercing, erupted from outside on the stairs. Then a series of shouts and shrill cries.

Stryver frowned and hurried out at a run. Etheos and Sir Humphrey followed.

They found an interesting scene. There was a knot of people grouped around someone lying on the steps, a single boot sticking out from the forest of trouser legs and Academy robes. "He's dead!" someone called from amongst them. "The Lord Overseer is dead!"

This was startling, but even more startling was the other group of people, not as tightly knotted, around the Lord Overseer's wife in her hideous lime green headpiece. She looked enraged, her hat askew, one of her gloves fallen off. She was glaring down at Wyona Wyncliff, who had apparently been pushed to the ground, her hair coming out of its bondage, some of the pearls falling out to roll down the steps, holding a hand to her face as if she'd been struck.

"You!" the Lord Overseer's wife shrieked. "You—you hussy! You killed my husband!"

Some in the crowd were trying to restrain the Lord Overseer's wife so that she didn't leap upon Wyona and tear her apart, others looked as if they wanted to seize Wyona and drag her off to jail.

Wyona, trying without much success to regain her composure, removed her hand from her cheek, which was now sporting a red bruise, to put one of her shoes back on. "I didn't. You did," she said. She stood. "If I could just look—"

"No! Keep her away from my husband! You've already done enough damage, harlot!"

There were too many people barring Wyona's way; she could not get to the Lord Overseer. No one, however, was watching Stryver. She saw him slide his way through the crowd on the steps. He was watching her closely too, his eyes unreadable.

"Lock her up!" the woman was still screaming. "Take her away and lock her up! No! Don't let her near my poor, dear Melvin!"

Wyona glanced about desperately. Stryver was getting closer. They were going to arrest her. In a moment she had made her decision.

She screamed, a very good impression of hysterics indeed, and if Sir Humphrey had not known her, he would have been fooled completely. As it was, the scream only served to confuse him, and Etheos as well. It seemed to confuse Stryver the most, stopping dead. He understood all too well in a moment when she threw out a finger to point at him.

"It's a Changeling! A Changeling! Look at his eyes! Heaven help us!"

And with that, she fainted.

It is amazing how quickly the temper of a crowd changes. Fleeting yet pitying looks were given to Wyona, lying on the steps, as their anger at everything, the death of the Lord Overseer and all the confusion, turned harshly onto Stryver. He stood still and blinked for a moment, hardly believing what had just happened. This, of course, turned his eyes white for a few moments, confirming his guilt.

Then he turned and ran.

He didn't get very far. Several of the chairmen's sons, trying to show their brave nature leapt at him, and they soon had him rather effectively pinned to the ground so that he could not move, much less change form.

He was manhandled to his feet and questioned by the mayor himself. When he gave no answers, he was slapped and, by one vindictive old lady, spit at. The ranking officers of Sir Galahad's Hall soon had a rather impressive guard called in to carry the villain Changeling away in a barred chariot, listening to shouts demanding his death all the while.

And all the time his eyes never left Wyona, who was still lying unnoticed on the steps, apparently in a cold faint.

After the barred chariot had driven away and the crowds began to disperse, congratulating themselves on upholding justice, Wyona sat up, looked about for a moment, and then went swiftly to the body of the Lord Overseer, covered with a sheet on the stairs.

"Is anyone about?" she asked, without looking over her shoulder at Etheos and Sir Humphrey. "The woman in the lime hat?"

"No," Sir Humphrey said. "She left in quite a hurry. Even left her glove," he added, picking up the article left on the steps and putting it in his belt. "What are you doing?"

"Looking for the genie," Wyona replied, searching his pockets. "It doesn't seem to be—AH!" She withdrew her hand quickly. Her fingers were swelling to twice their normal size and were already a rather bright orange color.

"What—"

"Pegasus sleep dust," Etheos supplied. "Some people keep it in their pockets to discourage pickpockets."

"But there's nothing *in* his pockets!" Wyona protested, staring forlornly at her hand. "Not even any money! And certainly no genie. Where could it be?"

"Perhaps someone slipped it away from him before now," Sir Humphrey suggested. "That...looks as if it's getting worse."

Her hand was now three times its normal size.

"It'll stop if you put some goat juice on it," Etheos suggested helpfully. "I have plenty back home. Come on. It isn't so far."

"No," Wyona said. "I can be back in Thieves' Den faster—"

"Not if one wing is five times as big as the other," Etheos pointed ed out.

Wyona frowned. "All right," she finally consented. "Lead the way."

"See, look!" Sir Humphrey said cheerfully. "It almost looks normal already!" Wyona's hand had been soaking in a bowl of rather foul smelling goat juice, which Etheos had taken from a shelf filled with such strangeness in his room, for about twenty minutes. "And my muffins will be ready anytime now." He was making an effort to be overly cheerful because Wyona looked particularly glum.

Her hair had completely fallen down now, hanging rather tangled down her back, not even making an effort to obscure her slightly pointed ears as it normally did, and if an enterprising young footpad had wished to follow them home, he could have simply to follow the trail of pearls that had fallen along the way. The red bruise on her cheek was beginning to turn funny colors as well.

The Lady Orville, perhaps thinking it indecent to have visitors at such a late hour, had retired to her bed in the coat closet and George was curled up at Wyona's feet, apparently asleep, though sometimes it was hard to tell. Etheos was sitting next to Wyona at the table, fiddling with his Magenta Medal of Merit absently while Sir Humphrey bustled about the kitchen.

"What's the matter with you?" Etheos asked Wyona finally.

"Besides having my hand in something called 'goat juice'?" Wyona asked.

"It's really made of—"

"I don't want to know," Wyona told him crisply. "Besides that, I've probably lost the genie, lost my one chance at—at finding a genie." Here she meant to say something else and stopped herself hurriedly. "And I've sold Stryver to the Knights for it."

"You don't like Stryver," Etheos reminded her.

"No, I hate him," Wyona agreed. "And he hates me—"

"Especially now," Etheos added.

"But selling out a fellow Changeling when we're both fugitives like this is—is wrong," Wyona finished.

"You both have a very interesting sense of right and wrong," Etheos observed. "Stealing from a dead man—and many living men in Stryver's case—is just fine, as well as deceiving poor old big-nosed city councilmen, but handing over a fellow scoundrel to the police is wrong? Is that what you're taught up there in those forests?"

"No," Wyona said scornfully. "Those fiends wouldn't know comradeship if it spat at them in the face. It's a sort of unwritten code. We're both in the same predicament. Even though we hate each other, constantly trick each other, sometimes try to kill each other, we'd never denounce each other for being who we are. We've had enough of that in the Changeling Forests, I'm afraid."

"What happened up there?" Etheos asked. "Why were you two banished?"

Wyona shook her head. "It was long ago."

Sir Humphrey, who had stopped his usual kitchen bustling to listen to the conversation, suddenly jumped. "The muffins!" he cried.

"They must be nearly burnt to a crisp!"

He jerked open the oven and tried to pull the muffin rack out with his bare hands, successfully scorching them. With a curse he grabbed at his belt for his oven mitts. Mistakenly, he managed to shove on the Lord Overseer's wife's glove he had put at his belt, and began to reach for the muffins once more.

Instead he was thrown off his feet by a large boom and a crack. When he looked up, he saw a strangely dressed woman standing before him, looking around the flat rather distastefully. She was wearing an exceedingly short plaid skirt and boots that laced up the front as well as a plain white blouse. Her brown hair was tied back in a common horsetail. Her skin was green.

Etheos and Wyona had both leapt to their feet. "The genie!" Wyona breathed.

"Well … *obviously!*" the genie said with a toss of her head. "And let me just say that compared to the last place I stayed at, this joint is a real dump."

"Aren't you supposed to be servile?" Etheos asked.

The genie rolled her eyes. "That's perpetuating an archaic stereotype. Here." She pulled a roll of parchment from nowhere on which something was written in a very scratchy language. "Article sixty-three, clause twelve of the Newly Revised Charter of the Jen states that although the genie is obligated to grant and fulfill three wishes stated by the master who released said genie, said genie is not required to share any opinions, philosophies, or crazy ideals held by said master nor act towards said master in any manner that would demean the importance or esteem of said genie. Nor is the genie required to take part in any aquatic ceremonial events." She rolled up the parchment. "But that's another matter entirely. So," she said, turning to Sir Humphrey, who still had the lady's evening glove on, staring at her. "I must say, you're a lot different than my regular customers."

"More hairy?" Sir Humphrey guessed, fingering his beard.

"No … actually more of a man. But if you want to wear the stylish lady's evening glove, that's fine with me. So, what'll it be?"

"You mean wishes?" Sir Humphrey asked.

"Of course," the genie replied. "Don't make me get the charter out again. You get three of them. So what'll it be? A haircut?"

"No!" Sir Humphrey cried, sounding horrified. "I'd like…" He frowned in thought. "I wish I hadn't burned my muffins."

"Piece of cake." The genie snapped her fingers and a plate of hot blueberry muffins appeared on the table. She picked one up and took a bite.

"They were banana…" Sir Humphrey protested.

"Blueberry is *better*," the genie said with her mouth full. "What's next?"

"I wish Stryver weren't in prison," Sir Humphrey said.

The genie nodded, snapped her fingers, and the door swung open to reveal a very battered-looking Stryver indeed. He stalked into the room and sat down across the table from Wyona. He had apparently lost his hair tie, because his black hair, having very much lost its shine, was hanging about his face giving him a very wild look. His purple coat was muddy, stained with dirt, soot, and a few drops of blood, and there was a very nasty looking burn on his left hand.

"That was exceedingly rude, bird brain," he said with mock polish and calm. "It quite disagreed with my constitution, I'm afraid."

"Better you than me," Wyona replied wearily, pushing away the bowl of goat juice as her hand had returned to normal size.

Stryver made a face at her and reached for one of the muffins. "Such reckless disregard. You were always the irresponsible one," he muttered under his breath. "Such—do you know that for *once* I didn't even do anything wrong?"

"You snuck into the ball without an invitation," Wyona replied coolly, but Stryver wasn't listening.

"*You* kill the Lord Overseer to get at his bloody genie and then blame me when I was just standing there, minding my own business and—these muffins are actually pretty good," he finished.

"Thank you," Sir Humphrey said, his cheeks going as red as his hair.

"I didn't kill the Lord Overseer," Wyona replied with a shake of the head. "She did," she added, pointing to the genie who was sitting on a countertop inspecting her nails critically.

Stryver turned and looked at her for a moment. "Oh, so you found the genie? Wonderful. Does—" He stopped and turned back to the genie. "Do genies usually dress like that?" he asked her.

The genie rolled her eyes and whipped out the charter again, holding it in front of Stryver's face. Stryver inspected it critically. "Article thirty-four, clause seven of the Newly Revised Charter of the Jen states that the genie may appear, dress, or act in any way that said genie chooses as long as said cultivated characteristics do not interfere with the occupation of said genie and the granting of the wishes. Said genie may not wear purple socks." She was about to roll the parchment up again when Stryver grabbed it from her hand.

"What are you talking about?" he demanded, tracing a finger over the scratchy script. "This is a menu for a seafood restaurant written in Troll Tongue. See?" he said, turning it around so that Etheos and Wyona could examine it. Wyona squinted at it for a moment and then nodded. Etheos nodded as well, though he had never bothered to learn Troll Tongue and hadn't the faintest idea what the scroll said.

The genie snatched the scroll away. "It is *not* in Troll Tongue," she replied as the scroll disappeared. "It just *looks* like Troll Tongue! It's the secret language of the Jen."

"Really?" Stryver asked with a raised eyebrow.

The genie folded her arms across her chest. "I don't think I like you. I think we'd be better off if the big oaf hadn't wished you out of prison. I bet you deserved to be in there."

"Actually, he didn't," Wyona replied. "Not this time, anyway. He was arrested for killing the Lord Overseer. Something, I believe, you had a hand in."

"Why would she kill her own master?" Sir Humphrey asked. "Are you allowed to do that?" he asked her.

The genie rolled her eyes again and looked as if she were about to take out her charter once more had Wyona not interrupted. "The Lord Overseer wasn't her master at all."

"Then who was?" Sir Humphrey asked, blinking in confusion.

Stryver sighed. "Look at the glove you're wearing, Sir Knight."

Sir Humphrey blinked down at the white evening glove. "Oh!" he suddenly cried. "His wife! But why would she want her husband dead?"

"It was her third wish," Wyona replied. "But, like her second wish—to get your dragon down from the curtains—it was rather an accident. She came upon the Lord Overseer and I talking on the steps. I gather that she's caught him being unfaithful to her in the past and I, I regret, assumed a bit too much. In her anger she distinctly screamed, 'I hate you, Melvin! I wish you would just die!'"

"Poor man," Sir Humphrey said with a shake of his head.

"But that doesn't matter anymore," Wyona said. "You've already wasted your first two wishes on muffins and Stryver—" Stryver threw her a murderous look. "So—"

"Here we go," the genie replied, rolling her eyes. "It starts."

"What starts?" Etheos, on his fourth muffin, asked.

"Every time there's a group of people present when someone finds a genie, there's always a series of long debates and arguments and pleadings with whoever happened to put on the glove or stick his head in the waste bin or whatever. It gets *really* annoying."

"I'm sure it does," Etheos replied, shooting Wyona a look. "And she should be ashamed, trying to use Sir Humphrey like that." He shook his head sadly. Then he turned to Sir Humphrey. "Maybe you could wish for a promotion for me. Nothing big, just Grand Wizard or something."

The genie groaned.

"I don't know," Sir Humphrey said. "I don't want to waste this wish. It should be something that could really help people. Maybe I could turn the Lady Orville human again!"

Etheos gave him a raised eyebrow. "And that would help people *how?*"

Sir Humphrey's face fell. "Oh. Right."

"If I were made Grand Wizard, it would help people," Etheos continued. "Those people being me…and you! I'd pay the rent on a *new* apartment. Somewhere nice. With a solid gold bathtub filled with treacle."

"I don't like treacle," Sir Humphrey reminded him.

"Well, I do," Etheos said.

"You can't waste it on *treacle*!" Stryver cried, standing, as the genie banged her feet against the cupboard she was sitting on and hummed loudly to herself.

"What if you used your wish to help us?" Wyona continued.

"Us?" Stryver asked, giving her a look. "I meant me."

"Think about it, Sir Humphrey," Wyona replied, ignoring him. "As long as we're forced to remain in this city, in this state, we're bound to be persecuted and hated. The townspeople will eventually kill us, probably for something we didn't do. Please, Sir Humphrey. If you'd just—"

"I asked you what you wanted before," Sir Humphrey replied. "Both of you. But you didn't have the time to tell me then, so I don't think I have the time to listen now."

"He's my best friend!" Etheos said to Wyona. "Why'd you think he'd listen to *you*?"

"Maybe because she wants something better than *treacle*," Stryver replied.

"I *like* treacle!" Etheos said defensively. "What do you people have against treacle anyway?"

"It's a stupid thing to waste a wish on," Stryver replied. "So are you for that matter."

"Hey!" Etheos said.

And so the argument continued, long and heatedly, Etheos defending treacle with every ounce of his being and Stryver bringing it up again whenever the argument veered because he seemed to feel it was a better topic of disagreement than any other. The genie began to bang and hum louder than before.

Sir Humphrey sighed, watching his friends fight. "I'm beginning to wish I'd never picked up the silly genie in the first place," he muttered.

The genie sat up straight. "Can do," she said. And before anyone could stop her, she snapped her fingers.

There was a flash of light and she and the white glove were gone, as well as the plate of muffins. Stryver was nowhere to be seen.

Etheos, Sir Humphrey, and Wyona stared at each other.

"You *idiot!*" Etheos said, sitting down dejectedly.

Wyona threw up her hands. "I was going to get that genie at the ball, you know," she said. "I'm a ballroom dancing *champion*; have you seen my card? I even put my hair up! And *you two* completely ruined it. Next time you feel the need to blunder into one of my careful schemes, *don't.*" With that she turned into a raven and flew out the window.

"I'm sorry, Etheos," Sir Humphrey replied. "But I know you'll be made wizard soon. You're too smart for them to ignore you much longer."

"I suppose I would've gotten sick trying to eat a bathtub full of treacle anyway," Etheos said bitterly. He stood. "I'm going to bed. Come on, George. I'll stop by the city hall tomorrow and see if the Death Cliffs Hang Gliding competition is still on, even with the Lord Overseer dead."

George, who had not shown much interest in being a mascot anyway, belched a puff of fire and rolled over.

The next morning's paper contained two articles of note that Sir Humphrey chose to save for his collection. One was about the prisoner seized for murdering the Lord Overseer, an unidentified man in purple, escaping without a trace from the dungeon. The other was a classified ad placed by the Lord Overseer's widow, asking if anyone had found her missing glove.

Misadventures at the Carnival

"This is probably even more idiotic than the time you made me go to the alchemist with you to hold your hand."

"He was pulling a tooth!" Sir Humphrey protested. "Do you know how much it hurt?"

"You're a grown man!" Etheos said. "You're—you're more than a grown man," he added, looking up at Sir Humphrey's face. "And you're a knight! Aren't knights supposed to be brave?"

"I'm brave," Sir Humphrey replied. "I can behead a unit of tundra beasts in under two minutes."

"And you can't bear to have a tooth pulled? I've seen you suffer countless injuries in the course of your duties but—"

"Can't you just enjoy the atmosphere, Etheos?" Sir Humphrey took in a deep breath. "Enjoy the fresh air?"

"No," Etheos replied, folding his arms sullenly. "This is a peasant attraction. It's demeaning to be here."

"Well, I have to be here," Sir Humphrey replied. "And I'm glad you've brought Lady Orville to keep me company." He smiled down at the pig, who was struggling at the rope Etheos had tied her to, trying to break free and run at a stand selling fried pixies. "It's a very serious job, you know," Sir Humphrey replied. "Keeping the level of crime down to a minimum at the carnival is—"

"Impossible," Etheos finished. "The entire thing is a scam designed to separate peasants and idiots from their money."

In essence, it was true. The carnival at which they stood was a collection of brightly colored tents and hastily erected platforms in a meadow outside the city. Any number of strange foods, goods, and spectacles could be found there as well as the usual jugglers, acrobats, and tarot card readers. Some of the performers had attained a level of skill, but most of the goods and, particularly, food were shoddy work indeed.

"I don't know," Sir Humphrey replied. "The fire-eaters are rather impressive. Look there. The one in the purple coat is rather extraordinary."

"I'm sure—purple coat?" Etheos turned to regard the platform near to their right. There were indeed a group of fire-eaters taking turns plunging the burning torches into their mouths. Most were stripped to the waist, their bare chests glistening with sweat from the heat of the flames. The one in the center, however, who seemed perhaps the most adept, also had the most style and stage presence. He was wearing an ostentatious purple highwayman coat, which he would throw carelessly into a dramatic pose before slowly, so as to increase suspense, dropping the crackling torch in his hand into his mouth. The crowd clapped for him heartily. He seemed to have the right amount of serious dramatic flare and reckless daring for their tastes. But it was Stryver.

"Sir Humphrey, you do recognize him, don't you?" Etheos said.

Sir Humphrey squinted. "Stryver? But what would he be doing here eating fire?"

"Who cares?" Etheos said. "You have to arrest him. He escaped from prison all those months ago so—"

"But he really shouldn't have been in prison in the first place," Sir Humphrey reminded him.

"Well—well he must be up to something!" Etheos said. "You know perfectly well he isn't a member of the carnival."

"And I can't arrest him just because of that," Sir Humphrey said adamantly. "Come on. Let's go find Lady Orville something to eat. She looks hungry."

They strolled through the labyrinth of brightly colored tents. Venders yelled unreal sale prices at them, which the three ignored completely, except Lady Orville who tried to make a mad dash every time she smelled something remotely like food.

"Here," Sir Humphrey said. "This is the best place. Can't go to a carnival without stopping at Friar Peterson's Fried Pixies."

"That's revolting," Etheos replied, making a face.

"No, it's delicious," Sir Humphrey replied, allowing Lady Orville to drag him towards the stand. It was made of wood and painted all in white. In the middle, behind the counter, stood a man dressed in the robes of a clergyman, a friar, except they were entirely white, with a straw hat upon his head. To one side of him was a large bird-cage wherein dwelt a multitude of pixies. They were quite crammed inside, squished against each other. They were screaming tiny, shrill curses in their own simple language, and a few of them tried to hiss and bite whenever someone's hand came a bit too near. On the other side of him was a large vat of deep frying oil.

"Hello there, good sir. What'll it be? A dozen? Two dozen to share with a friend?"

"Two dozen," Sir Humphrey replied. "And a small half-dozen for the lady," he added, nodding to Lady Orville, who grunted rather unappreciatively.

The man in the white friar's costume nodded and took a strangely-shaped net from beneath the counter. He plunged the net into the cage and caught a number of pixies, which he promptly pulled out and shoved into the vat. The pixies in the cage abruptly stopped and then, after a moment, began to make even more noise.

"Aw, shut up!" the friar yelled at them irritably.

It didn't seem to faze them.

After a moment the friar took the pixies out, separating them into a large container and a smaller container. They now resembled crispy fried nuggets without any discernible shape. Sir Humphrey paid the man and turned away. He handed the smaller container to Lady Orville, who gobbled it up so quickly Etheos wondered if she had chewed at all. Sir Humphrey put the other bucket under his arm and began to walk at a leisurely pace down the aisles of the carnival, plopping a fried pixie into his mouth every so often. Perhaps it was Etheos's imagination, but each time Sir Humphrey did so, he could've sworn he heard a tiny shriek.

"I think sometimes you're too proud for your own good, Etheos," Sir Humphrey said. "You're missing out on a real treat."

"Hey mister! Can I have one?" a scruffy-looking boy, no older than twelve, ran up to Sir Humphrey.

Sir Humphrey looked at him for a moment. "I suppose," he said.

"Here." He offered the boy the container so that he might choose which he wanted. The boy stared into it for a moment and then abruptly ran away.

Etheos immediately shouted a spell and the boy stopped, frozen in mid stride.

"Now, just what was that?" Sir Humphrey asked.

"He stole your purse," Etheos replied calmly.

"Oh yes," Sir Humphrey said, picking the purse in question out of the boy's pocket. "Now then boy, what are you doing at this fair? You're here to rob the peasants, aren't you?"

"No—no sir!" the boy replied. "I—I'm sorry sir!"

"I'm sure. All right, boy, who's the leader? We know the thieve network is operating here today. Just tell us where the leaders are and—"

"I don't know anything about that!" the boy assured. "I was hungry! But I don't want to eat that trash! And I don't have any money to buy anything decent." Sir Humphrey grumbled something under his breath and Etheos looked smug. "I'm not a bad kid, really sir. Just ask my aunt. She'll tell you. She's the fortuneteller. Her tent's right over there. I'm supposed to be drawing in customers for her you see— Ouch!" Sir Humphrey had seized him by the ear and dragged him over to the fortuneteller's tent. "All right boy," he said. "We'll see what your aunt has to say." He said it as if he very much doubted the fortuneteller, despite her occupation, would know anything about the boy at all.

He pushed his way past the beaded entrance into the dimly lit tent, coughing at the overpowering smell of incense. There before the crystal ball, wearing a beaded headdress and a colorful foreign scarf, was Wyona Wyncliff.

Sir Humphrey and Etheos held equal looks of complete astonishment. Wyona Wyncliff's eyes went wide for a moment and then back to normal very quickly. The boy whom Sir Humphrey was still holding by the ear looked up at him with a raised eyebrow.

"May I help you gentlemen?" Wyona asked. There was a new note of dramatic mystery in her voice.

"Who—what—do you know this boy?" Sir Humphrey finally

stammered out.

Wyona regarded the boy. "He's a pickpocket from a very sad, unfortunate upbringing," she replied after a moment in a manner that Etheos later described as absurdly theatrical. "Anything else, though, and I'll be forced to charge you."

"Charge—what—" Sir Humphrey stammered once more. "Would you like a fried pixie?" he finally asked, holding out the bucket.

Wyona looked into it, making a face. "No, I'll pass," she replied.

The boy at this point stamped on Sir Humphrey's boot to free his ear and scampered away.

"What are you doing?" Etheos demanded.

"Telling fortunes, what does it look like?" Wyona asked, dropping the mystical tone of voice completely. "Did you want me to look into your future?"

"No!" Etheos said. "You aren't a *real* fortune teller."

"Try me," Wyona said. "Go on, sit. I dare you."

Etheos glared but sat down opposite her.

Wyona took a deep breath, closing her eyes and holding her hands over the crystal ball before her. Then she opened them and gazed deep into the ball. "I see a long journey brought upon you by a rat, fraught with peril. I see a quest leading you far out into the wild, where strange things may happen. Watch the rose, for it always has its thorns. Watch the mountain, for it is made of the smallest pebbles. And watch the skies, for help shall always come from above. I see a strange enlightenment coming upon you. And beware of oats."

Etheos burst out laughing. "That's the most preposterous, improvised clairvoyance I've ever heard, and I've had Academy seers call me arrogant."

Sir Humphrey and Wyona exchanged a look. "That wasn't a seer; that was a janitor, remember?" Sir Humphrey replied, nudging him.

Etheos scowled. "What exactly are you doing here?"

"Telling fortunes," Wyona replied. "I just told yours. Pay up."

"What?"

"I'm charging five gold pieces a reading. There's a sign outside."

"I'm not giving you anything," Etheos said, standing. "Because you aren't really a fortuneteller."

"How do you know?" Wyona replied, standing as well. "There are plenty of things you don't know about me, Master Thaumaturge."

"I'd like to know what you're *really* doing here," Sir Humphrey said, folding his arms. "I'm here on business, Wyona. Keeping order. And when you're about, order is very often ignored."

"Perhaps that's only when we're about in the same place," Wyona suggested. "My plans usually work out well when the two of you don't show up. Now, if you'll excuse me, it's an hour past midday. Time for Mortimer the Magician." And she swept right past them out of the tent, leaving the beads swinging.

Sir Humphrey and Etheos looked at each other and followed, nearly choking Lady Orville as she tried to keep up.

"Tell us what's going on!" Etheos pleaded as they caught up with Wyona.

"No."

"Please?"

"No."

"It's all right, Etheos," Sir Humphrey suddenly said. "Stryver will tell us."

Wyona stopped suddenly. "Stryver?"

There was a shout from Friar Peterson's Fried Pixie stand. Friar Peterson was yelling and screaming bloody murder, as about five of his pixies had escaped, and were flying in the air baring their fangs and swooping down to bite people in the neck and suck their blood. In a moment they zoomed off to wreak havoc elsewhere in the fair. Wyona completely ignored them.

"Stryver?" she said again. "He's *here*?"

"Of course," Sir Humphrey replied. "Isn't he usually working on the same scheme you are, and then you just serve to get in each other's way?"

"That was *you* getting in our way," Wyona muttered.

"Wouldn't it be easier if you just worked together on things?"

"*No!*" Wyona replied with the true vehemence and feeling she only seemed to have in her voice when discussing Stryver. "Stryver and I collaborated once. Many years ago. He was nearly thrown into a Dread Portal of Chaos and I had to put my hair up *twice* in one week. Besides that, we were both banished from our homes, never to return on penalty of death. Stryver and I don't work well in groups!"

Sir Humphrey was slightly taken aback, as he had never heard Wyona shout so much before, except possibly at Stryver himself. "I—I'm—"

"Now where is he?" Wyona demanded. "Did he say anything about Mortimer the Magician to you?"

"No," Sir Humphrey replied. "He—he was with the fire-eaters."

Wyona rolled her eyes. "So typical. He does like to show off, you know, and since he hasn't any brains, that's what he has to fall back on. We'll have to watch for him." She shook her head and muttered something more. When she looked up again, she appeared to be calm and collected as usual. "Come, or we shall miss the beginning of the show." Wyona led them to the large stage where they had previously seen Stryver practicing fire-eating. Now it was set up quite differently.

There was a rather medium-sized crate, a pile of chains and manacles, as well as a smug looking man in a sparkly yellow cape. The elaborately painted sign bore the words "The astounding, amazing and most assuredly fantastic, Mortimer the Magician." The man in the sparkly cape, presumably Mortimer, was also wearing a very fancy cravat and a turban studded with large, fake jewels. He had a cunning little black mustache and thinning black hair. All in all, he was what has come to be expected from carnival fair shows: gaudy performers with third-rate slight of hand tricks, the sort that hadn't enough skill to get into a Wizard Academy and hadn't enough sense to seek out a better occupation.

Etheos wasn't impressed. "Wyona, what are we doing here? If you want to see card tricks or rabbits turning into fish I could *easily*—"

"It's not the show," Wyona scoffed. "And watch your purses, gentlemen. He almost certainly has someone working the crowd." She looked about at the gawking peasants beginning to turn up. "I don't see Stryver yet."

Mortimer the Magician, who had been previously busy setting up things on a small table covered with a magenta cloth, promptly surveyed the growing crowd and then walked off the stage.

Wyona smiled slightly. "Doesn't even make enough to have his own stage hands."

"Who is he?" Etheos asked.

"His name is Mortimer," Wyona replied. "A very old friend." But there was something about the way she said it that suggested the very opposite.

There was a bang and a puff of smoke, and Mortimer appeared on stage once more, coughing slightly.

The crowd applauded.

He began with a few simple sleight of hand tricks using coins and bits of string, speaking all the while in a terribly grandiose voice as if he were performing before the king. He went on to do some tricks with birds, making them appear in hats and empty baskets. They looked rather ill fed and dirty, and their release into the air was usually followed by assorted muffled cries as the pixies which had escaped from Friar Peterson attacked them. A few of the pixies lifted apples from nearby carts, which they proceeded to drop on people in the crowd. Sir Humphrey found this mildly entertaining, at least more so than the magic show, and gave the rest of his fried pixies to Lady Orville. Etheos was personally offended by the entire matter, muttering "Disgrace! Desecration of a noble art!" under his breath. Wyona's eyes only left Mortimer occasionally, and that was to search the crowd for Stryver.

"And finally, the moment you've been waiting for, my grand finale!" Mortimer proclaimed, raising his hands dramatically. "I performed this trick in front of the Sultan of the Desert Lands, and he was so stunned that he demanded to know how it was done. When I told him it was simple magical skill, he threw me on the rack. I was in his dungeon for six months." He sighed dramatically. "But I am not afraid!" he proclaimed grandly. "Not afraid to show it to you! For it is the greatest feat any magician has yet performed and you—you deserve to see it!"

A great cheer rose up from the crowd. Etheos muttered louder.

"I shall need a volunteer from the audience," Mortimer cried grandly.

A dozen hands shot up.

"You sir!" Mortimer cried, pointing at Sir Humphrey, who had been watching Lady Orville and hadn't even been paying attention.

"What? Me?" Sir Humphrey asked, puzzled.

"He's speechless!" Mortimer cried. "Come on up, lad. Don't be afraid."

Sir Humphrey snorted. "Afraid. Ha." Making sure to heft his battle-axe, he climbed the stairs to the stage.

Mortimer had to crane his neck to look up at Sir Humphrey. His turban fell off. A snake slithered out of it but no one noticed. "And what's your name, lad?"

"Sir Humphrey," Sir Humphrey replied. "Of Galahad's Hall."

"Ah! A knight!" Mortimer cried, as if he'd had no idea whom the man with the battle-axe could be. "Then you're well acquainted with these I expect." He handed the large pair of manacles to Sir Humphrey.

"Yes," Sir Humphrey admitted.

"Good. Be so kind as to put them on me."

It seemed he expected Sir Humphrey to gasp in surprise and refuse. When the big knight shrugged and did as he was told, Mortimer did not look amused.

"They're a little tight," he whispered.

Sir Humphrey shrugged. "Wouldn't want dangerous criminals to get away would we? Did you want some on your feet too? I have my own," he added, taking a pair of shackles from his belt beside the oven mitts.

"Very well," Mortimer said, seeming slightly annoyed. "And then you must tie me up in that rope, put me in that crate, and chain the crate shut. You'll notice, good people," he cried, addressing the crowd. "That on the whole of the crate there is only a single hole, on the other side—turn it for them to see, Sir Knight—and that is only large enough to allow fresh air."

The hole was slightly bigger than that. A small mouse could've crawled through.

"Put the box down, Sir Knight," Mortimer suggested. "And help me into it."

Sir Humphrey obligingly tied him up, making the ropes as tight as possible, Mortimer's face going slightly purple. He shoved him into the crate and chained the crate as best he could.

Wyona had a large grin on her face.

"I suppose," Sir Humphrey said as the crowd blinked at him. "He's going to try and escape."

"Try and escape?"

There was Mortimer, standing, just as before, his arms a little red from where the manacles had clamped around them.

"Open the box, good Sir Knight."

Sir Humphrey, giving Mortimer a strange look, opened the crate to reveal the rope and shackles, still clamped shut.

The crowd was properly amazed.

Mortimer bowed grandly, sweeping his sparkling cape.

Sir Humphrey regarded him with narrowed eyes.

Mortimer passed his turban around the crowd and earned a great deal of gold from it. The crowd began to disperse, and soon only Sir Humphrey, Etheos, Wyona, and the Lady Orville were left.

"There's something we might want to discuss," Sir Humphrey said to Mortimer.

"Oh?" Mortimer said, counting his gold carefully. "And what is that?"

"Just something I saw coming out of the back of the crate," Sir Humphrey said with a shrug. "You know, Mortimer— if that is your name—it's my duty as a knight of Galahad's Hall to arrest illegal and unregistered Changelings."

Mortimer's head jerked up. "What did you see?"

"Only a rat."

"You—you must understand, Sir Knight. I'm registered. Completely. I'll show you my papers. They're—they're in my tent."

"Then, by all means, lead the way," Sir Humphrey suggested, a firm grip on his axe.

Mortimer quickly hurried through the fair, Sir Humphrey following. Etheos, Wyona, and the Lady Orville were behind, Wyona with a very wry smile upon her face. Mortimer hadn't even bothered to glance at Sir Humphrey's companions.

"It—it's just here," Mortimer said. He pushed back the flap and then screamed, trying to jump back and hitting Sir Humphrey. "Sir Knight! Sir Knight!" he cried. "It—the—robbers! Robbers in my tent! I demand you arrest them at once!"

"There's only one," Sir Humphrey pointed out. "And you'd best get inside." He shoved Mortimer into the tent, beside Stryver who was sitting, waiting patiently and politely, with his usual feline grace, his purple coat slightly scorched. Etheos, Wyona, and the Lady Orville followed.

Stryver looked only mildly surprised to see Wyona as she took a seat next to his. "I thought you might have heard, bird brain," he remarked. "And dragging along the fool, the egotist, and the pig," he shook his head. "Tut tut, getting predictable."

"Wy—Wyona?" Mortimer stammered, beginning to sweat and pale considerably. "How—what—" He fell on his knees in a strange sort of genuflection at Wyona's feet. "Forgive my ignorance."

"It is a great thing to forgive," Wyona replied coolly.

Stryver smirked.

"You'd best get to your feet and explain yourself," Wyona continued.

Mortimer leapt to his feet. "I—I travel with the carnival now. It—it pays all right."

"And what brings you to the carnival?" Wyona asked.

"Well, I—I—"

"You should order yourself a nice set of business cards," Stryver replied with a yawn. "It would make this so much easier."

"I—I—"

"Have they banished you, Mortimer?" Wyona asked. "Did they catch you smuggling finally?"

"Or did they just get sick of you?" Stryver asked.

"I—they—they sent me—"

"Sent you?" Stryver asked. He and Wyona exchanged a raised eyebrow look. "Really? And why would that be?"

"To—to—" He fell on his feet before Wyona again. "Forgive me! Forgive me! I—I had no choice! They—they threatened my—"

"Money?" Wyona guessed.

"How much did they offer you, rat?" Stryver asked contemptuously. "How much, to spy on me?"

Mortimer slowly got to his feet. "But—but it isn't that!" he cried. "It isn't that at all! The council—the council did not know that you were together, though doubtless they should have guessed as much. But now that I know you are—" A very sly smile pulled across his face. "I wonder how much ransom they'd pay to get back the two of you—both wanted dead on astronomical charges."

Stryver stood in one fluid movement. "You wouldn't dare. The risk is too great."

"But the rewards are great as well."

There was a zing from somewhere atop the bookshelf and Wyona, who had stood, collapsed to the ground, a feathered dart in her neck. Stryver, glancing down at her, did not see the club in Mortimer's hand until it was too late.

Mortimer laughed, ignoring the presence of Etheos, Sir Humphrey, and the Lady Orville completely. He bent down on his knees and plucked the dart gingerly from Wyona's neck. "What would the council pay," he continued, throwing Wyona's ridiculous beaded headpiece over his shoulder. "For the felines' legendary Dark Prince and the aviators' Lost Princess?"

"What about them, boss?" came a grunting voice. An exceedingly small, stocky man, about three feet in height with a grizzly, pointed beard, leapt from the top of the bookcase. He had a cruel dagger at his belt and a blow dart gun in his hand.

Mortimer looked up sharply. "Who the devil—Oh, yes."

Sir Humphrey raised his axe. "I don't know what you think you're–"

Mortimer nodded to the short man who raised the blow dart gun quickly to his lips.

Etheos was faster. "*Cejjet!*" he shouted the spell.

Nothing happened and in a moment he had fallen to the ground.

Sir Humphrey roared, raising his axe and leaping forward. The short man—one of the numerous gnomes that dwelt around the city—leapt aside, releasing a second dart at the same instant that sent Sir Humphrey crashing down like a felled tree, landing on the desk, which collapsed under his weight.

The Lady Orville, who had previously been inspecting the contents of a bag marked "Enchanted Toadstools", took an appraising glance about the room and gave a great squeal of rage. The gnome tried to load another dart into his gun, but the Lady Orville was too fast, soon overtaking him, ripping at his leather jerkin in search of his throat. All he could do was thrash and shout.

Mortimer irritably raised his club, bringing the pig down on the second blow.

The gnome scrambled to his feet and edged away. "What is it, boss?" he asked gruffly. "That's no normal animal. It's wearing a sunbonnet."

"No," Mortimer agreed, peering at the Lady Orville speculatively. "If I'm not mistaken…" He blinked. "I do believe she's a Changeling. One of the swine varieties. How strange. I wonder where she came from." He nudged the Lady Orville with his foot. "Best to take her along too," he ordered after a moment. "It could be a link to more treachery than we had at first supposed."

"And them?" the gnome asked, jerking a finger at Etheos and Sir Humphrey, who was snoring loudly.

Mortimer waved his hand as if shooing away a fly. "Doesn't matter. They're only humans. Leave them. Have Stephan bring the wagon around. I must write a letter immediately to His Majesty."

Sir Humphrey yawned and sat up, stretching his arms and nearly braining Etheos in the process.

"Watch it!"

"Oh. Sorry." Sir Humphrey blinked in the darkness, looking around. "Where are we again?"

Etheos stood. "Well, we *were* at the carnival. But that was some hours ago. Looks like everyone's packed up and gone home."

There were still a few jostled tents standing on the darkened field and plenty of paper and food scraps lying about, but no one was in sight.

Sir Humphrey blinked. "Carnival…How come I don't—oh yes! Carnival. With fried pixies. And the magician and—" He leapt to his feet. "Where'd the magician go? With Stryver and Wyona?" He gasped. "Etheos! Where's Lady Orville?"

Not waiting for Etheos to answer, Sir Humphrey picked up his battle-axe and began to run about the field shouting "Lady Orville! Lady Orville!" madly. A few wild dogs howled back, but nothing else stirred.

"Humphrey! Sir Humphrey!" Etheos called, trying to stop him, but it appeared that Sir Humphrey intended to run all the way to the Frozen North shouting and searching, so distraught was he.

Luckily, as it happened, the group of escaped pixies that were still flitting about took that moment to drop a bag of horse oats on his head, cackling to each other before buzzing off.

Etheos ran over to him, shoving the bag off his back. "Sir Humphrey, listen to me—"

"No," Sir Humphrey said, rubbing his head. "That magician fellow, Mortimer, he kidnapped Stryver and Wyona. He must have taken the Lady Orville too! We've got to rescue them!" He stood resolutely and started off.

"Sir Humphrey!" Etheos cried, exasperated. "We can't just wander off and rescue them. We don't know anything about this. I mean, how much do we really know about Wyona and Stryver? Just that they're sneaky and greedy and somehow got in a lot of trouble. We don't know anything about this Mortimer and—and besides! They're already halfway up the Malignant Mountains by now. We'll never catch them."

Sir Humphrey stopped. "How do you know that's where they went?"

Etheos shifted his eyes. "Well—"

"Etheos!"

"Remember that spell I shouted at them just before that blasted gnome shot us?"

"Yeah. It didn't do anything."

"Even the best wizards can get muddled sometimes!" Etheos said defensively. "Besides, it *did* do something. It set a tracking spell on that gnome."

"So you know where they are?"

"Half-way up Malignant Mountain Pass. I suppose this means we're going to have to rescue them?"

"Of course it does," Sir Humphrey replied. "Come on, there's no time to lose."

And off he ran, his mail clanking in the still night air.

"Stupid pig," Etheos muttered, but followed just the same.

It was slow going. Etheos had persuaded Sir Humphrey to stop at an inn just outside of town to rent some horses, but when the innkeeper pleaded that none of his mounts could ever hope to accommodate someone like Sir Humphrey up the mountain, the big knight had become impatient and insisted that they continue on foot.

"It's all very well and good for you," Etheos complained between breaths, trying to jog in pace with Sir Humphrey but already beginning to fall behind. "But I was trained for better things than to be my own pack mule."

"It's good for you, Etheos," Sir Humphrey said. "Get some color in your face."

"Purple doesn't suit me," Etheos wheezed. "We have to stop."

"I bet you can't name all the Grand Masters the Academy has ever had in chronological order."

"I can so! Ignimus the Incoherent, Amos the Ancient, William the Wheezy, Icarus the Irritating…"

Sir Humphrey smiled to himself, but luckily Etheos could not see it in the darkness. "Wasn't he the one with the possessed table lamp?"

"No! That was Peter the Paranoid!" Etheos cried, appalled.

"My mistake."

The road became more difficult the farther they went, steeper, higher, and more twisted as it wound its way slowly up the mountain. It was not used often by traders anymore due to rumors of hostile ghosts and risks of landslides. Etheos, however, had always assured Sir Humphrey that these stories were groundless.

Still, as they climbed it now in the dead of night, even Etheos looked as if he were having doubts. Their footsteps seemed ominously loud in the silent spaces of darkness and the outlines of gnarled, twisted trees seemed to reach out to grab them from the sides of the road. The sky was cloudy and overcast; the edges and peaks of the Malignant Mountains hung above them like a haunting portrait with eyes that follow one about the room. There was no sound save their scrambling footsteps, the clank of Sir Humphrey's armor, and Etheos' heavy breathing.

"Stop! Stop!" Etheos finally cried, coming to a halt and bending over, panting. "Rest. Just for a moment."

Sir Humphrey grudgingly stopped. "But only for a moment. They must still be leagues ahead of us."

Etheos, frowning, straightened up. "No. No, they seem to be slowing down."

"Perhaps they're stopping for the night," Sir Humphrey said hopefully.

"Perhaps they met with trouble," Etheos countered.

"There's nothing to worry about," Sir Humphrey scoffed.

Etheos glanced at the shadows around him. "If you'd just let me light a little—"

"No!" Sir Humphrey said sternly. "If you lit the trail with blazes of mage light how would we sneak up on them? Don't worry about the dark. I know the road."

Etheos sniffed. "Wizards have excellent night vision," he replied loftily.

"Well, your ego seems to be back in place then. Shall we?"

But before Etheos could reply hotly, they heard a small, indistinct sound from somewhere off the path to their right, like the gasp of a dove. Both turned sharply towards it.

"What was—"

And then they were both bathed in a soft, almost ethereal glow emanating from somewhere in the trees, making the shadows move in a gliding, flowing dance across their faces.

"Etheos! I said no mage—"

"I didn't do anything!" Etheos protested. "It's something—someone in there."

Sir Humphrey tried to peer into the white light dancing among the tall trees but it was too bright to see much of anything. "We should probably go and—"

But Etheos, it seemed, needed no urging. He had already stepped off the path and into the trees, following the white light almost like a moth follows a flame. Sir Humphrey tried to grab his arm, but, in a moment, the big knight seemed to be entranced by the ethereal glow as well. The two wandered through the trees in a sort of absent, euphoric state, following the light as it bid them. They could now hear sounds of soft laughter floating on a light breeze that brought the scent of rose petals and lavender.

Finally the trees ended and they stepped into a wondrous garden, bathed in moonlight yet bright as day. It was enclosed by hedges and bespeckled with flowers of red and pink, blue and lavender, the colors seeming to flow, one into the other. In the center of the garden was a magnificent fountain in a fishpond strewn with water lilies, drinking in the light of the full moon. A pearly white tiger swam lazily about in the pond near a black swan, but it all seemed perfectly natural to the two, completely unaware of the danger. Their minds seemed to be trapped in that listless world between sleep and wake where the whimsical and confounding can be taken in stride so long as there is no discomfort to the senses.

Indeed there was not. The smell of rose and lavender was stronger still, and the light breeze caressed their tired limbs. The glowing, dancing shaft of light grew smaller and clearer as it flowed about the garden until it became a woman in a white dress that seemed to float about her. She danced, lighter than air on bare feet, and dew drops clung to the silvery blonde hair that flowed about her with the simplistic beauty of a leaf caught in a breeze. Her eyes were so dark as to be colorless, fathomless, and they were hard and calculating, even as she laughed gaily and smiled radiantly at them. But they were too far gone to notice such a thing.

No longer aware of their surroundings, of each other, of anything at all except the hypnotic dance of the woman in white, the wizard and the knight staggered forward towards her, reaching out to pull her towards them, to capture some of her beauty and magic for themselves. But she always laughingly eluded their grasp, and they would trip and fall, their limbs like dead weights as they tried to catch the dancing vision.

She climbed atop the edge of the fountain and at last stood still, gazing at them levelly. Sir Humphrey stumbled towards her, but she lithely moved aside, causing him to fall into the fishpond amongst the lilies. The water, strangely, hardly even rippled and did not interrupt the black swan swimming nearby. Sir Humphrey lay back in the water, floating contentedly as the smell of roses enveloped him.

And then Etheos moved towards her, the beautiful shining pillar of white. She smiled charmingly at him and did not dance away. Instead she held out her hand. He reached out to take it in his own and found himself instead holding a deep red rose, dark against her shimmering white.

"Hold it to your heart."

It was spoken in a deep, unfathomable, ageless voice, gently commanding like mothers never obliged while sweetly imploring like lovers never met. It was the same voice that had tempted weary, careless men to their fates for generations, and the same voice that sometimes intruded unwanted upon the midnight dreams of at least one long exiled prince.

Etheos, hardly even taking his eyes off her shining face, moved the rose closer to his heart.

But then something seemed to awaken inside him. Perhaps it was a lesson long forgotten from his first days at the Academy. Perhaps it was a blessing or a simple stroke of luck. Perhaps it was a young thaumaturge finally becoming a wizard. Whatever it was he felt it—a pricking around his fingers.

He looked down at his hand and saw that the rose's thorns had pricked him and a stream of blood was running through the creases in his palm and finding its own path down his arm. The spell was broken.

When Etheos looked up, he did not see an ethereal beauty in an ethereal garden. He saw a hag, gnarled and bent as the trees that lined the mountain pass, with a long crooked nose and ratty, torn rags thrown over her, standing on a rotting tree trunk. She had one good eye which did not blink and one bad eye which was not really an eye at all, but rather a mess of oozing, weeping scabs and scars.

She had only three teeth through which she hissed at him.

"You are not the strongest who has evaded me, little wizard, but it shall not be borne! His death because of it!"

And she disappeared in a puff of foul-smelling smoke.

Etheos saw that he was standing in the darkened forest once more, but the trees here were dead and rotting, fungi growing everywhere with a veil of decay. In his hand he held a long shard of glass, cutting deeply into his skin. He dropped it hurriedly and made to rip a bandage from the hem of his robes, but then he remembered Sir Humphrey.

He looked about him and was forced to summon a small sliver of mage light before he located the big knight, for only his head could now be seen. Instead of floating in a fishpond, Sir Humphrey was slowly sinking into a large pit of quick sand, strewn, not with lilies, but with rotting leaves. The swan had been replaced with a terrible black snake that rested in an overhanging limb, watching the dying man intently. And yet Sir Humphrey did not struggle, still locked in euphoric dream.

"Humphrey! Humphrey!" Etheos called to him, searching for a stick or rope. "Wake up!"

The knight sunk deeper.

"Blast it! *Zuequ!*" he cried, holding out his hands.

Sir Humphrey's progress into the bowels of the sand pit halted.

"*Evyqu!*" Etheos intoned, raising his still bleeding hand slowly into the air.

Sir Humphrey rose slowly as well from the pit and out onto solid ground.

The snake hissed angrily and, abruptly uncurling from about the limb, dove into the sand pit, which swallowed it up and then disappeared with a noise akin to a belch.

Etheos tried to shake Sir Humphrey, but found it too great a task when the man was so big and in chain mail, and so contented himself with shaking his hand. "Sir Humphrey! Wake up! Wake up!" He pinched Sir Humphrey's hand as hard as he could.

The knight abruptly sat up straight as a board, wrapped his arms around Etheos in a rib-crushing embrace, and kissed him full on the lips. It was only after the wizard was able to reach around and smack him on the side of the head that Sir Humphrey let off, looking around confusedly.

"Etheos? What are we—where'd the nice lady go?"

Etheos, who was wheezing again and looking like he was trying not to vomit, said, "There was no nice lady, you dolt! It was a wood siren!"

"But what—oh," he suddenly said. "Oh," he repeated again a moment later. "Well…" He abruptly stood, brushing dead leaves and slime off of his clothes. "This never happened."

"Right," Etheos agreed whole-heartedly. "And if I'm not mistaken, our kidnapped pig is that way," he added, pointing northward in the dark.

So the two started off once more, making a practice of not looking at the other, which caused Sir Humphrey to bump into three trees and Etheos to trip over a root and nearly give himself a concussion.

"Etheos, this is a serious rescue mission. I know that you aren't a knight, but can't you at least *try* to think about the safety of Lady Orville? Stop stalling and let's go!"

Sir Humphrey, who was ahead of Etheos, had stopped to turn back and admonish his friend, who was leaning against a large tree holding his side and trying to breathe.

"Sir Humphrey, I can't—"

"What, if you can't use magic it isn't worth doing? We have to catch up with them. You said we were close—"

"We are close!" Etheos replied, straightening. "That's why a little caution, a little slower of a pace would—"

"Just impede our progress. We don't know anything about this, like you said. We don't know what they want with Lady Orville. They could be *torturing* her!"

"Who would torture a pig?" Etheos asked irritably.

"What kind of maniac would *kidnap* a pig?" Sir Humphrey countered. "Besides, I'll remind you that she's a lady of court and as such might be desirable for ransom."

"For Merlyn's sake, they probably just wanted bacon for supper!" Etheos cried, throwing up his hands. "It's hardly worth dragging me all the way up this bloody mountain to rescue a useless, frivolous, *annoying* pig!"

Sir Humphrey stared at him. "Etheos, what are you saying? Don't you care about what happens to Lady Orville?"

"No!" Etheos shouted. "I *don't*."

Etheos' cry rang about them in the still night air, echoing off the mountain walls and the very clouds in the sky. There was a deep rumbling from above them.

"But—but—" Sir Humphrey was speechless.

Unfortunately, he had little time to collect his thoughts for the rumbling began to get louder and louder.

"It sounds like thunder!" Etheos yelled, holding his hands over his ears.

"It's not thunder!" Sir Humphrey replied, staring above them as the ground upon which they stood began to shake. "Look out!"

It was too late. The Malignant Mountains, long feared for rumors of landslides and avalanches, were indeed living up to their name. Etheos looked up in horror as a great wave of dirt and pebbles spilled down the mountainside in a deadly cascade to crush him. He tried to run, Sir Humphrey could see him muttering spells under his breath, but he barely had a chance before the mountain seemed to swallow him up.

And then all was silent. Sir Humphrey was looking at a patch of new earth. Etheos was nowhere.

He didn't know what to do at first. He stood, staring at the spot where his best friend had been. Then, with a great shout worthy of a battle charge, he sprang forward and began digging with his bare hands shouting, "Etheos! Etheos!" The dirt was easy to move aside, but he knew if the wizard were crushed, he was already too late. And then he reached for more earth and there wasn't any. What was this? Had he stumbled upon a cavern? An inexplicable patch of air? But no, there was the explanation.

It was Etheos, curled into a ball, covering his head, lying in a sort of domed cave. The earth was tightly packed all about him, but not a grain entered the air bubble he had created.

Sir Humphrey almost laughed for joy. "I do believe there is some advantage to being a wizard, isn't there, Etheos?"

Etheos shakily raised his head and looked about him. "It worked," he breathed, staring incredulously about him. "I mean, of course it worked. Had you doubt in me, Sir Humphrey? Why, every good wizard knows how to survive a landslide."

"Of course, "Sir Humphrey replied. "I should have known." He offered his hand and he had soon pulled Etheos out of the hole. The wizard brushed some flecks of dirt from his robes and Sir Humphrey looked about them warily.

"Well," he finally said. "You may not care what becomes of the Lady Orville, but I'm going after her, deeper into the wild and farther up the mountain."

"And since you insist, then I shall follow," Etheos replied.

Sir Humphrey beamed.

"What are friends for?" Etheos said with a half-smile. "Though I must say, Humphrey, it is a true friend that will accompany one up the Malignant Mountain Pass in the dead of night through landslides and sirens and other untold peril after three Changelings and a pig in a sunbonnet."

"Then you are a true friend!" Sir Humphrey declared. "Which way?"

"That way," Etheos replied, pointing farther up the pass. "And I do believe they have stopped moving."

Indeed they had. The two saw the fire through the trees before they saw the wagon. It wasn't the cleanest contraption, but it was serviceable and covered to keep the rain off. There were two horses tied up nearby and a tall, lanky man without a shirt, Stephan the Wagoner, stood near them with his whip. Around the campfire sat three people. Mortimer the Magician was there, his turban gone and his sparkly yellow cape as well. He was now wearing a simple, non-descript shirt and trousers, with thick boots. There was a sword and dagger at his waist. He was grinning, his eyes shining at his two prisoners.

Wyona and Stryver sat opposite each other, their hands both tied. Stryver had a purple bruise across his cheek and a patch of dried blood in his hair. His dark eyes were glaring hatefully, but it was hard to tell if this was directed at Wyona or Mortimer. Wyona was sitting, calm and serene as ever, staring levelly across at Stryver, sometimes granting a glance in Mortimer's direction. She seemed her usual self—except for the rope on her hands—and Sir Humphrey noticed, as he crouched in the bushes with Etheos, that Mortimer seemed to grant her a great deal more courtesy, as if he were quite afraid of her.

"Isn't it nice to have this little reunion?" he said to them both, sipping the mug in his hand. "Why, I don't believe I've seen you, Miss Wyona, since you were just a little one, learning how to fly."

"And failing miserably," Stryver put in. "Nearly broke her neck."

"Some of us have grown out of youthful bad habits," Wyona replied coolly. "Others have not. And as long as we're discussing the past, Mortimer—" she said the name with a hint of contempt. "You should address me as 'your highness'."

Mortimer chuckled. "You've been away a long time, Miss Wyona. I believe you've fallen out of touch."

"Well, you're the same as ever," Stryver said dryly as if such a thing were not a compliment.

"Yes, some things never change," Mortimer replied, glaring at Stryver as if this were not one either. "But then, some things do," he added, turning his full attention to Wyona. "I must wonder, Miss Wyona, what you're doing here with this—this—"

"Stryver," Wyona suggested. "His highness to you."

Mortimer smirked at her. "You are hardly in a position—"

"You should never criticize your betters, Mortimer. Leave that to those more equal to the task."

"And that is what confuses me, Miss Wyona. How you can even stand the sight of him after what he has done to you? Have you no respect for your family? Your name? Don't you remember anything of the past?"

"You, it would seem, do not," Wyona replied calmly. "Else you would remember never to turn your back on Stryver nor trust in the strength of his bonds."

And that's when Stryver, who had freed himself as Mortimer

turned his back and had stood behind the man for some time, threw the rope that had held him over Mortimer's head and pulled tight at the ends, strangling the man against him with a vengeful look upon his face.

Wyona watched impassively as Mortimer fell to the ground, his face blue. "Behind you," she suggested calmly.

Stryver ducked just in time to hear the Wagoner's whip crack above his head. He turned swiftly, drawing Mortimer's sword from the man's inert body and leaping forward. Stephan the Wagoner cracked the whip again, trying to aim at his face, but Stryver remained firm, dodging with seamless, feline elegance. Stephan tried again, this time wrapping the whip about the sword and wrenching it from Stryver's grasp.

Stryver seemed quite unperturbed, even as the Wagoner advanced upon him, bare chest heaving and a cruel look in his steely eyes. He reached calmly into his pocket and drew out a rather small silver pocket watch, inspecting it casually as if trying to discern if he was late for another engagement or not. Then, as Stephan drew ever closer, about to strike, he looked up and said, "There's someone who wants to meet you."

Stephan stopped, narrowing his eyes. But there was little time for the man to be confounded, for Stryver turned the watch so that Stephan could see the face.

Sir Humphrey and Etheos were not at a proper angle to glimpse the watch face as well, but a look of sheer terror registered on Stephan's countenance. He went white and his entire frame shook. Then, with a ghastly cry, he crumbled into a pile of ash at Stryver's feet.

Stryver sighed and put the watch back in his pocket. "Yes, Bruce doesn't make friends very well."

He retrieved his sword from the ground and turned back to the campfire.

"Not a step closer!"

There was the gnome with the grisly point of a beard holding his cruel looking dagger to Wyona's throat. Wyona was still sitting on the ground quite complacently as if she were taking a leisurely tea.

"I said not a step closer!" the gnome grunted once again as Stryver came forward still more. He dug the point of his dagger a little deeper into Wyona's skin for emphasis. Wyona made a small noise in the back of her throat but otherwise remained unchanged. "Unless you want me to slit her throat, you'd best come nay further," the gnome said gruffly.

"My dear fellow," Stryver replied with a jovial laugh. "Do you honestly think I care what becomes of her?"

The gnome grunted. "Don't believe you."

"No indeed, I've tried to kill bird brain many times myself; you'd, in fact, be doing me a great service."

"He is telling the truth, you know," Wyona replied complacently.

"Didn't ask for the opinion of the committee!" the gnome shouted, slapping Wyona across the face.

"How rude," Wyona muttered. "I think you shall pay for that."

"Oh really?" the gnome said with a snort of a laugh. "And who's to make me? Not this fellow."

"No indeed," Stryver replied. "If you're going to kill her, do hurry up about it. Things always have an annoying way of working out for her."

There came a great squawk and a large mass of white feathers fell out of the dark sky atop the gnome. A pointed beak jabbed forward, pecking out one of his eyes. The gnome shrieked and ran off into the underbrush.

Stryver rolled his eyes. "As I said…"

And then the stork quite promptly became a small, elderly man with a pair of spectacles perched precariously upon his nose and a balding head. He dropped to one knee and bowed his head before Wyona. "I bring you greetings from the Order, your most beloved highness." He stood, like a soldier at attention, though his slight paunch ruined the effect. "Earl of Westchester—at your service."

"Who is this nut?" Etheos whispered.

"Doesn't matter. Lady Orville must be in the wagon," Sir Humphrey whispered back. "Come on." Still crouching low, he made his way through the bushes towards the backside of the wagon.

Sadly, when one is approaching seven feet in height and can lift an ox over one's head, the skill of stealth does not come easily. It was definitely something Sir Humphrey lacked.

Wyona turned toward the noise and the little old man cried, "What's that?" and looked around hurriedly. He caught sight of Stryver, leaning rather lazily on his sword. "You!" he hissed. "Rogue! Villain! How dare you show your face in the presence of this lady? How dare you—" His wrinkled face was beat red with anger. He hastily drew the sword at his waist. "Have at thee!" he cried, running forward shouting, his sword recklessly thrown out in front of him.

Stryver yawned, took up his own sword, and with one deft swing and clash the chubby little man's own weapon went flying from his hands.

He stood still, looking forlornly after his sword. "Oh dear."

Wyona was still watching the bushes. "Sir Humphrey?" she finally said.

Stryver rolled his eyes. "Wonderful. Just what we need. Those two idiots."

Sir Humphrey stood. "We're here to rescue the Lady Orville!" he cried. "Where is she?"

"In the wagon," Wyona replied.

"No, she isn't!" Sir Humphrey insisted. "There's nothing in the wagon."

Stryver was frowning, searching the shadows around them. "Wyona," he said urgently. "Mortimer's gone."

Wyona turned swiftly and saw that it was true. "He must have gotten away."

"With Lady Orville!" Sir Humphrey cried forlornly. "Poor Lady Orville."

"What can the man be thinking?" Stryver asked, clearly perplexed.

"And what does he want with that pig?" Wyona said.

"Well, the pig is the smartest of the three," Stryver pointed out. "Do you suppose he thinks—no, even he's not that dense."

"Remember, it is Mortimer we're talking about."

"I'm not very likely to forget, am I, bird brain?" Stryver replied.

The little man, the Earl of Westchester, gasped, clearly scandalized. "Such—such disrespect! Why if I had my sword—"

"But you don't," Stryver pointed out. "Why don't you make yourself useful and run along?"

Westchester puffed himself up proudly. "I'll have you know, insolent wretch, that I am the Earl of Westchester, faithful servant of the royal lineage of the Aviator Clan for three generations."

"I'm sorry," Stryver corrected, rolling his eyes. "Why don't you make yourself useful and *fly* along?"

Westchester went very red in the face again.

"Would one of you gentlemen be so kind as to untie me?" Wyona interrupted.

The Earl of Westchester whirled around. "At once, your highness!" It took him a moment to undo the knot.

"Thank you," Wyona replied.

He bowed low. "It brings joy to my heart to be of service, highness. The Order shall rejoice that you are alive and willing."

"Willing?" Wyona asked with a raised eyebrow.

"To reclaim your rightful place, so unjustly taken from you," Westchester replied with a nod.

Stryver snorted derisively but everyone ignored him.

"Westchester … " Wyona replied, a strange expression on her face. "It's simply delightful to see you again. But perhaps—perhaps you should tell us how you got here. Shouldn't you be north in clan territory? Or have they started sending you out as diplomat again?"

"What about Lady Orville?" Sir Humphrey protested. Etheos had climbed out of the bushes and sat down near the fire, taking a link of sausage from one of his pockets and, putting it on the end of a stick, slowly roasting it. "We can't just sit here while she—"

"We don't know where Mortimer is headed," Wyona replied. "I assure you, I would like to catch up with him as much as you do, but we must not run into things too rashly. Especially not in these mountains. There are untold perils lurking at every turn."

"Truly," Stryver replied, glancing over his shoulder into the dark as he sat down next to Etheos, putting another sausage on a stick.

"I can see that the two of you have met with her."

"Who?" Etheos asked. "And where did you get that sausage?"

"Your pocket," Stryver replied nonchalantly. "And the wood siren. Pesky, isn't she?"

"We didn't meet with any wood siren," Sir Humphrey said, giving Etheos significant looks and sitting down near the fire himself.

"No, of course not," Stryver agreed with a sardonic smile. "She isn't so bad. I send her blueberry pie once a year."

Wyona rolled her eyes. "You shouldn't *tease* elemental beings of awesome power."

"Why not?" Stryver asked. "She can't ensnare me in her pretty little spells."

Wyona shook her head. "You're uncanny." She turned to Westchester. "You'd best tell us, Westchester. How did you come to be here?"

Westchester hesitated. He was dressed in a uniform blue with a strange crest upon it. It seemed to be a clawing hand on a dark field. "Much has changed since you left us, highness."

"Understandable," Wyona replied. "Is Kendall not a suitable king?"

"Your brother has—has disappeared, highness."

Wyona frowned. "Go on."

"We have not seen him in a number of years. We assumed he went to look for you until—until His Majesty came. Now we suppose he was assassinated."

Wyona shot Stryver a look but he was concentrating on the sausage.

"You knew me, highness, as a member of your father's council–"

"The most trusted advisor," Wyona replied with a nod.

"There is no council any longer," Westchester replied with the shake of the head. "No Council of Advisors, no Council of Clans. There's only—only His Majesty. He rules everyone, highness. All the clans must bow before his will. And no one has even seen his face. But his guards are everywhere, and they'll kill anyone who disobeys. The Forest is a dark place indeed. Our entire way of life is—is twisted and shattered since you left us."

"Since we were banished, you mean," Stryver replied, taking a bite of sausage.

"Villain!" Westchester hissed at him. "It's all your doing, I know it is! Some people have half a mind to believe that *you* are His Majesty the Tyrant and I wouldn't blame them."

"Even though it's entirely impossible," Stryver replied. "I was banished, same as bird brain. I've been wandering the world trying to make my way all these years. She'll vouch for that."

"It is true," Wyona replied. "Though he is a scoundrel and a cheat–"

"You are too kind to him," Westchester replied.

"He cannot be the overlord that plagues you now."

"Well, whoever he is," Westchester said, still glaring at Stryver. "His heart is as black as the night. We're little better than slaves. I myself have been lucky not to fall into the clutches of death like so many others of the old life. I retain a post as a clerk. I answer routine mail. It's a disgrace to my political skills, but it's better than being dead. I happened to receive a letter, hours ago, from a detestable rat, Mortimer. You remember him, the rodents' old councilman? He's risen to high places these days. He was writing urgently to His Majesty, saying that he'd caught the two of you. I knew what would become of you should you arrive at the Forest in his hands."

"Torture," Stryver replied. "And then they'd probably try to hang us again."

Westchester shook his head gravely. "His Majesty employs a much harsher punishment now." He shivered. "Thank God I have saved you from that fate. I hastened with all speed to come to your aid after sending word to the rest of the Order."

"What Order exactly?" Wyona asked.

Westchester reached under his tunic and pulled out a silver amulet on which was engraved with a crescent moon and a soaring falcon.

Stryver frowned at it. "That's odd. I've never seen the Aviator coat of arms and the Changeling Council symbol combined like that."

"It is the mark of our Order, highness," Westchester said to

Wyona. "Those who still hold true to the old ways, those of us who resist in secret to overthrow the dark Majesty. We have members from every clan of old, and now—now that you've returned to us… It is the first step in bringing down the evil one."

"That's going to be a problem, Westchester," Wyona replied quietly.

"It will be difficult but surely—'

"I don't ever want to go back to that accursed place again."

Westchester hesitated. "That—that does pose a problem, yes." But he continued to plead after a moment. "Please, your highness, you *must* return! You've no idea how your people suffer. You must help them!"

"They weren't exactly benevolent to me on our last meeting."

"That's in the past now, highness. Mistakes were made on all sides." Here he shot Stryver a look. "But we think that perhaps even then His Majesty was maneuvering for power. Your banishment suits his plans well and so if you—"

"You must find someone else," Wyona replied adamantly. "I find the Changeling Forest does not suit me."

"But you're the only one left!" Westchester cried. "Every other royal family, every other leader of old, has been completely destroyed, wiped out by His Majesty. You're the only one who survives! The only one of old who—"

Stryver began to cough loudly.

Westchester glared at him contemptuously. "You were never taken into consideration, being a filthy traitor. As far as the Order is concerned, the Feline House is dead to the last man."

Stryver threw up his hands. "Typical. I'm no less a traitor than Wyona!"

Wyona's eyes blazed. "Perhaps not by the standards of the council who sought to banish us, Stryver," she said evenly. "But I can assure you that should we ever have the time, I will not rest until I have your head on a pike."

Westchester was beaming at her and the side of Stryver's mouth twitched slightly. "I await the day," he replied. "That the irony and lies can be complete."

"Westchester," Wyona said, standing. "I accept your proposal to pursue Mortimer deeper into the wild and ever towards the Changeling Forest, oust the usurper from the throne and free the clans in a republic once more."

"Splendid!" Westchester replied, clapping his hands.

"Stryver shall accompany us."

"What?" both Stryver and Westchester said at once.

"He has proved useful in the past, Westchester, and, though I do hate to admit it, we shall probably need his help."

"But what if I don't want—" Stryver began.

"Stryver is coming," Wyona repeated adamantly.

"And so are we," Sir Humphrey said.

Everyone turned to look at him for, apart from Stryver who had been stealing Etheos' sausages, everyone had forgotten the knight and the wizard were present.

"We have to save Lady Orville," Sir Humphrey said defensively. "Besides," he added. "It sounds interesting."

"If I helped to restore order to the ravaged north, they'd have to make me a full wizard!" Etheos cried excitedly.

"That is, if you come back alive," Stryver reminded him. "The Changeling Forest is no place for pesky humans."

"It's no place for banished Changelings either," Westchester said, still glaring contemptuously at him.

"And by the sound of things, it's no place for anybody with the tyrant running it," Wyona said calmly. "That, gentlemen, will be our job to fix."

There were only two horses. Sir Humphrey took one and Etheos the other. They were wagon horses, not used to the fast pace but capable just the same. Wyona and the Earl of Westchester had transformed—Wyona into the silver banded raven and Westchester into the dignified stork—and both had flown off into the trees. Stryver watched them go, muttering darkly to himself, before promptly changing into the cat with the strange milky eyes and leaping atop Etheos' horse with him, sitting regally before the saddle. Etheos spent what time he could glowering at the cat, as, like most humans, Changelings made him edgy.

Still he had little time for that. Etheos was not a rider and it showed. He began to curse after only fifteen minutes that wizards had invented better forms of travel and why the devil didn't the world realize it? The cat just rolled its eyes and Sir Humphrey completely ignored him as he smacked up and down in the saddle. He should have been grateful; the horse made the descent down the Mountain Pass much easier, but then Etheos was not exactly the grateful type.

They rode long into the next day along the deserted road. It seemed to have been washed out recently in some places, and the trees about them grew thicker, higher, fuller. The sun barely showed itself all day, staying behind a veil of mist and cloud. There was hardly any sound in the woods around them save the occasional bird call, which Sir Humphrey turned his head towards sharply each time he heard it, thinking perhaps it was Wyona.

It was four or five hours after midday when they turned a bend and found Wyona sitting complacently on a rock by the side of the road, her legs crossed like a native.

Etheos, who had been complaining about hunger and the horse, broke off when he saw her. "Where's Westchester?"

Wyona gazed back over her shoulder into the trees and Westchester staggered out. His face was very red and he was breathing hard. Sir Humphrey was reminded of Etheos on the night before, but knew better than to say anything.

"I say—I say—" It seemed to be about the only thing the poor man was capable of repeating.

"There's a small outpost town up ahead," Wyona replied. "We shall find rooms for the night there. We can reach the Forest by noon tomorrow." She looked quite capable of flying the entire way and arriving before midnight, but the Earl of Westchester certainly did not. Etheos looked as though he too could use a rest—if for anything than to find something different to complain about—and Sir Humphrey was trained not to show such things, but his bones were weary as well.

The black cat leapt neatly from atop the horse and transformed into a man in an instant. He turned back to regard Etheos. "Perhaps," he told the wizard. "With all those robes, you would do better riding side saddle."

Etheos glared at him darkly. "I think I'm beginning to see why they banished you, Stryver."

"Nonsense, I'm sure bird brain would be more than willing to teach you."

Wyona was giving him a look again. It was the same look of controlled rage that she leveled upon him each time their banishment was mentioned. Perhaps she still blamed him for whatever happened, Sir Humphrey thought.

The town was indeed a small outpost. It was, as they called it in the city, the last bit of civilization before the savages took over entirely. "The savages" were anyone that wasn't a citizen on the king's land. These ranged from Changelings to native tribes to the pale-skinned traders of the north and all forms of other creatures and beasts. The people of these lonely outpost towns were said to be made of harder stuff than those of the city. They were brave and rugged and slept with pitchforks under their pillows. Sir Humphrey often wondered in his youth how they managed such a feat.

The name on the sign was Appleton, and indeed there were quite a number of vendors on the streets selling apples of all colors. Sir Humphrey, who was rather hungry himself, stopped Etheos from purchasing one of the orange ones, saying that it would give him nightmares. They wandered the one street rather raggedly; they had been riding for some time. Wyona seemed to know where she was going. She led them to an inn called The Grey Beard.

It seemed an odd name for an inn until Sir Humphrey stepped inside. It had a pleasant main room with high ceilings—nothing cramped and smoky like in the city—and wide windows, a large fireplace and three huge hound dogs as big as the Earl of Westchester lying lazily on the floor. There were a few men taking their early suppers in the common room at the long tables. They seemed to be the sort of good, honest townsfolk who took off their caps when they ate and always said a short prayer to whichever gods they happened to favor. And in the corner, each equipped with a long pipe, were four or five old men with long gray beards trailing down to the floor.

They had long narrow faces, which were so covered in wrinkles that the bags under their eyes seemed to stretch almost to their lips. They were whispering together, muttering sage thoughts by the fire and smoking their pipes calmly. One of them had a pink ribbon tied in his long beard, and another wore a wide hat with a ridiculous yellow feather.

"Don't ye mind 'em, lassie," the innkeeper, a round, red-faced gentleman who had a large mug and scrub cloth in his hand, said to Wyona as he gave her room keys. "They be a permanent fixture of this 'ere establishment. One of 'em's me own da. They sit there on most nights, talking and mumbling and telling stories of the past. Quite interestin' to talk to, if ye've got the time. They don't know much of anythin' a'tall, but that's a secret we don't let 'em in on, don't you know."

Wyona smiled at him. "Thank you for your hospitality, good sir."

"Oh, no trouble, no trouble a'tall. And will ye be wantin' to sup out 'ere directly?"

"Yes, if it isn't too much trouble. We've been traveling for some time."

"Oh, aye," the innkeeper agreed, peering around her at the others. "An odd bunch, that ye are. Might cause a right stir among the chickens, mightn't you?" He shook his head and did not wait for a reply, hurrying off to the kitchens to tell the cook—who happened to be his wife—that there were unusually strange guests come to stay.

They did indeed "cause a stir among the chickens" as the innkeeper had predicted. From the moment they all sat down at the long table to eat the simple meal of apple potatoes, applesauce, and apple pie, the other people in the room fell unusually silent and began to whisper to each other. It didn't seem to bother the party, for they ate in utter silence, too tired to say much of anything to one another, except Etheos, who kept a running commentary on how horrid the food was under his breath until Sir Humphrey pointed out the advantages of muteness with a few swift kicks under the table. The old men in the corner seemed particularly interested and watched intently through the meal, trying to discern who the strange visitors were, and waiting for one of them to introduce themselves.

When none of the party deigned to do so, the old men felt gravely insulted—they considering themselves the lords and masters of the simple hall. And so finally one of them—the one with the shortest beard and watery blue eyes—was pushed forward towards them hastily, just as the group had started on the pie.

"Ex—excuse me." He cleared his throat considerably. "Excuse me," he said more firmly. "But as a long and old resident of this hall I—we were wondering just who you all are?" He finished it off as a sort of question rather than a statement.

"We are travelers," Wyona replied calmly.

"Highway robbers," Stryver suggested at the same instant.

The grey bearded man looked from one to the other. "There is something here," he said quietly. The other grey beards still sitting in the corner put down their pipes and perked up their ears to listen. They had never heard him say such things before. He was usually the quiet one. "There is much here," he added.

Wyona narrowed her eyes at him. "What are you talking about?"

"Secrets and lies, deception, cruelty, a history unparalleled." He turned his eyes on Stryver. "And a sort of pain I have not seen in all my years of sitting in that corner."

"I don't suppose you would," Stryver said dryly.

"I can help you," he said. "They call me Sable here. And I can help you."

"You're blind," Wyona said suddenly.

"Almost completely," he replied with a nod. "But not many people know that."

"You have uncommon Sight," Etheos remarked, though he was not speaking of simple vision. "It is not unheard of for one to lose one's eyesight and gain another more intangible, imprecise yet glorious kind of sight."

Sable offered a wry smile. "Try it, boy. See what you think. But I can help you. All of you. The future is strong about you."

"Should we trust him?" Sir Humphrey rumbled. The knight did not put much store in fanciful palm reading.

"Yes," Wyona replied, staring intently at his face. "Tell us, good sir. Tell us what you see."

"But the glow, although it surrounds you, is still hazy," he said with a shake of the head. "No, you must tell me something first."

Sir Humphrey rolled his eyes, but now it was Etheos' turn to kick him under the table. "He's the real thing, Humphrey."

"Indeed I am, Sir Knight," Sable replied, his lifeless eyes not leaving Wyona. "Well? I grant you, opening the past to scrutiny is not easy, especially for the likes of you, but it is the only way for me to view your future with any clarity. What say you?"

Wyona paused for a moment. "Very well, sir."

Stryver sighed. "You're going to try and break my nose again, aren't you?"

Wyona ignored him for the moment. "You want the beginning?"

"By all means," Sable replied, taking a seat. "The beginning is the usual place."

Misadventures in the Past

"The world now knows me as Wyona Wyncliff, E.P.—adventurer, smuggler, spy, magician, and ballroom dancing champion, as well as many other things besides," she began, looking at no one but Sable, who stroked his gray beard thoughtfully. "But it was not always so. I was born as Wyona, sixth child and third daughter of the Chieftain of the Aviator Clan. I was not his favorite, that was my beautiful older sister—"

"The swan," Stryver muttered.

"Nor my mother's favorite either. That was my littlest brother—"

"The blue jay," Stryver interrupted again.

"I was nothing special. The biggest and bravest was Kendall, my father's heir."

"Condor," Stryver said, narrowing his eyes at the memory.

"He was intelligent and strong, the perfect hero, and we were all proud of him, everyone, even though he was prone to extravagance and showing off. The Aviators were respected at the Council of Clans, thanks to our brilliant representative, the Earl of Westchester," she nodded to the old man, "A close family friend. We lived in a palace in our city built in the high treetops well above the forest floor. Indeed, our people were rarely seen on the ground. I did not walk upon the forest floor until I was twelve years old. And that's when I met Stryver."

All eyes turned to Stryver. He was leaning back in his chair with a foot on the table, calmly eating his pie. He looked up at all of them. "What?" There was a pause. "Oh fine." He sat down correctly and said, "I was the only son of the Feline Chieftain. Awful man, really." He shook his head. "Cougar. It's my opinion that he was struck on the head as a child—not improbable being that I was then plagued with all sorts of burly uncles (not to mention their detestable offspring)—which caused him to be incurably paranoid from there after. He used to personally search each of my sisters' rooms before they retired for the night."

Wyona gave a wry smile. "Stryver had five older sisters."

"*Who* is telling this?" Stryver demanded. "Quiet!" He shook his head. "She always was the rude one," he added confidentially to Sir Humphrey who was seated beside him. "My father took politics very seriously," he continued. "It was all he thought about. I was not the most promising heir and, if he'd been given the chance, he probably would've bequeathed everything to one of my prissy, stuck up sisters anyway. Serious politics didn't help to dull his astute paranoia either. At the time, as I recall, the Aviators had a rather tenuous alliance with the Rodents against us. Oh, it wasn't war or anything," he said to Etheos, who had started to look interested. "Just a political alliance for defeating us in the Council of Clans. Of course," he added with a sly smile, "the Rodents weren't quick to forget that cats aren't the only things that enjoy the good mouse for dinner now and then."

"The alliance was filled with mistrust," the Earl of Westchester agreed with a nod. "Mortimer was their councilman and he did little to help it along. It's my opinion that even then he was working to serve His Majesty."

"So, as a good little kitten brought up by my father, I had learned to mistrust and hate everything that flew in the air or scurried along timidly on the ground."

"Somehow it's difficult to picture you as a good little kitten," Sir Humphrey said.

Stryver grinned. "Well, I wasn't. Otherwise, I never would've met bird brain over there at all."

"Tuna face," Wyona muttered.

"How did you meet exactly?" Sir Humphrey asked politely after a moment, as the two glared at each other.

Neither seemed willing to answer.

"You really must begin or we shall be here all night," Sable said quietly.

And, at this simple request, they relented.

It was a cloudy overcast day. The sun did not shine through the high treetops. There were few birds willing to sing so early in the morning, especially at the crisp beginnings of autumn, and the small group of boys moved almost unnoticed among the roots of the gigantic trees. There were four of them; the leader was a tall boy with sleek black hair and piercing black eyes. They were all rather lean and wiry, and each carried a short bow and a few arrows, which they had stolen from the armory. They should not have been out so early. They were breaking all kinds of rules.

"Come on, Stryver," one of them finally whined. "There's nothing about to shoot. We might as well go back and get some targets, at least."

"If we go back, they'll catch us and punish us," the leader, Stryver replied.

"We have to go back sometime," the other boy replied. "Besides, we're getting into Aviator territory. See the sign?"

The sign was high on the tree—so high that the boys had to crane their necks and squint to make out the soaring falcon crest.

Stryver grinned. "Gentlemen, we've found our target." He picked out an arrow.

"We can't shoot at the crest!" another of the boys said. "We'll get in so much—what if one of *them* is around? They'll gut us and leave us for dead! They're ruthless, you know."

"You're afraid of some stupid, feathery peacock?" Stryver scoffed.

"I heard that they come out at night and steal kittens from right beside their mothers," the youngest boy said. "Then they bring them back to their secret lair and put them all in this big vat where they cook them and drink their blood."

The other boys gasped. Stryver rolled his eyes in the annoyed, sardonic way that he was famous for in his older years. "Scaredy cats. They're just *birds*. Like the pheasant we had last night. It's not like they're smart enough or brave enough to do something like that. They taste good and they don't think much."

"Then how come your dad is so scared of them?" one of the boys asked timidly.

"He's not scared," Stryver said. "He's just—just cautious. I'm braver than he is. If there was an Aviator here, right now, I'd shoot it straight through the heart in one shot and pluck all its—"

"Shhhh!" the boys were motioning for him to stop, pointing up at the crest. "Look!" they whispered. "Look! We're done for now!"

Stryver looked up. There was a bird perched on the top of the sign. A black one. It didn't appear to have seen them, looking out instead upon the feline territory they had come from.

"Let's go!" one of the boys whispered.

"What, you're scared of that? It's just a little one!" Stryver said. "I bet I can hit it in one shot."

"Your father will kill you!" the boy insisted. "*They*'ll kill you. You can't—"

But Stryver had already taken aim and loosed his arrow.

It was actually a very good shot, striking the bird in the wing as it prepared to take flight. It gave a cry and tumbled off the sign, plummeting to the ground. But it was not a bird that landed at the base of the tree before them. It was a girl, their age, wearing white flannel pajamas, stained red at the shoulder from where the arrow had grazed her. She had long dark hair and skin almost as pale as the shirt she wore.

"It's one of them!" one of the boys screamed. "You've done it now!" They all dropped their weapons and ran.

"Cowards!" Stryver yelled after them.

He drew the short sword his father insisted he always carry with him and slowly approached the girl.

Her eyes snapped open and she tried to sit up. "If you dare touch me, my father will see to it that your entire clan is destroyed," she said, holding her chin higher.

"I'm not scared of the likes of you," Stryver said.

"I'm not scared of you either."

Stryver brought the sword point to her throat. "What about now?"

She glared at him contemptuously. "Only a coward would kill someone unarmed."

Stryver's eyes blazed. "I'm no coward." He bent and retrieved a second short sword, one that one of the boys had dropped, and handed it to her hilt first, moving back so that she could stand. "If you know how to use it."

She scoffed at him. "My father is the Chieftain of the Aviator Clan."

"We're even then."

He attacked first, slowly, testing her, but she replied in kind, quicker and more agile than he would have thought. Soon he threw all caution to the winds, caught up in the swift fight. She was good, perhaps his equal, but she always seemed to play rigidly by the rules, something Stryver had never been particularly fond of. As the fight dragged on longer and his shirt was stained with sweat, he leapt away, bent, and picked up a rock. Seeing an opening he threw it at her.

"Hey!" she cried as it struck her on her wounded arm, dropping her sword. "That's cheating!"

He brought his own sword point up to her throat once more. "Yes, I know."

"Are you going to kill me then?" she asked after a moment."

"No," he replied, much to his own surprise. "I'm not craven enough to kill a wounded bird. There would be no challenge."

She studied him for a moment and then said, "We shall meet again then, Stryver. And I shall bring you a challenge."

Then she turned quickly and ran off through the trees, leaving Stryver to stand and wonder how she had known his name.

"How *did* you know my name?" Stryver asked.

"I did my homework," Wyona shrugged. "Didn't your tutor ever force you to learn the names of all the current nobility?"

"Yes," Stryver reflected. "But I never bothered much with him."

"Lazy," Wyona chided.

"Tall!" Stryver yelled back, not being able to find a more suitable reply.

"No more so than you," Wyona told him sternly.

"Is there more pie?" Etheos asked.

"Have mine," Wyona replied, sliding it across the table untouched.

"So it all began with a fight?" Sable asked, pulling at his ear distractedly.

"And it shall end with one as well, undoubtedly," Wyona replied.

"Why?" Sable asked, turning towards her sharply.

"Because—because of what he's done!"

"The world knows of Mr. Stryver's exploits as the West Road Highwayman," Sable replied.

"No," Wyona said. "Before that. Long before that."

"Perhaps you would do well to continue."

It was five years later when next the two would meet, quite unexpectedly indeed. Rumor and news had spread that an adventurer hired from distant lands had brought back to the Rodent clan something they called "The Sacred Pear" and prized very highly. They showed it great reverence and veneration, often bowing to the very building it was encased in if they should pass it in the street. No one knew quite what it was, as few had seen it, but all agreed that such a thing was priceless.

And so it was no surprise that, should anyone have been up in the late hours of the night, they would have seen a strange black cat scaling a tall tree opposite the temple where the Sacred Pear was kept. Nor should it have surprised anyone to see on the opposite side of the building a small raven alighting on a windowsill. The habit of the two to arrive at the same place at the same time with the same scheme in mind, which would inconvenience them countless times in the future, was just becoming apparent as each in their own way snuck into the sacred tower temple of the rodents to steal the Sacred Pear.

Stryver crept along the darkened corridor, his soft boots making no noise. Although a cat would be smaller and harder to discern in the shadows, a cat, he knew, was no welcome guest in Rodent territory. No, it would be far easier to talk his way past as a man should he be caught. He came to the end of the corridor and frowned, leaning against the wall in the shadows. Which way was it? Left or right? He couldn't tell anything in the dark and so, finally, decided to guess at random and turned sharply left.

It was the wrong choice. He ran headlong into someone in the shadows and both were sent toppling to the ground. He leapt to his feet in an instant, drawing his sword. His opponent had obviously done the same for there was a slim saber glinting at him from the moonlight coming from the window. He'd been caught. There was nothing for it but to attack or run.

So he attacked. He was, after all, the greatest swordsman in his father's hall, and he had known no equal with the blade in some time. If he couldn't best a simple guard, well…

But it seemed he couldn't. Whoever it was—for he still could not see clearly in the darkness—was meeting him blow for blow. No matter what feints he tried, his opponent was always on par, his equal.

"You're good," he remarked.

"Indeed."

He frowned. A woman? And she seemed far too tall for a Rodent, who were prone to being rather short and squat. He took a leap backwards, landing in the moonlight streaming from the window he had entered through. She took a step into the light as well.

"Stryver?"

"You!"

"It's Wyona, actually."

Even though it had been half a decade, it was impossible not to recognize the pale Aviator girl he'd shot out of a tree all those years ago.

"Just what are you doing here?" he demanded.

"I could ask you the same question," she replied calmly.

"Don't you know it's dangerous to be sneaking around in here? They have three units just here, guarding that Sacred Pear."

"Yes, I know," she replied. "I also know where they're keeping it, which, it would seem, you do not."

"How do you—"

"I memorized the plans for this building. Don't you ever study? Or do your people not have a library?"

"At least my father isn't going back on a long alliance with the Rodents. My father isn't a traitor."

She raised her sword once more, dark eyes flashing. "Your father isn't fit to lick my father's boots! He doesn't know I'm here and if he did, he'd probably disown me! He's a noble, honorable man, something the likes of you wouldn't understand."

"The noble, honorable man who raises his daughter to break into their neighbors' sacred temple to steal their sacred relic?"

Wyona let out a cry of rage and leapt into battle. Her practiced, serene demeanor vanished entirely. Her eyes snapped, alight with a vengeful wrath. She fought with a sort of fire that he would not have thought her capable of, for though he had barely spoken three sentences to her in his whole life, he thought he'd known her sort. True, he had only given his tutors passing nods over the last few years, but, due to his father's increasing paranoia, he had come to know at least a little about the Aviator clan. He didn't know much about Wyona, though why should he? She was not the heir to the throne, nor a great beauty or scholar; she had little to no influence at any council and, though her name was recorded in one of the clan's great books, next to her name was only a date of birth. There was nothing more of import about her. She simply was, quietly and obediently. The way she had fought previously, rigid and particular to structure and form, only confirmed this opinion he held. But then, what sort of obedient little princess would sneak in here, after a sacred relic, for no more purpose than to cause some trouble? It was rather like himself.

So surprised was he at her anger and intensity that he barely noticed that she had backed him against a wall until her sword was pointed squarely at his throat.

"Is that enough of a challenge for you?" she demanded.

It took him only a moment to remember. "You'll do, I suppose. Nothing like a master with the blade but—" He choked as she stuck her sword harder into his skin.

"I am your *equal*, nitwit."

"Bird brain."

She rolled her eyes. "We've had the same instructor, obviously."

Stryver blinked. "Old Master Nwin of the Serpents?"

Wyona nodded with a wry smile. "Rather odd that he is so good with his hands—"

"When his other form has none," Stryver finished, staring at her incredulously. It was the same thing he used to tell his friends after particularly long sessions with the old master.

Before Wyona could reply to this, they heard a voice and saw a light moving along the other hallway. Wyona had leapt into the shadows opposite him in an instant and he himself pressed further against the wall, making no noise, trying to not even breathe as the two men passed them. Their outlines were visible against the light of the torch one carried. One was short and moved with a sort of shuffle—definitely a Rodent, Stryver decided. The other was only slightly taller, but lean, and moved with a sort of bobbing sway. Stryver frowned, not being able to place it.

"It will be safe to talk here. No one is allowed in the same chamber as the Sacred Pear," the rodent said.

The other nodded. "It is nonsense," he added.

"Indeed, but convenient."

They continued on down the passage. And, as Stryver stood still in silence, the shadows across from him began to move after them.

He caught her hand. "What are you doing?"

"Following them, of course," came the answer. "That was the Rodent councilman, Mortimer. He always struck me as a rather dubious character. I would like very much to see what sort of secret meetings he's conducting in the dead of night. Was it any of your business?"

But as she moved to leave, she noticed that he followed right alongside her. She paid it no mind and, sticking to the shadows, the two made their way towards the inner chamber of the Sacred Pear, where the most clandestine of conversations was taking place.

It was a circular room with a ring of candles surrounding the pedestal on which the pear stood. It was just that, a pear. It was also made of solid gold. The two men were standing next to it, within the well-lit circle, while their two watchers crouched in the shadows along the wall. Mortimer was a short man with dark hair and eyes and a rather strange twitch about his fingers, as if he were perpetually nervous. His companion wore puffy pants and a simple vest, all of a shiny green that glinted in the flickering light, with red hair done back in a horse tail and large, wide eyes. Stryver still couldn't place him.

"Now," Mortimer said in a businesslike way. "Here is what you must do." He took a rolled parchment from a pocket. "Deliver this to the Canine grand vizier. Don't bother going to the councilman; he's got some funny ideas about loyalty. The vizier has more sense. Explain to him that it is in everyone's best interest."

The other man didn't seem convinced. "In your best interest you mean," he said quietly. His tone could have been mistaken for servile if one ignored what he'd said. "In your clan's best interest. I fail to see how this senseless killing will help anyone else."

"That is because you are *blind*!" Mortimer replied through clenched teeth. "Blind to the future, to the present situation! Don't you see that they have too much power?"

"You are their allies, sirrah."

"Oh, no. We are their tools. They will use us against those accursed Felines until they've all the power, and then the two will simply destroy each other. Don't you see what a war of that magnitude would do to our home? They are too powerful as it is. In this way, all those responsible will be eliminated to leave room for more democratically-minded fellows."

"Like you," the other man guessed. "The chieftains, perhaps. I concede that such a thing may be a proper course of action. But what of the children? Innocent of—"

"No man is innocent, fool. And they will only be in the way. Our ally insists—"

"The Avia—"

"No, fool! *Our* ally! We have a comrade in this plan, one with much power who will see to it that a greater good is achieved. He supports us. You must learn to trust his wisdom as I do. He will not allow us to fail."

"As you say, sirrah."

"You will see!" Mortimer snapped. "Just deliver the message! We will continue this later." He turned on his heel and was gone. The other man stood for some time in the empty room, next to the Sacred Pear. Then, quite suddenly, he turned his face towards the shadows and both Stryver and Wyona had the sensation of being suddenly seized from behind.

"Bind their hands," he ordered quietly as he walked out the door. "And put them in the carriage. I shall question them myself. Spies shall not be tolerated."

There were grunts of acceptance from behind them, and Stryver didn't even have to look at the two bulky forms to guess their clan. Swine. They usually had a distinctive smell about them.

It was as they were being dragged from the room through the door the strange man had taken that Stryver chose to attack. He had no wish to be questioned or even recognized. He turned swiftly, tripping the man who held him with a sweep of his foot and a tug of his hands. He drew his sword—for he had managed, as was a particular talent of his, to slip free of his bonds—and lunged at the other, who held Wyona. Although they were strong, they didn't appear to be the fastest of thinkers, and, when surprised, it took them some time to recover. Time that they did not have. In a matter of minutes, each was lying on the floor and a little stream of blood was pooling at Stryver's feet.

Wyona stared at them coolly over her shoulder. "You certainly made quick work of them."

"I don't like being tied up."

"How did you break free?" she asked, struggling with the rope that bound her own hands.

He shrugged, cutting her bonds with a swipe of his sword. "It's a trick my father taught me. We'd best leave by way of the forest."

Wyona agreed and, as quietly and quickly as possible, they made their way to the window by the large tree.

"Watch that third branch down there," Stryver cautioned as Wyona climbed onto the windowsill. "I think it's dead."

Wyona gave him a wry smile. "I don't believe I have to worry about it." And then a small raven stood on the windowsill in her place, giving him a rather amused look.

"Well," he said defensively and immediately transformed into the black cat. He leapt atop the windowsill alongside her and took a swipe at the little bird with one of his paws.

She was too fast for him, leaping into the air just out of his reach, giving him a very reproachful shriek.

He yawned in her face and polished one of his sharp teeth with his tongue.

She flew off towards the forest and he leapt off the window and onto the tree, quickly making his way down. Stryver ran quickly through the shadows until he was under the deeper darkness of the trees once more. Yet the moment he stood as a man he felt something leap upon his back, arms nearly choking him. He cried out in surprise, throwing his attacker off. The attacker was soon dislodged, but instead of offering blows, slapped him across the face.

"That's for trying to eat me."

Stryver laughed. "But I wasn't really considering it… very seriously. You are the enemy, you know."

Wyona's face, or what he could see of it, became suddenly serious. "No. No, it seems we've another enemy."

"Yes," Stryver agreed. "That is a problem."

They walked through the dark woods in silence for some time. He couldn't see Wyona anymore, even though she was standing right next to him.

"What shall we do?" she finally asked. "Warn our parents, surely?"

Stryver frowned. "I'm not sure that would do any good. My father, you see, is already paranoid about everything. He already thinks there are about fifteen plots afoot trying to assassinate him. And everyone in our clan is so used to it that they wouldn't take me seriously if I tried—"

"You've got to try anyway. I'm going to talk to my fath—my mother." She frowned. "Perhaps Kendall. Kendall will listen to me. And Father will be sure to listen to him. Yes. Yes, that will work."

"What are you going to say? Our allies are making secret treaties to murder us all in our beds with the help of the Canines and a 'secret ally'?"

"Exactly."

"Who do you think it is anyway? This secret ally that little rat is trusting so much?"

Wyona shook her head. "Someone like him. Someone who wants

power." He heard her stop. "I have to head off that way now," she said. "Flying. Else I'll never make it back in time."

They both paused, not knowing exactly what to say.

"Thank you," she finally said. "For getting us free back there. You really aren't so bad for a complete scoundrel."

"And you really aren't so bad for a complete birdbrain."

He didn't even have to see it to know that she was scowling at him. "I'll see you tomorrow night, then," she replied. And there was a rustle of wings and he knew she was gone.

"What was tomorrow night?" Stryver asked.

"You don't remember?" Wyona replied, blinking. "The autumn session of the Council began two days afterwards."

"Oh," Stryver replied rolling his eyes. "That's right; the bloody formal function—what was it called?"

"Welcoming," Earl of Westchester supplied. "It was very tense that year, as I recall."

Stryver snorted. "An understatement. I was arrested!"

"You're always arrested," Wyona replied.

"Yes, and things always work out for you," Stryver said. "I don't see how that's fair."

"Sometimes life isn't meant to be fair," Sable interjected. "It makes us stronger. I take it that, though you warned whom you could, it was for naught?"

"Yes," Wyona said. "How did you—"

"I have heard many such stories before. Sadly, it oftentimes takes a great cataclysm indeed to oust some from their set opinions."

"Yes," Wyona agreed. "I have met many such people myself, but I thought it strange that Kendall, my dear brother, should be one of them."

"He wouldn't listen to you?" Sir Humphrey asked.

"Oh, he listened," Wyona said. "He seemed sharply surprised, so surprised that I was afraid he wouldn't believe what I told him. But he stood quickly and said, 'Don't worry, little sister. I shall see to this at once'. But then he did nothing."

"Odd," Sir Humphrey commented.

"Yes," Wyona agreed. "I think he must have become distracted and forgotten. Kendall was a wonderful person, noble like our father, but he was easily distracted by simple things, like a new sword or boots. Sometimes you'd find him sitting, staring at the same painting for hours on end, daydreaming. But he was too dear to us for anyone to reproach him for it much."

No one was looking at Stryver, but if they had, it might have raised some very interesting questions with some very interesting answers. He had been sitting fingering his pocket watch—the one he had shown to Stephan the Wagoner that had turned him to dust—ever since Sable's talk of fairness. Now it was in the palm of his hand, and he was squeezing it so hard his knuckles were white. A careful observer would have noticed indentations and scratch marks on the surface as if he were in the habit of doing this often.

"It is a great loss indeed," Westchester said with a sorrowful shake of the head. "And an untimely demise that I'm sure you shall make His Majesty pay for in the end."

Stryver coughed loudly.

Westchester glared at him. "It isn't as if the likes of you would understand such virtue."

"No," Stryver replied, though all could hear the carefully caught anger behind his voice. "I'm not the sort of man to live up to Kendall's *virtue*."

"I take it you don't care for Wyona's brother?" Etheos guessed, having finished his pie and becoming slightly bored.

"You'll learn sometime, wizard, not to mention Wyona's family," Stryver said, his eyes never leaving her face, which, it should be noted, she was struggling to keep calm and neutral. "It's about the only subject that can easily break down that schooled calm into something you don't particularly want to face unless you have a good sword and know damn well how to use it."

"You are offensive, sir," Westchester said coldly, trying to retain some of that calm manner that had been practiced by royals for generations.

"And you are old and have a funny nose," Stryver replied entirely without malice.

Westchester looked as if he were going to leap up and challenge Stryver to a duel, which doubtless would've ended very badly for the old stork, but Sable, who seemed to prefer to listen to everyone in their turn, said, "And pray, what happened at this formal function? If there were men out to kill you, it would be dangerous indeed."

"It was," Wyona replied, still watching Stryver carefully. "Though not for whom you would suppose."

If anyone had the right to be nervous, it was surely the Chieftain of the Rodent Clan. It didn't help that he was usually edgy by nature, for tonight he visibly shook, as it was his year to host the welcoming. Delegates and nobility from all the clans of the forest had come that night, and everyone could feel the tense air push against their skin as they entered the grand ballroom. The chieftain just knew something terrible was going to happen. The fish people would probably get into their usual fight with the burly bear delegates, and he was praying that the wolves didn't get drunk again. But what he was most worried about were the Felines. What Rodent wasn't afraid of them? The delegates and the royal family had all arrived on time, all tall with, it seemed to him, long sharp teeth. They moved with a sort of agile grace that he found unnatural and rather frightening. He didn't trust them. They were the enemy.

Not that he trusted his supposed friends either. The Aviators scared him almost as much. For years now, Mortimer, the councilman, had been whispering in his ear how tenuous the alliance was, and by the look in the Aviator chieftain's eyes as they shook hands, the chieftain didn't doubt it. As Kendall, who was right behind his father, came upon the little man—his transformed state was that of a mole rat, but there was very little difference in human form—the chieftain's hand was shaking so much he spilled his drink all over the young man. He let out a small shriek of surprise. Sure that Kendall would leap for his throat, he began immediately muttering apologies, almost cowering before the prince. Only when Kendall smiled wryly and said, "Not to worry, old chap. I didn't like this tunic much anyway. Here, I'll get you another drink," did he begin to calm down, although Wyona, who was right behind her brother, did not do much to improve his mood with her eerie calm that even then she had become quite skilled at.

For something called "the grand ballroom" it wasn't much, though no one was crass enough to say so. Its ceilings were actually rather low, making it seem smaller and darker, though it was rather small and dark to begin with. It was not at all difficult for Stryver to find Wyona standing by a window. She wore a long dress of midnight blue and her long hair was done up on top of her head in curls. She was scowling. Stryver, on the other hand, was grinning widely. He was wearing a strange coat, the make of which she had not seen before, in an ostentatious purple, while everyone else in the room—with the exception of a few Reptile delegates—was dressed in dark colors.

"You look in a foul humor," he commented.

She scowled deeper at him. "And you're annoyingly cheerful. Why are you wearing that ridiculous thing?"

Stryver shrugged, leaning against the wall and watching the finely dressed individuals mill about in the same way as he might watch an opera—with an exceedingly skeptical look on his face. "It was my grandfather's. He traveled, you know. Out into the world."

"To study?" she asked.

"No," he replied. "To steal things from rich people. But think of the grand adventures he must have had."

Wyona laughed a rather humorless laugh. "My mother says adventures are for commoners."

Stryver laughed too. "But you don't believe that yourself."

"How would you know?" she demanded.

"Because if you did we wouldn't have met at all last night, would we? Speaking of that, have you seen any dark shadows wandering about wielding butcher knives?"

"No," Wyona said, rather angrily.

"Just what *is* the matter with you?" he asked.

"My hair," she replied, in a barely audible voice.

He frowned, looking at the curled mass of dark hair with narrowed eyes. "It looks…like a cloud," he finally decided.

"Really?" she asked.

"That's trying to eat your head," he added.

Her scowl returned. "I *hate* putting my hair up."

"Yes, and I hate the man who's trying to brutally murder us. Have you seen him?"

"Mortimer?" Wyona asked. "He's over—he was near the chieftain," she replied as she looked over towards the nervous man. "I don't know where he's gotten off to."

Before Stryver could comment that it was probably to carry out some nefarious scheme, the two were accosted by a slender woman with very little hair and an amazingly smooth face. "Well, isn't this just darling?" Her voice had a strange, bubbling accent and was too squeaky for anyone to listen to for long periods of time.

"Excuse me?" Stryver asked.

"You two. I'm so proud. Not being tied down by the social expectations of your respective clans. It's just wonderful."

"Dolphin delegate," Wyona whispered to Stryver.

There came a sort of chirping noise from one of the violins, and then, of a sudden, the minstrels in the far corner burst into music. Considering the rather uncomfortable room, the music wasn't half bad, except for the pounding dulcimer, which seemed to be having trouble keeping up with the others.

"Well, don't just stand there skulking in the corner!" the delegate suddenly cried, grabbing each by the arm. "You're young; go out there and have some fun." And then, before they could protest that Wyona's hair really looked too carnivorous and that Stryver's coat wasn't fit to be seen in public, she had pushed them both out onto the dance floor, and they had no real choice but to begin dancing or be run over by the large stag couple that was already doing so.

It has been observed that Stryver and Wyona dance in the same way they would fence—with a sort of easy, careless agility that almost befuddles their observers with the unpracticed elegance and grace.

Of course, in reality, it wasn't entirely unpracticed.

"I don't think my father would be very happy if he knew that Master Nwin was teaching you as well," Stryver commented mildly as he turned Wyona on his arm.

"He'll be a great deal more upset when he sees us now," Wyona replied, casting a glance over her shoulder. "Not to mention my father and the Earl of Westchester and—is anyone watching us?"

"Don't be stupid—everyone's watching us," Stryver replied nonchalantly.

"Well, then don't step on my dress," Wyona said.

"I wasn't planning on it."

"They're going to be so angry with me when they catch me later."

"Well, then don't think about later. Think about what you're going to do when that thing starts growling and flies off to eat people."

"I *hate* putting my hair up," Wyona muttered.

"It doesn't look that bad," Stryver said. "You look radiant."

"Liar."

"Well, if it gets you to shut up about—"

"My father was right about you people. Crass and rude and untrustworthy, the lot of you."

"Then why are you still dancing with me?"

She was silent.

"Ah yes, and then the bird brain's secret came out. You're in love with me."

"I'd sooner fall in love with a cod fish."

But Stryver went on undeterred. "Tell me the truth. Is it my suave charm?"

"Cod fish," Wyona repeated.

"Devilish good looks?"

Wyona rolled her eyes.

"Ah yes. The purple coat." He shook his head sadly. "You aren't the first innocent, naïve little thing to be drawn in." He sighed as the dance ended, still keeping her hand as she shook her head at the absurdity. "But I must apologize. It's not meant to be." He raised her hand to his lips in a rather dramatic theatrical fashion, not realizing that the Aviator chieftain and Kendall were directly behind him.

Wyona saw them, though. Her eyes went slightly wide. Her father, she could see, was furious, even though to any passing observer he would seem only slightly agitated. Kendall looked curious.

But in a moment the dance and even the rather risqué gesture was forgotten. A cry rose up and shouts of "He's dead! Dear Lord!" rose up. Everyone turned.

The Rodent chieftain had fallen suddenly to the floor, in the middle of his conversation with the heir to the Equine throne, his wine goblet lying beside him, and the dark red liquid trailing among the feet of those that surrounded him, an ominous sign indeed.

"It looks like blood," Wyona breathed.

In a few moments it was apparent to all that the chieftain really was dead. And the physician, called in quickly from another part of the fort where he was seeing to a broken leg among the stable hands, soon pronounced the cause. "Poison," he said. "A good one. It could have been administered almost any time in the last day. It's hard to tell with these things."

Wyona turned to Stryver. "But I thought they wanted to kill us. Why would Mortimer murder his own chief?"

"But his highness has been too ner—excited to eat anything today," Mortimer, who was nearby, said. "Except—except when he had luncheon with the Felines."

His eyes turned on Stryver.

Stryver looked about the room quickly. His father and sisters were nowhere to be seen. Where the devil had they gone? All eyes in the room were turning to him, accusing, glaring hatefully.

He turned to Wyona, who was simply staring at him curiously, wondering. "It seems it's time for me to depart."

And then he ran.

The Earl of Westchester laughed. "Didn't get very far though, did you?"

"No," Stryver replied, rolling his eyes. "Not even to the window. It was that dog-man. Jumped right at me. You know," he continued reflectively, "that was the first time I've ever been thrown in prison. And I didn't even consider stopping to savor the moment."

"Could they simply arrest you like that?" Sir Humphrey asked, frowning. "Without even bothering to prove you were really guilty of anything?"

"Under normal circumstances, no," Wyona replied. "Mortimer

told of the events at the luncheon, mentioning all the possible times Stryver could have slipped something into a glass or bit of tuna. I didn't find it terribly convincing, but there was something in Stryver's manner that insured his guilt."

"They could see he was a no good scoundrel!" the Earl agreed.

"I think it was because he ran," she supplied. "And the fact that the rest of the Felines had strangely disappeared."

Stryver shook his head. "I never saw any of them again. Whatever became of them? Were they killed?" he asked the Earl of Westchester, as if he were inquiring about the old man's pet fish.

"Your father was for certain, in battle, as to your sisters … no one really knows. Either they've been murdered or are being held prisoner in His Majesty's dungeon. God knows how many missing souls survive down there." He shook his head. "A cruel fate."

"Crueler exist," Wyona murmured.

"But who *did* poison the Rodent chieftain?" Etheos asked. "If it wasn't Stryver—"

"Who said it wasn't Stryver?" Westchester demanded. "Why would Mortimer poison his own chieftain?"

"It wasn't me," Stryver said adamantly. "Though I cannot say for certain it was not my father; however, poison was not his style. It would be far more like him to suddenly draw his sword and impale the chieftain in the middle of the crowded hall. He was never very subtle, you see."

"As if we should believe your lies!" Westchester hissed.

Stryver spread his hands. "On the contrary, Westchester, I don't make a habit of lying."

"No?" Westchester asked, raising an eyebrow.

"No, not if I can help it. It's mostly just cheating, stealing, and piracy."

"I am curious," Sable murmured. He did not speak very loudly. He didn't have to. "I am curious as to what you think, Miss Wyona. Who do you think poisoned the chieftain?"

Wyona paused in thought for a moment. "I do not think it was Stryver," she said finally as the Earl of Westchester gave her disapproving looks. "For, whatever he is, he is not a coward—he takes great offense to the accusation, indeed—and poison is the most cowardly way I know of to kill an enemy. I don't know who really did. Perhaps Mortimer, scheming for more power. Perhaps his secret ally. I hardly know more than I did then."

"What did you know then?" Sable asked curiously.

"I knew I didn't think Stryver was guilty," she reflected. "But I knew he wasn't entirely innocent either."

Sable smiled slightly. "So you set him free?"

Wyona was slightly startled. "Well that's not…exactly how it went."

It did not help that the Rodent guards were all frightened of Stryver. They had all heard the horror stories of Felines, turning into wild cats at a moment's notice and massacring whole villages down to the last mouse without the slightest provocation. Kendall saw it was going to be a problem immediately. "Father, they're never going to hold him," he pointed out. "Perhaps it would be best…" he left it hanging, hesitantly.

The Aviator chieftain frowned. He had no wish to become badly entangled in this business, but at the same time aiding their allies in a fight against their enemy would strengthen the bond between them. In the end he made the decision that, in the eyes of the Forest, doomed him to death thereafter.

"It is with respect for our mourning brethren, just now coping with the loss of their beloved chieftain, that I take the responsibility of this vile blackguard upon myself. We shall hold him in the Aviator dungeon tonight, and he shall be executed at dawn."

The Rodents did not contest this. Everyone knew the harshness of the Aviator prison, suspended hundreds of feet above the ground, and there would be no doubt that the firm chieftain would keep his word to the last and execute the villain. It made everyone feel safer to know that the criminal was out of their city.

"Executed, Father?" Kendall asked, a frown marring his handsome face. "Are you sure? Without a trial? The Felines will not—'

"They are the enemy, boy," his father replied sternly. "And they are absent. No, it will go far better with the Rodents if we kill him."

"He's their only heir, Father," Kendall pointed out quietly. "Surely, you—"

"Unless one of his own comes to plead a case, I will not be dissuaded," he said firmly. "By their flight they show their guilt. And if he is not the culprit, his death shall punish them enough."

"Very well then," Kendall said, with equal firmness. "I shall travel to the Feline clan. I shall tell them what has transpired. One of them will surely return with me to save the poor chap."

"You'll never make it back in time."

"Then do me this one favor, Father, and postpone the execution a day. It can do no harm. Why, the night's almost spent in any case. Everyone shall be more prepared, and surely, if you're to make an example of the fellow, you want as many in attendance as possible."

His father frowned, conceding that it was so. "Be careful," he said. "You cannot trust them for a second, nor turn your back upon them. Keep your wings always ready."

Kendall nodded and turned swiftly, making his way from the hall. On the way out he caught the eye of his sister, who was still standing by herself in the middle of the dance floor, eyes still wide with shock. He nodded to her, smiling slightly, and was gone.

"Are you all right?" Sir Humphrey suddenly interrupted. He had noticed, perhaps they all had, the increased feeling in Wyona's voice as she spoke of her brother. Was she on the verge of tears? Stryver, though no one bothered to look at him, had a face black as thunder.

"Yes," Wyona replied, swallowing hard. "I'm fine. It's just— Kendall … "

The Earl of Westchester leaned over and patted her hand. "A fine man he was."

"These years apart have not been easy," she said, shaking her head. "I have always felt like—like a coward. Running from my responsibilities and duties. But it always gave me hope to think that Kendall was the chieftain, doing best by the clan. I loved Kendall–" She shook her head, looking at her hands. "So much. It was difficult, growing up amongst so many. It seemed like there was never any time for me, and I was often alone. I didn't mind it so much. I've learned now to like loneliness—as it is preferable to some company—but no matter how much work Father had to do with the state, and no matter how my mother's back ached from the weight of the latest child, Kendall—Kendall always had time for me."

The loud honking noise of Sir Humphrey blowing his nose into a handkerchief embroidered with an E broke the melancholy silence that had descended over the group.

"For Merlyn's sake, Humphrey!" Etheos cried. "Pull yourself together! And—is that my handkerchief?"

"I know what it's like!" Sir Humphrey wailed. "My family is so large—I have forty-three first cousins!" He began to howl, almost like a dog, as large tears splashed down his cheeks. "My old gran couldn't even remember my name from the others! She—she always called me Shirley!" he wailed.

"I can't believe you steal my handkerchiefs!" Etheos exploded. "I thought George was eating them!"

Sir Humphrey sniffled. "Want it back?"

"No," Etheos said carefully. "No, on second thought, you keep it."

Stryver raised an eyebrow. "Shirley?"

"We didn't have a lot of money," Sir Humphrey shrugged, calming down. "Sometimes I had to wear my older sisters' clothes."

"Indeed," Stryver replied, somewhat confounded. "She must have been a formidable young woman."

"The kindest, most formidablest woman that ever lived," Sir Humphrey agreed, brightening considerably.

"Prince Kendall was always too kind-hearted," the Earl of Westchester replied with a shake of the head. "Lord knows he could've met his doom amongst those mangy felines."

"As opposed to the rest of my family," Wyona replied, her large eyes suddenly taking on a haunted, dead look. "Who—"

"If you're going to get confused and emotional and tell it out of order, you'd best let me," Stryver interrupted. "Women," he added to Sir Humphrey, rolling his eyes. "Always crying at the drop of a hat. No offense, Shirley," he added with a roguish grin. "In any case," he continued, before Sir Humphrey could look up sharply. "I was then placed in Aviator custody, which was not at all good for my well-being. Rodents are very easy to escape from, especially given my knack with ropes and irons. Aviators are a different story. Even if I did manage to escape the prison—not a chance unless I could fly, and even then…risky—do you know how far that whole blasted city was above the ground?" He shook his head. "I was in hot soup indeed."

The large cage was suspended by a series of ropes over the ground. He was definitely uncomfortable with the way it rocked when he moved the slightest bit. He spent the better part of those early, half-lit hours of the morning sitting very still, and trying desperately to think of some kind of plan. That was probably why he didn't hear the guards, stationed on the nearest platform, ready to transform into fierce hawks or eagles should they see anything amiss, walk away. He didn't hear the soft wings, and was only aware that something had landed on the top of the cage when he was staring at a pair of boots.

He stared up into the just-visible pale face of Wyona. There was no question that he was surprised. Not that he was going to show it. "Come for a little chat with your friend in the cage?"

"No," Wyona replied, swinging one foot lazily and making the enclosure creak back and forth. "The thing is, I'm not sure you're my friend or not."

"Well, don't worry overly much about it. This time tomorrow I'll be dead."

She frowned. "I'm not so sure about that. I don't know if you did it or not."

"Does it matter?" he asked. "They're going to kill me just the same. But, no, I didn't do it, if it makes any difference."

"It does," Wyona replied. "Because I'm not about to let them kill an innocent man. Although I don't believe that you're entirely innocent either."

"I didn't poison him," Stryver replied, looking up at her. "I swear it. Poison is a coward's tool. And my father raised no cowards. Except

Julia," he added after a moment. "She's scared of everything."

Wyona scrutinized him for a moment.

"But then, why should you believe me?" Stryver shrugged. "I'm the enemy, aren't I?"

Wyona was silent for a moment more. "In any case," she finally said, "it would be a crime in itself to kill such a fine dancer as you. Hold still a moment."

She stood on the cage, and, strangely, it hardly moved at all beneath her, drawing a knife from her boot. She frowned at the knots in the rope system holding it suspended. "I think this'll work, though I warn you I've never sprung a murderer from my father's own prison before."

"You don't happen to have a hairpin, do you?" Stryver asked.

Wyona blinked and shook her head hard, emphasizing the waves of dark hair falling loose down her back.

"Yes, I thought not," he sighed mournfully.

"Oh, wait." She drew a handful of hairpins from her coat pocket. "I forgot my sister borrowed my coat last week. Here."

He took the hairpin and stuck his arm out through the bar, picking the lock in a matter of seconds. Swinging atop the cage—and causing it to bounce precariously back and forth—with the agility of a gymnast he was soon standing beside her.

"Handy," she said. "Hold on to that rope." She added, indicating one of the ones tied to the top of the cage. "And please try not to scream."

That being said, she raised her knife and hacked at the other bits of rope until the cage was only hanging by one—the one they were holding onto—and they were sent swinging wildly through the cool air like a pair of monkeys on vines, until they finally hit the large trunk of the tree the rope was fastened to. The cage made a loud clang that rang in his ears as it hit.

"And I'm sure they heard that," Wyona said, when they could both hear again. "We'd best hurry."

Without further preamble she became a bird and circled elegantly towards the ground while he transfigured into a cat and climbed his rather precarious way down the gigantic tree trunk.

It was perhaps half an hour later that he found himself, strangely, running through the trees beside Wyona.

"You're crazy," he finally said. "You should turn back now. Then when they catch me, at least you won't be in trouble."

Wyona shook her head. "I didn't just go to all the trouble of setting you free to see you captured again."

"And how does your being here help me run faster?"

"Whose idea was it to take the long way back to Feline territory?"

"Yours, and I still think it's daft."

"They'll never expect it," she insisted. "They'll never consider that you'd take this way. Not only because of the curse but because it's in the wrong direction."

Stryver slowed. "What curse?"

Wyona shrugged. "There's some old legend that once this part of the forest belonged to a goddess whom we stole it from. One of my ancestors pushed her into a well or something. She laid a curse upon the land, saying that no one could walk upon it and live. The well's even supposed to be around here still, carved with the words *And all shalt be made into Chaos*, supposedly the last words she ever spoke. It's utter nonsense, of—"

Stryver stopped abruptly and, in a moment, so did she. There, in the center of four tall, leafy trees that almost shaded it from outside view, was an old stone well, a wooden bucket still attached to the moldy old string. And at the base the words *And all shalt be made into Chaos*.

"Utter nonsense?" Stryver asked, raising an eyebrow.

"Well…we're still alive, aren't we? There's nothing to be afraid of, I'm sure—"

A deep glow that pulsated with the colors of red and orange and gold began to emanate from the very depths of the well.

"Do you ever get tired of being wrong, bird brain?" Stryver asked.

"Maybe we should turn around," Wyona suggested.

And then the well began to sing in a language that neither of them understood, though Etheos surely would have. It was, they later realized from wisdom gained on their respective travels, the language used for sorcery and spells, though an exceedingly ancient form of it. It seemed to go on forever, in the deep voice that boomed from within.

Finally, Stryver bent and picked up a rock, throwing it over the side and into the well. The light and sound abruptly stopped.

"Is throwing rocks your answer to everything?" Wyona asked irritably.

"It worked, didn't it?"

Then there was a loud boom as the well exploded. The stonewalls blew away in a sudden burst and the hole that was left expanded so rapidly that Wyona barely had time to take flight into the branches of a nearby tree. Stryver was not so lucky. He was soon waist deep in the oozing, pulsating orange, yellow, and red glow that filled the hole, forever moving and changing, contorting and spinning into almost hypnotic designs.

And it was eating him alive.

He stayed very still, trying to slow the sinking process, but it didn't seem to matter; he felt his legs grow cold.

"What the hell do you think you're doing?" Wyona yelled at him from her perch atop the tree. She had become human once more, sitting astride the branch.

"Struggling only makes you sink faster," Stryver said, trying to move his mouth as little as possible.

"That's quicksand, you dolt!" Wyona shouted. "This is a Dread Pool of Chaos! Struggle! Struggle for all you're worth or you'll end up in *her* world."

Stryver blinked.

"A world of sheer and utter chaos!" Wyona cried, exasperated. "Nothing is at it seems, pain and torment run amuck—for the love of—you really don't have a library, do you?"

Stryver was at least struggling now, trying to swim for the side, but he wasn't making much progress. Cats are not notorious swimmers and it wasn't exactly water either. The numb, cold feeling was all the way to his waist.

Wyona drew a thin rope from one of her pockets and edged out further on the branch, tying one end to it.

He was up to his shoulders now, and could barely keep his head above water.

"Catch!" Wyona called.

"Can't!" Stryver called back, and then he disappeared beneath the dancing surface of the Dread Pool of Chaos.

Wyona stared wide-eyed at the spot where he had been for a moment. Then she let out a small cry and, taking the rope firmly in hand, dove neatly off the branch and cut the surface of the pool like a knife, disappearing the next instant. The forest waited in silence. And then a hand reached out of the Chaotic waters, grasping the rope as firmly as possible. In another instant, Wyona was tugging Stryver onto firm ground, both covered in the strange liquid, with the heavy substance of melted butter that burned the skin to the bone.

"Stryver," she said, hitting him. "Wake up, dolt."

Stryver opened his eyes wide and Wyona cried out, leaping to her feet in dismay. His eyes were no longer the cynical, mocking black; they had gone completely white. He coughed and sat up, as if nothing of the sort were wrong.

"Stryver, you—"

"What?" he asked, looking up at her.

But his eyes were black again.

She stared at him in complete consternation. He blinked a few times and they went milky once more.

"Your eyes!" she cried. "They keep…changing."

Stryver blinked once more, in surprise, his eyes going black again. "Really? How so?"

"Changing to white—"

"Oh. Sort of like that streak in your hair?"

"WHAT?" Wyona seized the hair, still dripping with the chaotic liquid, and saw that it was true. A few streaks of white stained the perfect midnight. "It—we've been tainted," she finally said. "Tainted by chaos."

"Yes, and you look rather like a skunk now." And he began to laugh. He continued to laugh as he tried to wipe the burning substance from his face.

Wyona muttered something that sounded a lot like "Ungrateful maggot" and sat down, trying to tug one of her boots off. "Stupid Dread Pool of Chaos. Seeps in everywhere. Even in these bloody–"

"Here." He took her boot in his hand and gave it a good tug. It came off, spilling a surprising puddle of the glowing, pulsating liquid onto the ground in the process. "And I really *am* grateful," he added, handing her back her boot. "You saved my life, and I'm not going to forget it. I'll pay you back sometime."

"Better make it quick. Because you've only got a few more hours, cur!"

Stryver looked up, just in time to be knocked senseless as a rock came soaring out of nowhere to land on his head.

Wyona stood, nearly crying out in surprise when five large eagles dropped out of the sky, and another, the one who'd spoken leapt out of a tree. Two of them seized the unconscious Stryver.

"Don't worry, your highness. You're safe now," one of them tried to assure her.

"Safe?" Wyona cried, pulling her arms free of them. "What are you doing here?"

"Rescuing you, of course," he replied. "From this mangy Feline. We're still not sure how he got out of prison, but you don't have to fret, because it won't happen again. He's to be executed at dawn, and we'll have a good watch on him all night. He won't be kidnapping you again."

"Kidnap—no, you don't under—"

"It's all right, your highness," another of them said, helping the others to lift Stryver upon a large net lying on the ground. "She's just a little shaken," he added to the others. "The distress of being kidnapped by this rogue. Are you safe to fly, highness?"

Wyona stared at them all despairingly. "Yes. Yes, I'm fine. Executed at dawn, you say?" she asked, looking determinedly at Stryver. "Then we have little time, don't we?"

The guards all transformed, taking a corner of the net each in their talons, and took flight. "Very little time indeed," Wyona said, transforming herself.

The moment she touched down on the platform, her mother ran

out, sobbing, and embraced her. Wyona choked at the sudden grip and nearly fell over the side. It was some sort of planned public display; her mother was not an emotional person. "My sweet, sweet child! Thank God you're safe! That filthy wretch didn't hurt you, did he?"

Before Wyona could answer her mother pulled her inside, still weeping, with a soothing hand on her shoulder.

The minute the door was closed behind them the woman transformed once again into the mother Wyona had always known: tall, stately, and always perfectly, unshakably calm. There were no traces of the tears or concern, simply a tranquil face that gave nothing away, a look that Wyona would strive to mime, though not entirely master in years to come.

"Come, your father wishes to see you."

Without so much as a look at her daughter, she continued in the dignified way down the corridor and into one of the family rooms. Her father was there, looking particularly tall and stern today. He did not frown at her, but he didn't look particularly pleased to see her. The look told her full well that he and her mother did not in the least believe that she had been kidnapped, though he made no mention of it.

"It is good to know that you are safe," he said after a moment. "And you needn't worry about the bandit escaping again, unless he thinks he can cut through steel chains. The guards will perch atop the cage and watch also from the platform. You are quite well protected from him. And at dawn tomorrow it shall all be over."

"Father, he—"

"I know it must have been a trying day for you, Miss Wyona. Attempt to put it from your mind. Forget him."

"But I don't think he's done anything wrong!" Wyona protested. "That's why I—"

"He kidnapped my daughter and murdered the Rodent chieftain," her father said stubbornly. "He is the enemy, Wyona. You must always remember that. You are dismissed."

"But—"

"Dismissed!" he thundered.

She shook her head, turning to go, wishing Kendall were there. Kendall would listen to her. Kendall, who believed Stryver was innocent. Perhaps there was still hope, if Kendall returned in time. That gave her a new idea.

"And Wyona," her mother added as she was leaving. "There's no reason to fret. Your father will post a guard outside your door tonight. You're perfectly safe."

The glare she flashed them both, which she would repent terribly later, was filled with hate. "Thank you for your concern."

A guard did indeed follow Wyona back to her room from supper. He was big and surly, and didn't look like any amount of persuasion would get him to budge. She frowned, thinking hard. She couldn't go to Kendall herself and urge him to all haste, but she could do the next best thing.

Of course, the guard was suspicious when the cheerful, blond haired young man—perhaps four years younger than Wyona herself—appeared at the door to see her.

"Who are you again?" he growled.

"The name's Crispkin, milord. James Crispkin."

"And what's your business here?"

"Carrier pigeon, milord. The Queen's fastest."

The guard scowled and knocked on the door he had been set to guard.

"Oh, my carrier pigeon!" Wyona exclaimed when she opened the door. "Yes, I'd nearly forgotten. Here you are." She handed Crispkin—who, it should be noted, had been enamored with her since she'd begun giving him tips on his fencing—a small envelope with the blue wax seal used by her family. "Thanks, Crispkin."

Crispkin winked slyly, a broad grin on his face.

"And what's this?" the guard asked.

"Just a letter to my Uncle Norrington," Wyona shrugged. "It's his birthday next week."

Before the guard could ask any further questions, Wyona had shut the door and Crispkin had turned into a pigeon, carrying the letter in his beak.

Wyona waited, silently, until very late. She heard the guard slump against the door, no doubt worn out from being so gruff all the time. Then, with her usual quiet elegance she slid open the small window in her room. It was not large enough for a normal Aviator to fit through, even in their transformed state. Indeed, her family tended towards large, regal birds—except her youngest brother the blue jay who was destined to remain a baby and a pet all his life—while she herself was a simple, ordinary, if not unusually small blackbird. Perhaps her father had forgotten that.

It was a bit of a squeeze, but she did manage to fly free of the window and high into the tree tops, much higher than was usual for those in the city going to and fro. She couldn't afford to be seen. It was a quiet night. Nothing moved in the still air as she made her way across the city to the prison, landing in the branches high above the cages. She peered down through the shadows, spying a cage done with chains instead of rope. But where were the guards? There was nothing perched atop it. It was too dark to see much more.

Gingerly, trying to move as little as possible so as not to attract attention, she glided down to a lower branch, and then another. What was that creaking sound? She floated down ever further until she was nearly even with the cage. Then she saw it.

There was no one in the cage. The door was open, slowly creaking back and forth. And there were no guards anywhere. She perched on the branch, dumbfounded. Stryver could pick locks easily, that much could be said. Perhaps—though it would be a frightening trial—he could even walk across one of the chains in his feline form. But where were the guards? Could it be that he had tried to escape and they had moved him, awaiting his execution, in precious few hours? Or had he found some way to best them or fool them?

She stayed there a long time, watching and waiting, though nothing happened. Then, as the dark of night turned slowly to gray, she shook herself from her stupor and took flight as quickly as possible back to her room. She dressed hurriedly in formal attire, though hers was not so fine as some of her siblings, looking like a nice imitation of the wingmen's livery. Then, with a sigh, she turned to the mirror and began putting up her hair. Morbid or not, the execution of such a prisoner was a formal occasion and it was required of her. The fact that the prisoner wasn't in prison was something she had to pretend she didn't know for the time being.

It surprised her that she was the first of her family to arrive. The long row of seats for all her brothers and sisters was empty. Even her father and mother's chairs. She frowned. Usually they tried to be seated there before any of their subjects to forgo the useless standing and trumpets. But she was the only one there. A formidable crowd had already gathered, staring at her questioningly, wondering where her family was. She stared back at them with an equally confused look.

And then the young sparrow hawk plummeted out of the sky, landing and transforming in an instant atop the gallows.

It was a guard, and he was breathing hard. "It's Stryver!" he cried. "The Feline prisoner! He's murdered them all! The royal family is no more!" He collapsed, obviously not remembering Kendall, lost somewhere in Feline territory, or Wyona, staring at him with wide, horrified eyes. Under the circumstances, nobody bothered to correct him.

Wyona stared at the table for some time, and no one could decide if she was angry or about to cry.

Everyone was silent, shocked. Even Sable, who had maintained the same, contemplative expression, jumped in his chair. Sir Humphrey turned to Stryver. "You didn't *really* do it, did you?" he asked incredulously. They all knew Stryver to be a no-good scoundrel, but a cold-blooded murderer?

Stryver was staring, expressionless at the table as well. No one could see, but beneath it he held the silver pocket watch, his knuckles white against it. "I did." There wasn't even a trace of regret.

"But—but *why?*" Etheos asked, just as shaken.

Stryver opened his mouth to say more, but the Earl of Westchester interrupted him. "Because he is a villainous, treasonous blackguard!" he exploded. "The enemy! He should never be allowed anywhere near her highness—"

"I've had many chances to kill Wyona before now—"

"And made many attempts," Wyona added. "Have you been following me all these years to finish the job?"

Stryver could have argued, was about to in fact, but then just sadly shook his head and looked down once more.

"They were all asleep in their beds," the Earl of Westchester said after a moment, as neither seemed able to continue. "They were found there, eyes open, deep knife wounds in their chests. Same place on all of them, right over the heart. He was good at it. No one saw or heard him till the maids came to rouse the King and Queen—usually they did not need to be awakened, you see—and found them like that, and this wretch locked in their safe with a long, stained knife, and blood all over his fingers. Seems he'd decided to rob them after he'd killed them, only to be locked in when the theft mechanism kicked in. You can imagine the hysteria."

"It was a flurry of noise and movement, sheer chaos everywhere," Wyona continued quietly. "Everyone rushed right and left, sending messages to foreign embassies, to other clans, to Kendall, all saying that the royal family had been murdered in their beds—except for the prince. They all forgot I was still there, I suppose. I admit, I forgot about myself as well. I wandered around in a sort of daze, not seeing or feeling anything around me. I didn't even grieve—that came later—because I was too caught up in the extraordinary luck and irony. If I had not been outside the night before, trying to free Stryver, he would have murdered me too."

She looked up at him carefully, and he simply shook his head again. "It was a long time ago," he said.

"It doesn't matter," both the Earl and Wyona said at the same time, the Earl furiously and Wyona evenly.

"I walked off by myself," Wyona continued. "Contemplating that. I was in shock, I suppose. It's rather strange to go from having such a large family to no family—save one—in a minute. Perhaps it was a good thing I sat down on the edge of the platform and stared off into space. Because it was there I saw the black cat making its hurried way down the tree."

She glared across at Stryver.

Stryver shrugged, still not meeting her eyes. "They were in a great rush and panic. They forgot I was a special case, and simply tied me up. You can imagine how long I let that last."

"So you ran?" Etheos asked.

"His solution to almost every problem," Wyona said bitterly.

"I ran," Stryver agreed. "Not just back to my own clan but out of the Forest altogether. I had to get away. Everyone, it seemed to me, was mad. I had to escape."

"And you—you followed?" Etheos asked of Wyona.

"He was getting away," Wyona replied, narrowing her eyes. "Of course I followed. I'm not above vengeance. I'm still waiting for it, in fact."

"But then how were you banished?" Sir Humphrey asked.

"I discovered it when I was making my way back, after chasing Stryver to the very edge of the Forest, and five hawks dropped out of the sky, armed and ready to arrest me for conspiratorial murder and regicide. They had a warrant signed by Kendall himself. I tried to explain but … they wouldn't listen."

"And news of you killing five of our guards did not do much to help your reputation," the Earl of Westchester chided gently. "It was too suspicious," he continued. "After they realized that her body was not among the bloody corpses, they decided she had been spared. And when she and the criminal went missing at the same time, well, everyone jumped to the most logical conclusion, remembering how it had happened before. It surprised Kendall more than anything when he got back. He refused to believe it of her for some while. But, when she didn't turn up, he relented and was persuaded to sign the warrant."

"I have no case," Wyona replied with a shake of the head. "If I tell them I missed the knife to rescue the murderer, my story will be little better than the one they made up for me. And so I have remained, banished, making my way and fighting against him for all these years."

By this time the fire was dying down and even the grey beards had all retired to bed. It was dark outside and raining.

"Is that enough past to suit you, old man?" Stryver asked.

"Yes, more than enough," Sable replied. "And I can see now that yours is not an easy path. Your suffering weighs great upon you."

The Earl of Westchester snorted, rolling his eyes.

"The end is in sight," Sable continued. "But it may be no less painful. You may find that when you release your demons, their absence burns as well. Keep a sharp eye on your wings, for I can see your known enemy tearing them off—twice."

"He doesn't have any wings," the Earl of Westchester muttered.

"You, sir, are set in your ways," Sable replied, turning his head sharply to the Earl. "But if you do not learn to open your mind, it may well be your death."

The Earl of Westchester, startled by this beyond measure was, for once, silent.

"You, Sir Knight," he said to Sir Humphrey. "Never lose your strong heart or your strong axe. Both shall be indispensable in the day to come. There is much strife where you go." He paused for a moment and then turned to Etheos.

"You are arrogant, wizard, but you will stay true. Do not think it above you to be guided by the advice of others, or you shall fail at your endeavor. Your fondest wish is nearly in your hands if only you would accept the help of others and always, always remember H. P. Nortonus."

Etheos frowned, thinking hard.

"And you," Sable finally said, turning to Wyona. "You who seemed to have been punished for nothing. You who fear and deny what will be—you feel it yourself that it will be, and try to change it—even though it is inevitable."

"It is terrible," Wyona murmured, staring at him with wide eyes.

"Perhaps you think so now," he agreed. "It seems so. But in the near future you will learn." He shook his head at her. "You too carry great pain. I cannot tell you that it will be lessened, but you shall have your long awaited revenge."

Stryver jerked his head up and Wyona stared across at him, her face unreadable. "I think," she said finally, "that you are wrong, old man. We have wasted our time in talking with you."

She stood and left the room, climbing the stairs to the chambers above.

Sable smiled a strange, half-smile. "She doesn't understand," he said simply. "She will in time."

"Thank you," Etheos said, standing as well. "It is an honor to stand in the presence of a true master." He bowed as he left, admonishing Sir Humphrey later for not doing the same.

The Earl of Westchester, glaring at Stryver, made his way up the stairs as well, leaving the scoundrel in the purple coat with the blind man. They were both silent for a long time. Finally Stryver stood in the dark—as the fire had died completely—and walked over to sit beside the old man, trying to peer into his face. "You know, don't you?"

The old man nodded slowly.

"I thought so," Stryver said. "Why didn't you tell them?"

Sable didn't answer for a long moment. Then he reached up a gnarled old hand and lightly, with the educated touch of the blind, felt Stryver's face. He ran his fingers along the bridge of his nose and his small black goatee, across his broad forehead and even back to the black horsetail of hair. "Tell me," he finally said, "what does it feel like to live such a lie and walk such a paradox? Shall it consume you one day?"

It was a thoughtful question.

Stryver bowed his head, and said nothing.

A Final Misadventure

Sir Humphrey had lost one of his oven mitts. It was very distressing to him, being that they were his favorite—green with tiny yellow chicken print. They'd been a Christmas gift from one of his numerous rosy-cheeked sisters, who all seemed to have married dairy farmers for one reason or another. He realized it was gone when he was fastening his belt over his mail that morning in the dim light of the room he shared with Etheos, who was, at that moment, sleeping soundly in a geometrically precise diagonal. During the night, he'd somehow managed to not only steal all the covers, but also both pillows and Sir Humphrey's nightcap. The big knight had half a mind to think his friend had also taken the missing oven mitt, but when he tried to wake him, the wizard only muttered something incoherently, a few sparks drifting lazily out of his dangling fingers to make small scorch marks on the rug.

Sir Humphrey had learned rather quickly from living with Etheos—who was definitely worse in the morning—that waking a wizard is not a good idea unless one would rather have a rutabaga instead of a nose. So he tugged on his boots and clunked out of the room, fully intent on searching downstairs and possibly grabbing a bite to eat in these gray hours of the morning before attempting to awaken Etheos again.

He didn't quite make it.

For he wasn't the only one accustomed to arising early in the morning.

"Go away."

There was no mistaking the calm, collected voice of Wyona, and Sir Humphrey jumped at it being so near. He looked around, thinking she was addressing him, but she was nowhere to be seen. Then he saw the door a little further down the hall, slightly ajar. He stepped a little closer, curious, peering inside.

There was Wyona, standing before the small mirror hanging on the wall, parting her long midnight hair with an ebony comb. She was fully dressed in her Sky Rider's garb, except her feet, which wore only a pair of black and white striped stockings, her boots lying in the corner. She was glaring in the mirror at someone she could see behind her. Sir Humphrey realized who it was in a moment.

"No," Stryver said, just as complacently. He was standing inspecting her saber, which he had picked up from a chair. "Are you sure this is balanced correctly?"

"Yes," she said, an increasingly irritated edge to her voice. "Go away."

"Nonsense, there's no one else awake to bother," Stryver yawned. He set down her sword where he had found it and plopped down on the bed, bouncing slightly like a little boy who knows that jumping is forbidden. "This is a lot nicer than mine," he said reproachfully. "Probably had less fleas too."

"Unlike some people, I don't make a habit of bringing my own."

"Feather brain."

"Mangy, flea-ridden cretin," Wyona replied, running the comb through her hair. "I should kill you."

"Yes, but you won't because you can't," Stryver replied with a slight smile, taking out his pocket watch and fiddling with it absently. "You *need* me," he added, emphasizing the word with a smug grin.

"You know, any decent sort of person would least try to redeem himself for his unspeakable past," Wyona said, exasperated.

"But then I'm not really a decent sort of person, am I?" Stryver asked, raising an eyebrow. "But then neither are you."

"I'm not a murderer."

"So I suppose your knife just happened to slip its way into the Archduke of the Centaurs' back? Or what about that pirate—what was his name? Blood something, I think—or—"

"That's different," Wyona said.

"I don't see how."

"I had *reasons*."

"The pursuit of money and power. Always admirable, that. Really noble of you. Bet Kendall's proud." He said it surprisingly maliciously.

Wyona turned with a cry of rage and flung the comb at him as if it were a throwing dagger. It missed his head by a few inches, striking the wall behind him and falling harmlessly to the blankets. Stryver picked it up and threw it back.

"You're going to need that," he added. "Still look like a skunk after all these years."

"I don't," Wyona replied, regaining her composure and turning back to the mirror, running the comb through her hair once more. "I dyed it out."

Stryver shrugged. "It's still there though. *I* can see it at least."

"That's because you've been tainted as well," Wyona replied. "A curse has been placed on the both of us. Everyone can see it in those eyes of yours."

"Really? And I thought they were rather fetching myself."

"It's a curse of—"

"Chaos, I know," Stryver replied. "Since we were both immersed in the Dread Pool. It's why chaos follows us around—an effect, which I've noticed, you don't altogether care for. I think it's splendidly useful myself."

Wyona narrowed her eyes at him.

"What do you take me for?" Stryver asked innocently. "Some sort of dimwit that's never set foot in a library?"

"It's not just a curse upon us," Wyona replied with a shake of her head, finishing and putting the comb into a pocket under her tunic. "It's a curse upon the entire Forest." She removed her sword from the chair and sat down, pulling her boots on. "It must be. Because we disturbed the Dread Pool and let it loose. That's where this— this His Majesty came from and all this trouble. That's why we— the both of us—have to go back and set things right. It's our fault."

"I beg to differ," Stryver replied, shaking his head, his eyes gleaming though Sir Humphrey could not say why. "If you recall—as I'm sure you do since you just finished telling everyone the delightful tale downstairs—there was scheming and plotting against the council far before we had the hapless luck of falling into that well."

"What are you suggesting?" Wyona asked, pursing her lips with a frown.

Stryver was grinning outright now. "Someone else found the well first. Long before us. That's the root of all that scheming and killing and—"

"Who do you suppose it was?" Wyona demanded. "His Majesty? The dictator?"

Stryver shrugged. "Whoever it is, it's not going to be a pretty fight. Do you know what happens to people who've been utterly consumed by chaos?"

Sir Humphrey would have liked to know, because he found this conversation quite interesting, and leaned in a little closer—even though he knew eavesdropping was not exactly gallant and noble—so that he might hear better. Alas.

"Sir Humphrey! Sir Humphrey, what's for breakfast? Are you making crumb cake?"

Sir Humphrey nearly jumped out of his boots at the sound of Etheos' sleepy, yawning voice directly behind him. The two voices in the room next to him were abruptly silent as well.

Sir Humphrey turned to see Etheos, his thick hair tousled from sleep and his green eyes still rather hazy, the blanket he had taken full possession of during the night draped about his shoulders like a king's ermine cape.

"Etheos, why don't you go get dressed," Sir Humphrey suggested. "I'll find us some breakfast downstairs."

Etheos yawned again. "All right," he said. "But nothing sunny side up. Not since the hurtling fireball of death incident." He turned and shuffled barefoot back down the hall.

Sir Humphrey breathed a sigh of relief. When Etheos was half-awake, as he was most mornings, he was liable to mutter spells by accident and turn chairs into ferocious, fire-breathing marmosets, which were a pain in the knee to get rid of, not to mention the window-repair bills for the entire building.

That's why he gave a yell and tried to heft his axe—until he remembered it was back in the room—when Stryver poked his head out of the door behind him and said, "Hurtling fireball of death incident? That sounds strangely familiar."

"What?" Sir Humphrey cried, between eavesdropping and Etheos' groggy conversation, becoming understandably confused. "What did—"

"I said," Stryver clarified. "That it sounds like I could've had a hand in it. When exactly?"

Before Sir Humphrey could answer, Wyona came up behind Stryver, who was leaning precariously in her doorway, and gave him a firm kick, sending him careening out the door to run headlong into the big knight, crying out as he struck Sir Humphrey's mail, and landing in a heap on the floor.

"Now go wake the Earl of Westchester and see that the innkeeper gives us a quick breakfast," she ordered from the doorway. "We have to leave soon, so hurry up." Then she slammed the door.

Stryver, growling in a way that was particularly feline, clambered to his feet in a way that particularly wasn't. He had a strange red chain mail imprint on his forehead. "Who does she think she is?" he complained, loud enough for Wyona to hear through the door. "The bloody Queen?"

"Isn't she?" Sir Humphrey asked, still feeling rather perplexed.

Stryver scowled at him. "You're no help! Go wake up the Earl of Westchester." Then he stomped down the hall—indeed making such an effort to stomp that he nearly tripped over his own boots at the top of the stairs. He cast a contemptuous glance over his shoulder, as if warning Sir Humphrey not to say a word, and disappeared down the stairs.

"Who does he think he is?" Sir Humphrey muttered. "The bloody King?"

"Not while I'm alive." There was the Earl of Westchester, closing the door softly to his room across the hall, fully dressed, his eccentric wisps of white hair even more unsettled from a restless night. "Her highness may insist that he is needed, but there is no way that I, as a senior member of the Order, shall see that villain on the throne!" He spoke with such accusing vehemence that Sir Humphrey raised a hand to assure him that he'd been suggesting no such thing. "That fiend should be shot!" the Earl continued, his face growing red. "He is not fit to rule and I'll be hanged before—"

Sir Humphrey got the feeling that the Earl had been thinking about this all night. Indeed, he probably had, because the rant continued all the way downstairs, all through the light breakfast of bread and cheese—indeed it seemed to intensify over the meal with Stryver leaning lazily back in his chair, swinging the silver pocket watch recklessly by its chain—and would surely have continued for the rest of the day had not Wyona finally told him to hold his tongue, which he did, still glaring hotly, before turning into a stork and flying away next to the white-streaked blackbird.

Sir Humphrey found that he didn't like the Changeling Forest. It was as dark and foreboding as whispered rumors in the city made it out to be. The trees stretched high into the sky and covered the forest floor in an unnatural dimness that made Sir Humphrey squint to see long distances. It was eerily calm, unnaturally calm. Not a bird sang nor breeze rustled in the trees. Sir Humphrey didn't like it. He felt the gaze of a thousand silent eyes staring at him from the treetops above, and he convinced himself that every shadow was an assassin ready to leap out from behind a tree. He felt enclosed, trapped by the enormous, silent trees that seemed to stretch forever in all directions, even when he turned his head up to try to see the sky. His warrior's senses were alert, his hand tingling, longing to reach onto his back and unstrap the axe. There was danger near.

Etheos didn't seem to sense anything. He was still yawning and grumbling under his breath, glaring daggers at Stryver, who was sitting exceptionally straight, his tail twitching. His curious white eyes were shifting constantly, searching out the shadows and the trees, recalling a flood of memories he had pushed away over the years since he had left.

"I should be in my alchemy class," Etheos grumbled. "They're going to have a fit. I don't think they're going to believe the excuse that my friend's pet pig was kidnapped by Changelings and gnomes either."

"She isn't a pet," Sir Humphrey replied quietly. "She is a lady of court and therefore liable to be ransomed."

Etheos shook his head in disgust. "But they don't know she's a lady of court! They think she's just a stupid pig—"

"Unless they think she's a Changeling!" Sir Humphrey suddenly cried, forgetting his attempts to preserve the silence. "That's it, Etheos! They think the Lady Orville is a Changeling! And she—she sort of is, I suppose."

Stryver rolled his eyes, and Sir Humphrey had no trouble understanding what he meant by it because Etheos said at about the same moment, "No she isn't! That's preposterous. A Changeling is someone who can change from human to animal form whenever they choose. Lady Orville's just been cursed."

"Well, it's their mistake, not mine," Sir Humphrey said defensively. "Maybe it means she's still alive."

"How do you suppose that?" Etheos asked sourly.

"Because I have to hope, Etheos," Sir Humphrey said. "And have you seen my oven mitt? I'm missing one."

"What would I want with your oven mitt?" Etheos snapped. "I still don't see what you want with them, carting them everywhere like you do. It's silly and grossly improper for a knight, especially one as respected as you!"

Sir Humphrey shrugged and went back to watching the shadows. He was not, however, the first one to see the strange shape flying at them at a surprising speed through the trees. Stryver was the first to sense its approach, and jerked his head up, standing in an instant with a hiss. Etheos and Sir Humphrey both looked in the direction of his gaze—straight ahead—and soon saw the gray speck, hurtling towards them.

"What is it?" Etheos cried, alarmed.

"I don't know," Sir Humphrey cried back. "But—"

Before anymore could be said, Stryver gave a perturbed yowl and leapt off the horse as the gray speck hurtled straight towards Etheos, knocking him in the chest and landing before him in the saddle where Stryver had been seated. It took Etheos a moment to realize that it was a pigeon. A moment was all he had, for in the next, there was not a pigeon, but a sandy haired young man with blue eyes and a wide grin facing him on the front of his horse.

Etheos gave a yelp and his horse abruptly stopped, giving the newcomer time to leap nonchalantly off it before Etheos could shout a spell. He brushed off his dark cloak, which bore an embroidered crest of a clawing hand in gray thread, and smiled winningly at the two astonished humans.

"Terribly sorry," he said in a jovial voice. "I didn't expect you to be this far along. I never supposed you lot to move so fast."

"Who are you?" Sir Humphrey demanded, having already taken out his axe. "How did you know we were coming?"

The young man blinked. "Oh, but Westchester told me," he said, breaking into his jovial smile once more. "Terribly sorry," he repeated. "My name is Crispkin. The Queen's fastest." He bowed rather floridly, taking off his hat, which was floppy and had a point in one end. "At least I was once," he added, coming back up. "And I daresay I will be again soon too." He looked down at the embroidery on his cloak, said "Bah!" and made a face as if it were a habit. Then he turned back to the two by now rather confused humans and smiled again. "And whom do I have the pleasure of addressing?"

Sir Humphrey was still watching him with narrowed eyes. "Sir Humphrey," he finally said. "Knight of Galahad's Hall." He offered his hand, which Crispkin took in both his own, shaking heartily. "And this is Etheos, Thaumaturge of the Merlyn Academy."

Etheos inclined his head imperially.

"Oh, and Stryver—" Sir Humphrey looked about, frowning. "Where did he get off to?"

"Here," Stryver replied. He was leaning against a nearby tree, regarding Crispkin with a level, calculating gaze. "What brings you here?"

"I could ask you the same question," Crispkin replied. His jovial smile had faded. "We thought you were dead."

"Wishful thinking," Stryver said with a bitter smile. "Though bird brain has certainly tried."

"And where *is* Wyona?" Crispkin asked, his smile returning suddenly in full force.

Stryver cast his eyes skyward. "She'll be here in due course I should think."

Sure enough, in a moment the white-banded raven came streaking down from on high, transforming in the air and landing quite soundly on her feet.

"Crispkin!" she said at once, smiling for the first time in some while.

Crispkin grinned even wider and did his florid bow once more. "Your highness. Or should it be 'your majesty'? I must say, I'd nearly given up hope of ever seeing you again."

"Yes, but it's been—" She stopped. "But just why are you here, Crispkin?"

"Oh, didn't Westchester tell you?"

Wyona glanced upward for a moment and then shook her head.

"Well, then it stands thusly," Crispkin explained. "I am the head of the Order—of which dear old Westchester is a senior member— made up of delegates from each clan to bring about the end of His Majesty's vile reign. We shall have you back in your rightful place in no time, highness, and things will finally be as they were."

At this moment the stork—Westchester—fell out of the sky, transforming a moment later, panting.

"Oh, your—your highness! You mustn't turn so—so sharply like that! I feared—Oh, I must say– I feared—"

"Westchester!" Crispkin exclaimed happily. "Good work, old sport! Here you've found us our missing princess!"

"And some others, less welcome," Westchester grumbled, shifting his eyes towards Stryver, who ignored him completely.

"But we'll need all the help we can get," Crispkin replied, smiling wider for all Westchester's gruffness. "Especially a real wizard— I must say, I've never met one. Do you really wear those ridiculous-looking hats?" he suddenly broke off, looking questioningly at Etheos.

"Only the old masters do," Etheos replied. "On special occasions. The rest of us think they're preposterous."

"Quite right. Quite right," Crispkin replied with a laugh. "Rather gnomish, you know. And frightfully dangerous. You could poke an eye out if you happened to trip over those funny robes—anyway," he continued, shaking his head and trying to find his wayward point. "A real wizard and a brave knight, the kind we have all heard tales about, will certainly be of invaluable use to us in the day to come."

"But surely the Order—" Westchester began.

"Alas, we are far too sparse," Crispkin replied with a shake of the head. "Our best man—besides you of course, good fellow—was captured just yesterday by His Majesty's guards. He'll be executed tomorrow at dawn."

Westchester shook his head. "Poor Ziggy."

"Sorry to interrupt," Stryver said casually, "but do either of you brave gentleman have a plan?"

"None that involves you!" Westchester said vehemently. "If you think we'd trust you after—"

"Need I remind you," Stryver replied. "That there are only five of you—including the dimwit and the egotist, both of whom will invariably muck things up. You need me. If bird brain sees it, I should think it would be obvious to the rest of you."

"Such—" Before Westchester could begin his rant about the disrespect, Wyona cut him off sharply.

"Stryver's right," she said firmly. "And there will be no more arguments about it. Crispkin, how is His Majesty's fortress fortified?"

"Well, just see for yourself," Crispkin suggested. "It's not but a few minutes farther. He has built a new city, you see, where they say he looks down from his high tall tower, though, as I've said, we've never seen him. Sometimes I've glimpsed a dark shadow standing at the highest balcony, but that is all even we of the Order have ever discovered. Come, but carefully. We do not want a brush with his guards."

"No," Westchester agreed fervently, his face pale. "No, we most certainly do not."

The city was indeed just through the trees, and what a sad, desolate place it was. It was certainly large enough, houses with tiny windows and shops with dark fronts stood stoically along the straight, perfectly designed streets. But everything was grey and silent, like the trunks of the giant trees that rose up around them, sheltering the city in a perpetual twilight. Rising in the center, far above the other buildings, was the tower, a single pillar made of solid, unyielding stone, pointing towards the sky as if it would rival the trees in height. A few narrow slits of windows dotted its impassive surface and near the very top, where Sir Humphrey had to crane his neck to see, was a square-cut balcony, jutting out from the tower. There was a single, giant torch lit atop the tower. The rest of the city was dark and silent in the coming night. Not a soul moved about on the streets and the darkness slowly crept further upon them, as if even it were afraid of what might happen to it out alone.

It was a surprising sight to all, except Crispkin and the Earl of Westchester who were used to the grim shadows. Sir Humphrey and Etheos, each used to the bustling, busy life of their happy city were shocked at the emptiness of this one, and Stryver and Wyona were startled at the change that had come over their land.

"It is a curse," Crispkin said, and for once he was not smiling. "A curse that we shall break tonight. Come. Quietly."

And they slowly made their way into the place, watching the shadows over their shoulders and creeping along like bandits or criminals—as indeed they were. Sir Humphrey held his axe firmly, ready to swing at the slightest noise, and Etheos was muttering protection spells under his breath, but so quietly that nothing came of it. The Earl of Westchester appeared to be the worst off. He was shaking, his eyes darting about frantically.

Crispkin stopped at a crossroads for a moment, carefully looking both ways before emerging from the shadows and making a left, continuing down the street. As Sir Humphrey turned, his mail gave off the slightest creak that seemed louder than a shout in the still air. The Earl of Westchester jumped, whirling, his spectacles falling off his nose and shattering on the pavement.

Everyone froze, staring around in horror, waiting for the shouts of a battle to envelop them. Nothing happened. The silence returned and a fog began to roll in.

Crispkin let out a sigh of relief. "That was bloody close."

Sir Humphrey's nostrils flared and he spun around, facing the foggy street behind them. "Show yourself!" he shouted. "I challenge thee as a knight of honor!"

A moment later, a small, emaciated dog trotted towards him, tongue lolling out and wagging his tail.

"It's only a stray, Humphrey," Etheos said, rolling his eyes.

And then the dog turned into a bear, towering over even the big knight and letting out a roar.

"Guards!" Crispkin cried, pulling a dirk from somewhere in his sleeve. "I'm afraid this *is* a spot of bad luck."

The bear roared again, lumbering forward. Sir Humphrey swung his axe as he leapt aside, cutting into the great animal's side. The bear bellowed and staggered, nearly falling on top of the Earl of Westchester, who seemed paralyzed with fear. It transformed into a goat and then fell on its side, bleeding in the middle of the street. It became a fish, a chipmunk, and then a python in quick succession, and finally, it was a snail that shriveled up and died at the Earl's feet.

Wyona, her slim saber glinting in the tenuous light, stared at it with wide eyes. "What manner of Changeling—"

"It is no Changeling," Crispkin replied, firmly stepping on the snail with his boot for good measure. "They are His Majesty's guards. Spelled or enchanted in some fashion to transform into whatever they so choose. They have no human form."

"Why not?" she asked.

"They have no need," he shrugged. "They communicate with each other by means of telepathy. Which is why now we must run."

There was no need to tell anyone twice for the flutter of wings met their ears and a screech that came from no bird. Everyone fled down the street, weapons drawn, following Crispkin into a dilapidated shop with boards over the windows—everyone, that is, except the Earl of Westchester.

"Westchester!" Wyona cried, stopping suddenly. "Westchester, come on!"

Stryver, who nearly ran into her, rolled his eyes, muttered a pirate curse, and doubled back, seizing the Earl of Westchester by the elbow and dragging the terrified old man after him.

And then they saw it. A cloud, a dark cloud of wings and teeth and eyes was rapidly gaining on the Aviator and the Feline.

"Bats!" Sir Humphrey cried, standing in the doorway of the house. "Run, Stryver!"

They were gaining rapidly, bearing down upon them.

"Move!" Etheos cried, trying to shove Sir Humphrey out of the way. "Move! I can help!"

Sir Humphrey stepped aside and Etheos leapt out into the middle of the street. He raised his hand and cried "*E Elzyulrqu, qurm rfyqu fevyu!*" Whatever his intended effect upon the bats, nothing happened to them. Instead, there was a loud bang, and Etheos was thrown backwards several feet, landing hard on the cobblestones.

The bats nearest to the two helplessly fleeing fugitives transformed into giant eagles—larger than any such bird those present had ever seen—seizing the lagging Earl in their talons and taking flight into the air once more in the same horde, leaving Stryver to arrive next to Wyona, doubled over and panting, empty-handed.

"They're headed for the tower," Wyona said quietly.

"Get inside!" Crispkin hissed, motioning hurriedly.

Sir Humphrey pulled Etheos to his feet and guided him towards the door.

"I don't understand it," Etheos muttered, holding his head.

"It's all right, Etheos," Sir Humphrey said. "Everyone gets muddled under pressure."

"I was not muddled!" Etheos insisted. "It's like my spell—like it bounced right off them."

"It makes sense," Stryver replied with a shrug, tugging the door closed behind them and bolting it. "They seem to be made purely of magic after all."

They found themselves in a low-ceilinged, cavern of a room with countless dusty boxes piled all about them and the scuffling sounds of burrowing rodents in the corners. Crispkin lit a lamp and sat down atop an overturned bucket while his guests found seats on the floor.

"They were composed of layer upon layer of spells," Wyona agreed. "I'm surprised you did not see it."

"Then how can they be killed?" Etheos demanded incredulously, clearly frightened at the thought of his spells being useless.

"Seemed to work fairly well for me," Sir Humphrey shrugged, fingering his axe.

"Perhaps at the heart of the spells is the last glimmerings of the life they once had then," Stryver said off-handedly. "In any case, I'm certain that you'll have plenty of time to study them in a few minutes when they come back for us."

"I must speak quickly," Crispkin said. "Obviously our aim is to kill His Majesty. It is the only way, all must agree on that. It is a difficult task, for his tower is guarded by the beasts that we just saw, terrible things."

"I could simply fly up to his balcony," Wyona said.

Crispkin shook his head. "I myself have tried. There are spells upon it. You cannot get within ten feet. There is a way in, though, that I have … sought out."

"And it is?" Stryver prompted when he didn't continue.

"There is a girl who bakes the bread that feeds the prisoners in His Majesty's dungeon whom I've become very … acquainted with. She can be trusted. Once inside the fortress, you have only to follow the stairs to the top, where you shall undoubtedly find him."

"What do you mean?" Wyona asked. "Are you not accompanying us, Crispkin?"

"Inside the castle, yes," Crispkin said. "But I have a different task. I must free Ziggy—that's my best man, you know, fine fellow—from the prisons."

"The Earl of Westchester," Sir Humphrey rumbled. "What about him?"

"We shall have to rescue him as well," Wyona agreed. "Then, if we fail in killing our adversary, at least he will be free."

"Best to send *them* along to do that," Stryver said to her, waving his hand at Sir Humphrey and Etheos. "You know they'll just get in our way."

"If the Earl were here, he would tell me not to go anywhere alone with you, Stryver."

"Well, the Earl isn't here," Stryver pointed out. "And it isn't as if you would've listened to him anyway."

"Just a minute," Etheos said indignantly. "I will *not* get in the way. You should be grateful to have a wizard—"

"Thaumaturge," Wyona murmured.

"—At your disposal. Do you think you'll just be able to run up there and stick a sword in him, no trouble? Besides," he continued. "I'm no use against those guards as you saw. Perhaps I could be of use against His Majesty. Send Humphrey; Crispkin will surely need his axe."

"And you will come with us?" Wyona asked, raising a skeptical eyebrow.

"Bad idea," Stryver said adamantly.

"Perhaps separated they will not be as much trouble," Wyona replied. "Are you prepared, Crispkin?"

Crispkin nodded. "Yes, highness."

"Then we'd best go and see this young woman whom you are very acquainted with."

The girl, whose name was Ellen and could turn into a mouse if she chose, told Etheos to shut up. "There's no use you going on so," she chided him. "It's not as if there's anyone about to see you."

Etheos glared at her. "Easy for you to say," he muttered. "You aren't wearing a dress."

"As a matter of fact I am," Ellen replied. "If you hadn't noticed. And you're wearing one of mine. So don't get it dirty. Now pick up that basket and let's go. Your friend doesn't complain at all, does he?"

"He can't complain," Etheos said, picking up the basket in which Stryver, Crispkin, and Wyona were hiding. "If he speaks, he'll break the illusion."

The three were walking through the narrow alley, the tower looming before them. Ellen had seen to everything at once in a practical no-nonsense way. She immediately seized one of her own plain gray dresses from a drawer and tied Etheos into it, placing a simple coif upon his head before the wizard had time to protest. Then she had ordered the three Changelings to transform and climb into the basket in which she normally carried bread. Crispkin, once he became a pigeon, seemed rather wary of hopping into such close quarters with the white-eyed cat whose tail was twitching slightly, but when Wyona jumped in unhesitatingly he meekly followed.

Sir Humphrey had been the only problem. The knight obviously could not fit in the basket, and he was far too big and bulky to pass off as Ellen's companion. So Etheos had preformed an illusion spell, after much huffing and complaining. He explained that it was very simple, like invisibility except with a picture painted on the subject. A red haired young girl with a bowed head walked silently between he and Ellen, her hands clasped as if in prayer.

Ellen made her way confidently towards a back door to the tower. There was a single guard, in the form of a boar. It grunted suspiciously when it saw her companions.

"Cousins of mine," Ellen told it. "Here to aid me. I fear the task of feeding so many has become too much for me."

The boar grunted again, but moved aside.

Ellen tugged open the heavy door and led them into the dripping darkness beyond.

She walked down the corridor, the two following, turned a corner, and then stopped. "This is where we part," she said. "Put the basket down."

Etheos did as he was ordered, eagerly tugging the coif from his head. Soon the Changelings were among them again in human form, Crispkin eyeing Stryver warily.

"I swear he was thinking about eating me," he said.

Stryver grinned in an all too cat-like way. "Would I do that?"

Crispkin didn't see fit to answer, simply made sure to keep a careful distance between them.

"The stairs to the upper floors are just there," Ellen said, pointing. "The rest of you may follow me."

She turned and continued walking down the corridor.

"Good luck, Etheos," Sir Humphrey rumbled.

Etheos glared at him. "Who ever heard of a wizard saving the world in a dress? It's disgraceful, that's what it is. You are *never* telling the Academy about this detail, you hear me, Humphrey?"

"Oh, I don't know," Wyona replied in her calm voice. "I think it looks rather fetching."

Etheos glared daggers at her. "Bird brain…" he muttered. He felt a slight blow to the head, caused by Stryver swinging his pocket watch carelessly in the air.

"So sorry," he said. "Shall we continue? Wouldn't want to keep His Majesty waiting."

They started up the stairs they found just where Ellen had indicated. Etheos found he had trouble keeping up with his swift, long-legged companions, especially in the difficult folds of the dress. They went ten floors up, climbing the straight staircase, which doubled back on itself every so often, until it ended completely, turning into a small spiral stair that made Etheos dizzy. The climb seemed endless, and he lost all track of the distance he had climbed in the forever-twisting stair. Just when he thought that perhaps it was one of those infinity tricks he had read about in the library once, like the never-ending passage, he came, breathing heavily, to level ground.

They were standing before a large pair of double doors with the threatening crest of His Majesty: the clawing hand on the dark field. Wyona drew her sword with a steely ring and Etheos began to conjugate verbs in that strange tongue of incantations in his mind. Stryver, however, did not reach for a weapon before he took out his small silver pocket watch, tugging the clip free and holding it by the chain in his left hand, drawing his own sword with his right. Etheos was too distracted to notice, and even if he had, Stryver was known to be rather strange.

Wyona looked from one to the other, then nodded, and pushed open the door.

The room they stepped into did not match the astute, silent grey of the city below them. The floor was covered in colorful rugs from a desert land, and the walls were draped in ancient tapestries, darkened with age, depicting eerie forest hunting scenes. The furniture was walnut and richly upholstered in red velvet with tiny gold tassels. There was a fireplace, a number of bookshelves, and a liquor cabinet filled with interestingly shaped glass decanters. The glass doors to the balcony were thrown open and a tall man, his outline lit by the giant torch on the roof, was standing at it, his hands resting on the rail. A slight breeze was blowing this far up, rustling his rich blue cape. He did not turn at the sound of the door's opening.

"Welcome." The single word rang in the space between them.

Wyona frowned and Stryver fingered his pocket watch.

"Surrender now," Wyona finally said. "Surrender now and perhaps we shall be lenient."

"How does one kill someone leniently?" Stryver muttered through the side of his mouth, but Wyona didn't answer him.

The man on the balcony stood still for a moment, and then he squared his shoulders, his hands dropping to his sides. "I think you mean to kill me."

He turned and took a step forward then, his face glinting in the dying fire in the hearth. He had a strong face that did not look evil at all, rather open and kind, generous and caring. His wide blue eyes looked out at them with an earnestness that quite took Etheos by surprise.

Indeed, at the sight of him, Stryver's eyes went white for a full two minutes, but Wyona was by far the most startled.

She dropped her sword with a clatter, shouted "Kendall!", and before Stryver could fling out his hand to stop her, she ran towards him, throwing her arms about him with wild, unthinking joy.

His expression didn't change at his long lost sister's embrace. In fact, neither Stryver nor Etheos saw him move a muscle. But then Wyona staggered backwards, staring with wide eyes at her brother, who casually took out a handkerchief and began cleaning the blood off his dagger. Wyona tripped over her own feet and fell to the floor at Stryver's, clutching the wound in her stomach and gasping for breath.

Stryver dropped his own sword and swiftly began to mutter in a strange language—one Etheos recognized from somewhere before—kneeling beside her.

Etheos leapt forward with a spell on his lips, ready to disarm His Majesty, but with an idle flick of the man's fingers, he was pinned powerless against the wall.

Stryver's chants, which Etheos realized were the same he had used to bring her back from the dead in the King's bedchamber so long ago, appeared to be useless. Wyona lay still.

His Majesty looked down at her and then laughed shortly. "I was wondering if I would ever see you again, sister dear." His eyes danced. "And you too, cat? What brings you both here together?"

Stryver continued to chant, unabated, the pocket watch still firmly clasped in his hand. His Majesty—Kendall—saw it and his eyes glinted.

"Ah, so you are still carrying that burden about the world?" He gave a short laugh. "I'm glad to see it."

Yet still Stryver went on.

"It does no good," Kendall said after a moment. "She is dead. You can't bring her back."

"I have before and I will again," Stryver said. "Unless you'd like to kill me too."

"In good time," Kendall said. "You shall have to wait till dawn, I'm afraid. The people supposed they would see one traitor executed, not four. And two foreigners. It's wonderful. Perhaps I can start a war."

"Four?" Stryver asked, looking up for the first time.

Kendall laughed. "Did you honestly think your friends could just walk into my dungeon and free my prisoners?" He shook his head. "Can't allow that. Ah, here we are."

Three guards, in the shape of large gorillas stood in the doorway.

"Take these to the dungeon," Kendall ordered. "Executed tomorrow at dawn with the others."

One of them seized Etheos and threw him over his shoulder, dress and all, like a sack of potatoes, lumbering out of the room. The other two reached for Stryver, but he immediately seized Wyona's body with both hands, until they were forced to carry her down to the dungeon too, leaving drops of blood to mark their path.

Ellen was weeping inconsolably into Crispkin's shoulder. The sound filled the dank dungeon, echoing off the narrow walls. None of the other prisoners, in their own wretched cells, showed any sign of hearing. Sir Humphrey was playing a dispassionate game of rock-parchment-broadsword with the Earl of Westchester, who was in the cell beside them. He had a nasty bruise on his forehead, but otherwise seemed unharmed. He had not, however, resigned himself to being executed. Even after the guards had come and captured Sir Humphrey and Crispkin, he still remained adamant.

"It matters not," he said with a little laugh. "Her highness will soon rule again and she shall get us out of this prison. She would never let us suffer such a ghastly fate."

"Hanging?" Sir Humphrey suggested.

"Oh no, no," the Earl of Westchester replied, his eyes going wide. "Far, far worse. Far, far worse indeed. But there is no cause to worry. Her highness will no doubt outlaw such—such villainy."

His faith in Wyona's skill did not ebb in the least when he saw her corpse, growing cold, thrown into a cell across from them for Stryver would not let go of it, his eyes looking rather insane as they turned white.

"You braggart! Villain! Traitor! It's your fault! You killed her!" the Earl began to yell at Stryver, his eyes filling with tears.

Sir Humphrey went to the bars of his cell. "Etheos? Are you all right?"

"Yes," Etheos said. "Yes, but Stryver isn't. I think he's gone mad, Humphrey. It—it must have been the shock."

"Is Wyona really dead?" he asked.

"Yes," Etheos called back. "Yes. But Stryver didn't do it," he added in the Earl of Westchester's direction. "It was His Majesty. It was Kendall."

The Earl of Westchester reeled back and was silent for a moment. Crispkin and Ellen both looked up, disbelieving.

"Kendall?" the Earl of Westchester finally said. "Impossible. You're mistaken, wizard."

"Well, I don't think Wyona would be," Etheos said. "She ran right at him when she saw him."

"I can't believe it. I won't believe it," the Earl of Westchester said. "Kendall was always—"

"Killing the Rodent chieftain," Sir Humphrey interrupted incredulously. "Yes! He did! You remember in Wyona's story, how he got him another drink. That's where the poison was!"

"That's preposterous," the Earl of Westchester said.

"No," Sir Humphrey said. "I see it a lot. I am a knight, you know."

"Really? It isn't as if you've shown it before now." It was Stryver's mocking voice, as he looked up from Wyona's still form. "Wizard!

Get over here! I need you."

"There's nothing you can do," Ethos replied with a shake of the head, looking down at Wyona. "She's dead. You can't bring back the dead."

"I have before!" Stryver shouted at him.

"That was different," Ethos said. "A life for a life. She saved your life and so you saved hers. But unless she's saved your life twice—"

"You're wasting time, wizard!" Stryver said, standing. "I have done it before, I know the way. And you have the power to help me."

"You're crazy," Ethos said, taking a step back.

Stryver stepped carefully over Wyona, his white eyes boring into Ethos' skull.

"You're crazy!" Ethos repeated fearfully, his back to the bars. "There's no way to bring her back!"

Stryver's hand shot out and grasped Ethos' throat, lifting him off the floor. "You'd better hope there is, wizard, because I shall kill you in a moment."

Ethos struggled, swinging his feet wildly, his dress flying.

"Think back, wizard. Think back on everything you've studied, everything you've learned in that pathetic little Academy. There must be something to close the wound, to bring her back. And you'd best think of it soon."

Ethos coughed and spluttered. He choked out something unintelligible.

"What was that?" Stryver asked, lowering him to the floor.

"H. P. Nortonus," Ethos said, coughing. "H. P. Nortonus. He—he—they said he was crazy."

"And?"

"He devised a spell to bring people back, but—but it never worked."

"It'll work this time," Stryver said, seizing the collar of his robes and shoving him forward. "Do it."

"I can't!" Ethos said irritably. "I hardly know the proper—and—and besides…where are we going to get a vial of snake venom down here?"

Stryver's eyes flashed and he looked as if he were about to break

Etheos' neck when a ponderous voice said from the shadows of the cell beside them, "Snake venom, do you say? You're in luck, sirrah."

Stryver turned swiftly, peering into the shadows. "Who are you?" he hissed. "I've heard that voice before."

But it was not the shadowed man that answered. "Ziggy!" Crispkin cried from across the way. "I'm glad you're all right."

"For the moment, sirrah," the man said, stepping forward. His red hair, done back in a horsetail, glinted in the wavering light, as did his puffy pants and vest.

"You!" Stryver said. "You were Mortimer's henchman."

"That was long ago, sirrah," he said with a bow of his head. "I serve a different order now. I am Zighain of the Salamander clan. Is this what you need, little shaman?" He pulled from a pocket inside his vest a vial of a clear, syrupy liquid.

"Yes," Etheos said. "Snake venom."

He handed it to Etheos through the bars. The wizard unstoppered the top, held his hand over the liquid and said a few words. Then he turned it over and poured it carefully into the open wound of the body.

"This is never going to work," he muttered.

"You'd best hope it does," Stryver said. "Or I'm going to make sure she has company." He was watching Etheos carefully, his eyes white and unblinking.

Etheos swallowed hard and held his hand over the wound, muttering spells in a steady voice that varied in pitch, wiggling his fingers slightly in the air and closing his eyes. It was the longest spell Sir Humphrey had ever seen him perform, and everyone seemed to hinge on his words, though they did not comprehend their meaning, motionless, expecting.

If Stryver saw the wound slowly close and color return to her dead cheeks, he said nothing, and Sir Humphrey and the Earl of Westchester were too far away to discern much in the dim shadows. All they knew was that suddenly she sat up, nearly knocking heads with Etheos, gasping for breath. Etheos fell back, panting, sweat pouring down his face. Wyona completely ignored him. She leapt to her feet, ignoring also the joyous shouts of the Earl of Westchester, rounding on Stryver.

For someone who had acted so mad moments before, it was an astounding change, his eyes had gone black again and he looked completely unperturbed.

"You *knew*," she spat at him. "You knew who he was! You knew all the time and you said nothing!"

"Yes," Stryver agreed, fingering his pocket watch distractedly.

"Were you in league with him?" she demanded. "Were you acting on his orders to kill them? How could you—how could you—" Wyona seemed to be beyond words. She leaned against the wall, her tall frame shaking. "You're a monster."

"Some thanks I get for saving your life," Stryver muttered.

"Why does it matter?" Wyona said, shaking her head. "He's just going to kill us at dawn anyway."

"It matters." The silver chain made a clinking noise as he slid it between his fingers.

"May I ask," Etheos said after a moment as Wyona bowed her head, "what manner of watch is that?"

Stryver said nothing.

Etheos took a step closer. "Because it has spells all over it," he added.

"There's a demon in it," Stryver suggested after a moment. "Name's Bruce."

Etheos blinked. "Do demons normally have names like Bruce?"

Stryver shrugged. "Mine does."

"He must be a very different sort of demon."

"Well, you've met him," Stryver said. "In the king's bedchamber. He was the one that killed Wyona the first time."

"You imprisoned him in a watch?" Etheos asked, remembering vaguely how the demon had ended up trapped in a mirror.

"Yes," Stryver said. "What's wrong with that? It doesn't tell time, but it can do lots of other interesting things."

"Like kill people," Etheos supplied.

"Yes, there's that."

"There's just one problem," Etheos continued, not taking his eyes off the watch.

"What would that be?"

"The red spells are for the demon," he said, pointing at the watch, though Sir Humphrey later verified that there was nothing colorful about it. "But what about the black ones?"

Wyona jerked her head up and stared at the watch Stryver held.

Stryver said nothing though his eyes gleamed.

"You, sir," Etheos concluded satisfactorily, "are part of the Black Magic Guild."

Stryver grinned his feline grin. "Not me," he said with a shake of the head. "Though the maker, certainly, as you well know."

"What do you mean?" Etheos asked, frowning.

Stryver opened his mouth as if he were about to elaborate, but then, after a moment, seemed to change his mind. "I can't say."

Etheos was still pondering his previous remarks, for renegade wizards were a preoccupation peculiar to his trade. "I haven't met any members of the Black Magic Guild!" he protested.

"I have," Sir Humphrey supplied from across the way. "Arrested him turning chickens into watermelons."

"That hardly seems like Black Magic, Humphrey," Etheos chided.

"No, it's the law," Sir Humphrey said. "By Royal Decree, any practitioner of higher magic not registered at the Academy is a member of the Black Magic Guild. I could arrest poor Mrs. Malone in the flat below for bewitching her crumpets if I had a mind."

Etheos' eyes widened. "Then there is someone."

"Who?"

"Kendall."

All eyes turned to Stryver. He was still holding the pocket watch, his eyebrows raised rather high.

"Stryver," Wyona said, standing. "Who killed my parents?"

"I did," he answered.

"Really?"

Stryver hesitated. "I did," he repeated after a moment.

"Etheos," Wyona said distractedly. "What sort of spells are the black ones?"

Etheos frowned, peering at the watch still in Stryver's hand. "I've seen something like it before. It was a mind control exercise. It ended up going wrong and causing the professor's foot to explode."

"Mind control!" Stryver said defensively. "And you call yourself a wizard!"

Etheos scowled. "Speech control then! Inner city street gangs use it on their members all the time."

"A little more sophisticated than that," Stryver suggested, looking down almost admiringly at the pocket watch.

"But that's the gist of it!" Etheos insisted. "I'm a wizard! I *know* what I'm talking about."

"That's hard to believe," Stryver commented, swinging the pocket watch.

"So…Kendall put a spell on Stryver's pocket watch so that he wouldn't tell anyone that he was really His Majesty?" Sir Humphrey asked.

"And many other things as well, I should think," Wyona replied, still watching Stryver closely. "How long have you had that, Stryver?"

"It was my father's," Stryver replied.

"Then you could be hiding all sorts of things from us," Wyona said.

"Well, it isn't as if it's my fault, is it?" Stryver said indignantly.

"I'm not so sure it's not."

"It doesn't matter!" Ellen wailed. "They're going to—going to displace us all at dawn!" Her face disappeared into Crispkin's shoulder again, and all the Changelings fell abruptly silent, leaving Etheos and Sir Humphrey to wonder exactly what sort of fate awaited them in just a few hours.

The Earl of Westchester's snoring was keeping Etheos up. He was too tense to sleep much anyway, but the noise was beginning to grate against his ears, sometimes sounding like a loud whine and other times towering to an unbearable roar that filled the dank dungeon. He wondered how the others could ignore it. Ellen had finally cried herself to sleep in Crispkin's arms, and whether he was sleeping as well over in the shadowy corner or simply trying not to disturb her was impossible to tell. Sir Humphrey, who was known to snore himself on occasion, appeared to be sleeping soundly, his fist flexing slightly as if trying to grip for his axe. He was used to sleeping thusly, Etheos knew, when he was given lonely guard duties late at night. He could see the faint outline of the mysterious Ziggy in the cell beside him, sitting cross-legged on the floor of his cell and taking deep, long breaths.

The only one who appeared to be awake, in those fleeting gray hours of the morning, was Stryver, who was staring off at the small, barred window, rubbing his pocket watch absently with one finger. He and Wyona were sitting side-by-side, leaning against the stone wall. Wyona's eyes were closed, and her head kept slowly lolling down towards Stryver's shoulder, but each time she jerked up abruptly until a few moments later when it would happen again.

Etheos, who was leaning against the bars, glared down at the gray dress that fluttered about him, wishing that, if he had to die, it wouldn't be in this ridiculous thing. He found it surprisingly like his wizard's robes, a fact he would not admit to anyone at all.

"You meant it was Kendall, didn't you?" he heard Wyona say quietly. He looked up slightly. She was staring at Stryver, who appeared to be ignoring her. "You meant it was Kendall yesterday when you said that someone before us had unleashed the curse in the well."

"Yes," he said simply.

She shook her head and turned away. "I never would have thought it of him."

"Because you don't think like a scoundrel," Stryver said with a half-smile. "You care far too much for our line of business, bird brain. Always have."

"Yes, and I'm not so sure that you don't either," Wyona replied. "I was sure I was done for, that time after the ghosts, but you didn't slit my throat, did you? You keep saving my life, Stryver. I don't understand it."

He said nothing.

"Thank you, anyway," she continued after a moment. "I don't think I ever said that."

"You're only saying it now because we're going to die in half an hour."

She smiled slightly. "Perhaps. Or perhaps it's because I'm really going to miss you. Tuna breath." Then she leaned over and kissed him on the cheek.

Stryver broke out into his grin. "Westchester's going to be very put out," he said, teasingly.

"Westchester isn't here," Wyona replied, folding her arms across her chest and closing her eyes once more. "And it isn't as if I'd listen to him if he was."

It seemed like only minutes later to Etheos when he heard the door to the dungeon bang open and a series of gorilla guards stormed in, looking taller and stronger than before. One tugged open the cell next to Etheos and threw Ziggy onto his shoulder, dropping his turban. Another took the Earl of Westchester—jerked out of his sleep with much protest—and two more for Ellen and Crispkin. Two were assigned to Sir Humphrey, probably due to his general size, one for Etheos, and two each for Stryver and Wyona, who must have been considered too shifty to take chances with. They were dragged into the dim light outside the dungeon and into a square before the tower. There was a platform in the middle of the square, upon which stood Kendall himself, to everyone's surprise.

A sizable crowd was already gathered, looking on silently. Those that may have recognized Kendall were too prudent to say anything. When they caught sight of the prisoners, however, some hushed whispers went through their ranks. The Earl of Westchester was obviously well-known, as was Crispkin to a select few. Many recognized Stryver, as tales of his villainy were still circulated, and a few were even wise enough to guess Wyona for a member of the Aviator Royal House, though even in her own day she had not been prominent. Kendall, indeed, seemed the most surprised by her presence. He climbed down from the platform and strode towards where his guards were keeping a tight hold on her.

He stared at her for a long moment and then at Stryver, nearby.

"Well," he said. "You really did it. Lord knows how, but you did." He shook his head. "A pity to waste someone so useful." He turned back to Wyona. "But it matters not, sister dear," he added with a faint smile. "I shall just kill you again. Or displace you, rather. Which will be ever so much more fun."

"Monster," she spat at him, sounding very much the same as when she had said it to Stryver a few hours before. "I'm almost glad you killed them. It would break Father to see you now."

Kendall gave a start at this. He looked from Stryver back to Wyona. "So," he said after a moment. "Truth at last. Too bad it's a little late." He smiled. "Dear Wyona. You always were the slow one." He turned swiftly, said something to one of the guards, and then returned to the platform. He addressed the crowd for the first time in his long years of oppressive rule.

"I promised a traitor to be displaced today," he said to them. "And so we have him. Zighain of the Salamander clan." He looked over his shoulder at the prisoners. "But there are others, other traitors, ones of much higher standing and malice than he. We have today Crispkin, once a carrier pigeon, the leader of the so-called 'Order'. They sought to replace me with one of the two bandits and murderers you see—Wyona of the Aviators or Stryver of the Felines. Both, as you well know, are villains of the highest degree. I hope you will see today, good people, that no one—*no one*—will contest my authority and live."

An ominous silence followed this speech as his words echoed back from the grey city and the tall trees. Kendall smiled satisfactorily. He made a curt gesture with his hand and the guard holding Ziggy pulled him forward and onto the platform.

Ziggy stood in the middle, still and unafraid, staring calmly out at the horizon. "I shall be avenged, sirrah," he said quietly.

"By whom?" Kendall laughed. Then he held out his hand and a deathly quiet fell over everything. He was mumbling under his breath, and his words became louder and louder until he was nearly shouting. A wind rose up, rustling everyone's hair and clothes, throwing leaves into people's faces, and making a noise equal to Kendall's words, as if the two were fighting for supremacy.

"It's Black Magic!" Etheos shouted to Sir Humphrey. "Of the darkest kind, whatever he's doing."

And then there was a pop and the wind died abruptly. In Kendall's outstretched hand was a small, green salamander with a scarlet head, wiggling slightly. Ziggy stood stock still for a moment, and then he fell to his knees, gasping as if not only was he suffocating, but his lungs had disappeared altogether. Then the salamander ceased to wriggle, lying still and limp in Kendall's hand, and a terrifying ripping scream escaped Ziggy's throat, as if his very soul had been torn from him. Then he fell on his face, dead. The salamander turned to dust in Kendall's hand.

There was a stillness about the world as everyone in the crowd bowed their heads at the hideous sight. Not only was Ziggy dead, but his animal form, a full half of his identity, had been torn from him—the most painful, torturing fate a Changeling can be made to suffer, or so they said.

Then Ellen let out a wracking sob.

Kendall made a second curt gesture and a guard cleared away the remains of Ziggy, while two others brought forward Wyona. She stood with the same stateliness as Ziggy had, but said nothing at all to her brother. Kendall raised his hand and Stryver looked at the ground, shaking his head.

He began the incantation again, and the same great wind rose up as before, blowing Wyona's hair across her face and making the flaps in her strange tunic ripple. Just as it seemed that Kendall could shout no louder, that the wind could whistle no fiercer, Etheos distinctly heard a great roar, louder than both, coming from somewhere above the trees.

Others in the crowd heard it too, looking up fearfully. Kendall did not pause, continuing his spell. But he found, a moment later, that his subject was gone. A great blue streak fell out of the sky, seized Wyona, and carried her off before he could blink; and there were more of them, exchanging roars and calls. People screamed, wondering what manner of beasts were now attacking them. Etheos started for a moment, thinking it must be dragons—long-believed extinct—but then, as he got a closer glimpse of one of the humans on their backs, he suddenly smiled. "It's all right, Sir Humphrey," he said. "It's the Sky Riders."

There must have been fifteen or twenty of them in all. The beasts they rode were cousins, perhaps, to the dragons and their contemporary models like George. Each was only about the size of a horse with large, feathered wings like those of a bird. Their lean, scaled bodies came in various colors, varying shades of blue and green, some silver, and one a menacing black. Their calls seemed to be a mix of a bird's squawk and a thunderous roar, and they soared and dove in the air almost like otters playfully gliding through the water. Their riders appeared to be quite skilled, moving seamlessly with their mounts, and gripping the feathery manes of their necks with one hand, while drawing swords with the other. The Sky Beasts themselves were at no loss for weapons, as Etheos saw clearly in their calls, for their mouths were filled with sharp teeth.

The one who had scooped up Wyona from the platform, a man with a weather-beaten face and a long scar on one cheek, turned his mount after setting the Aviator down on solid ground to make a second pass at it, this time raising his sword towards Kendall. At the last minute the dictator leapt away, landing in the thick of his guards on the ground, who were already being harried by the other Sky Riders, transforming into various large forms—elephants, rhinos, and lions—in an attempt to fight off the attack from the sky. Kendall stood easily and began to run for the cover of the tower, his blue cape snapping. The Sky Riders, who were too busy with the guards, did not see him escape.

Stryver leapt forward, and his pocket watch was in his hand in an instant. "Kendall!" he called, and something in his voice made Kendall stop and turn. "Do you remember long ago when you freed me from prison?"

"I saved your life," Kendall said. "You should be grateful."

"Oh yes," Stryver said, his eyes flashing. "Allow me to repay the gift. There's someone here who wants to meet you." He raised the pocket watch in his hand and smashed it to the cobblestones. It flung into a thousand pieces, silver mechanics glittering in the morning sun. A large puff of red smoke billowed out as well, and there in the courtyard, larger than the Sky Beasts raiding from above, stood Bruce.

Actually, his real name was Gorthnak Man Masher, and he was known throughout the seven realms of the underworld as quite the hot head, one of the most feared demon warrior chiefs. It had been some time since he had been summoned to kill the king, at which point Stryver had imprisoned him in the watch he had carried about the world for so long, relying on the teachings of a crippled old shaman who always smelled like anchovies he had met in the Wawakill Desert. Gorthnak Man Masher had put up with quite a lot during his time in Stryver's watch. Months at a time without food, the constant annoying humming of the spells with which he shared his confines, and, most maddening of all, the absurd insistence of the daft pseudo-shaman to call him 'Bruce'. Gorthnak Man Masher was not exactly a happy demon.

And Kendall, not expecting such a thing to appear out of the watch, what he saw as his best handiwork, made the mistake of looking into its eyes.

Stryver grinned and Wyona looked on impassively as her brother fell to the ground, dead.

But that was not the end of Kendall.

His body immediately liquefied into a strange substance almost like quicksilver, changing color from red to orange to yellow and changing shape along with it, from the body of Kendall to a sphere, to a strange octopus-like being with too many tentacles. It convulsed in this way, momentarily stopping the fight and the shrieks of the crowd from the courtyard as everyone looked on in wonder at the convoluted mass of pure Chaos.

Then there was a piercing crack and the air around the shape began to glow a fiery red that smelled of sulfur and pushed back everyone, save Wyona, whose hair bore streaks of white once more, and Stryver, whose eyes had not been black in some time.

"It's the curse," Stryver said, "that Kendall opened so long ago."

Wyona seemed to be mesmerized by its pulsating glow. She took a step towards it. "How do we get rid of it?"

Stryver drew a dagger from somewhere in his sleeve and threw it at the ball of pure Chaos, but it simply receded and relocated slightly to the left. A low, cackling laughter filled their ears.

"I'll hold it still," Wyona suggested, reaching out a hand.

"No!" Stryver said. "It will consume you too."

"Then how—"

Stryver drew from his pocket an oven mitt, green with yellow chicken print.

"You stole my oven mitt!" Sir Humphrey yelled indignantly, but Stryver ignored him. Putting it on, he reached forward and, in one swift movement, as if he were seizing a trout from a stream, grabbed hold of the roiling mass. It struggled, convulsing wildly, trying to be free of his grip.

Wyona drew her slim saber and, without hesitation, plunged it into the twitching, struggling, changing ball of Chaos that had plagued them for so many years. For a moment it was perfectly still. And then it exploded, showering all present with tiny flecks of red or gold, and filling their ears with a ringing for some time afterward.

But then it was truly over.

His Majesty's guards all exploded as well, one by one, except for the last two, which simply melted into little puddles. The people who had filled the square, busy hiding in shops or behind a stack of crates on one side of the courtyard began to peer out at the sudden calm, even as the Sky Riders landed, dropping gracefully from the air. The man with the weather-beaten face astride one of the blue mounts, who, Etheos noted, had a gold crest sewn onto his jerkin— a close replica of Wyona's—landed nearest them, dismounting in one easy motion.

Wyona smiled when she saw him and threw her arms about him. "I don't know how to thank you, Amos," she said. "You've saved my life once again."

Amos smiled, his gruff face looking rather pleasant. "No trouble, Miss Wyona. Always willing to help out a friend. And the best damned navigator we ever had too."

"But just how did you know about the execution?" Wyona asked.

"Truth is, we didn't," Amos replied. "We were in the area helping out another old friend." He turned over his shoulder, adjusting one of his leather gloves. "Fleet! Over here!"

A younger man, probably no more than fifteen, jogged over to them, saluting Amos—obviously an officer of some kind—as he arrived. "Sir."

"And where is your precious cargo, fledgling?"

"Just here, sir." He went over to the black Sky Beast, his own mount, and came back carrying a strange pink and white bundle. It took Sir Humphrey a moment to recognize her, being that she was wearing a ridiculous white feather headdress but when he did—

"Lady Orville!" he cried.

The pig hopped down from Fleet's arms, allowing the big knight to embrace her warmly before admonishing him in a series of grunts and snorts for allowing himself to wander so far afield.

"She's a little different than the last time we saw her," Amos said to Wyona. "But still the same tyrannical little lady if ever I saw one."

"You knew the Lady Orville?" Etheos asked. "When she was human?"

"Of course," Amos laughed. "Her da funded our first garrison."

No one noticed the Earl of Westchester and Crispkin's whispered conversation until they were both standing before them, smiling and silent, Westchester holding something wrapped in brown paper. Ellen gave a little cry when she saw them thusly, then took a handkerchief from her pocket, licked it, and stood on her toes to wipe a smudge of soot from Wyona's cheek.

Wyona had returned to her habitually calm, impassive front, though she still wore a slight smile, and completely ignored this.

"We—Crispkin managed to salvage what he could from the Aviator palace," Westchester said. "Before it mysteriously burned down. So—so if you wouldn't mind, highness, as—as the highest ranking member of the old court present I'd like to—to—" He unwrapped the brown paper, revealing a few rather tarnished plain circlets of wrought silver. One had a "K" engraved in it, which Crispkin hurriedly seized and hid behind his back before anyone could notice.

"So, if you wouldn't mind kneeling…" the Earl of Westchester suggested.

Wyona, with a wry, humoring smile, bent her willowy form down on one knee, bowing her head. After a moment, in which the Earl was busily fumbling with the two remaining circlets, she reached up a hand and resolutely tugged Stryver down beside her. He scowled darkly. "Making me a king, are we? I don't think I shall ever forgive you…"

Wyona continued to smile wryly. "If I'm trapped, you will be too."

Westchester, when he finally looked up, scowled darkly at Stryver, but did not protest, placing the finer of the two upon Wyona's head after a ceremonious, long-winded speech and a kiss on her brow, while dropping the other, rather tarnished one, atop Stryver's crown of dark hair with hardly a word spoken.

They both stood then, to the applause of those present—the Sky Riders, the people beginning to appear from their dark houses, Etheos and Sir Humphrey, as well as Crispkin and Ellen. Wyona smiled at them, thanking those closest to her politely. She turned to Stryver and stopped short, then solemnly offered her hand. He shook it, and then suddenly burst out into his grin.

"Wyona, I didn't kill your family. It was Kendall. I think mayhap he's up to no good…"

Wyona gave him a look, but it didn't seem to stifle Stryver's joy.

"And you've no idea how long I've been waiting to say that!" he said gleefully. "Oh," he added. "And also this." He leaned over and kissed her, right on the lips. Amos began to laugh, a deep full-bodied laugh, and Etheos blushed for no discernible reason while Ellen started to cry. The Earl of Westchester made a noise in the back of his throat, seized the circlet with the "K" from Crispkin's hands and began to beat Stryver over the head with it.

Wyona started laughing.

Sir Humphrey smiled. "Well, Etheos," he said, lifting the Lady Orville into his arms. "Maybe it's time to go home."

Post Script to the Second Edition

A nd so ends the grand adventure, which I was fortunate enough to participate in, and it always thrills me each time I read it. But Stryver was wrong—not as though he'll admit it—for we, all three of us, were indeed of use in the end: Etheos' power, the Lady Orville's royal connections, and my oven mitt. Although I myself don't think any of us did much of anything out of the ordinary—except perhaps Etheos' astounding application of H. P. Nortonus, which the Academy has yet to explain to anyone's satisfaction—it was gratifying and rather encouraging to be hailed as heroes in the months after our return. Wyona wrote a letter to the king and the Masters of the Academy, which—whatever was in it—arrived two days before us in the city, probably thanks to Crispkin. So it was that when the three of us rode wearily through the gates, we were greeted with a fanfare and crowds of people cheering our success.

It was amazing how many turned up to greet the heroes of the city, as *The Frog Prince Post* called us, people who only days before would have been terrified of Changelings. The king was there and made a rousing speech about loyalty and bravery, and somehow related our success to the controversial fish tax increase in a feat of wording I've yet to comprehend. They wanted to knight us all, until they remembered that I was one already, at which point they decided to do it again for good measure. So I became the first person in the city's history to ever be knighted twice, an honor I am even prouder of than the second-in-command position I later received.

The Masters of the Academy, present in their admittedly ridiculous pointy hats, refused to allow his majesty to knight Etheos, protesting most vehemently that such a thing was not fitting for one of the magical profession. After much debate among themselves, they assented to granting him a similar honor, and thus Etheos was made a wizard on the spot. It was a rather informal induction into the higher orders of magic—the elder was obliged to use an umbrella instead of a golden staff and a flagon of whiskey donated half-heartedly by my own commander instead of a chalice of wine—but Etheos informed me that a few days later, after the Masters had read his dissertation on H. P. Nortonus, they performed it a second time in the usual way, this time offering him a professorship. So Etheos became the youngest professor—by a number of decades—that the Academy had ever seen, and even after the talk of our adventures in the Forest had died down, Etheos' fame at the Academy was still well-established thanks to tales of his seemingly miraculous raising of the dead, an occurrence that, to my knowledge, has never been repeated by Etheos or anyone else. His classes were always sure to be filled with the curious, and it was strange not to have at least three or four young women fall desperately in love with their mysterious numerology professor who quite appreciated his not having a long, graying beard, a fact that he had so often lamented in the past.

As for the Lady Orville, the king publicly apologized to her when we first arrived for her long exile from the palace and invited her back to stay as she pleased. It was a great surprise to all of us when she snorted derisively and turned up her nose at him, insistently following Etheos and I back to our old humble lodgings. The king never repeated this offer, probably because of the political cartoons appearing in *The Frog Prince Post* the following day.

It surprised me at first, how crowds of people suddenly heralded us as heroes for helping overthrow a man they had never heard of for two people they never knew in a land they feared filled with people they hated. I realized after a time that it wasn't so much what we did, it was that we did it, and we were just like them. Everyone needs someone to look up to. And so, because of public pressure and my own curious desire, I began to pen our adventures till now, our strange dealings with the Changelings. Etheos provided his differing points of view, and Wyona provided me with all the help she could. It was this very work, as you've no doubt deduced, which sold wildly in its first edition, beyond my comprehension. Perhaps we gave them hope. And as I once told Etheos, one must always hope.

As for me, I had immense hopes for Stryver and Wyona in their forest. The Earl of Westchester sent Etheos and me a signed certificate expressing the crown's thanks, something I was positive he had concocted all on his own, as it was far too silly to come from the practical mind of Wyona and far too nice a gesture to have anything to do with Stryver. Crispkin and Ellen sent the three of us an invitation to their wedding, which we were all more or less happy to attend (though Etheos grumbled the entire way there). I didn't hear a word from Stryver in all six years since the adventure, but Wyona wrote me regularly, once a month, describing her continued efforts at rebuilding society as well as Stryver's seemingly counterproductive escapades—including the now infamous incident involving the fishing trip and the dynamite.

It sounded as if, from all her letters, the two of them were getting along just fine, known simply as the king whose eyes were known to turn white when angered and the queen whose hair sometimes held flecks of the same color—though all were assured that it was due to stress caused by the king. Therefore I suspected nothing when I received the following:

Dear Sir Humphrey,
Greetings, old friend, I hope all fares well with you.
I fear there are strange, urgent matters that much vex my
mind. It would do well if you were here to aid us.
Wyona Wyncliff

And so I made plans to visit the Forest, where I had not set foot in six years, dragging Etheos and the Lady Orville along after me.

We arrived in Wyona's new city to find the Forest different than it had been. It was not so deathly quiet and still, and the trees were no longer ominous but sheltering. I felt a sense of peace, and wondered what matters then could be so distressing Wyona. After waiting for fifteen minutes in an anteroom, we were shown into a comfortable sitting room, the door closed behind us.

There was Wyona, seated at a magnificent wooden desk, writing something with a dark feather quill in her slanted hand. She looked the same as always, her face calm and serene, but she was not dressed in her typical Sky Rider's garb, rather a slim dress of midnight, the silver circlet still gracing her brow. It took me only a moment to recognize the cover of this book lying beside her on the organized desk. Stryver, I realized after a moment, was seated off to the side playing chess with himself. He, too, was different only in attire, wearing a fine suit that did not really suit him at all.

Wyona stood and set her quill aside after gracing the bottom of the parchment with a hurried signature. "Sir Humphrey," she said, smiling, coming forward to embrace me. "It has been too long since we spoke last." She turned to Etheos, who was scowling beside me, and resolutely pulled his nose, before curtsying most becomingly to the Lady Orville who accepted it with a bow of the head. "I'm most pleased that you could come so quickly."

"What is it?" I asked. "Has the curse—"

"No," Wyona said quickly. "Nothing like that." She turned to Stryver, who was leaning back in his chair watching the proceedings coolly. "Would you like to explain?"

He stood, drawing a rolled parchment from his pocket and handed it to me. "We received this a month ago," he said. "Found in a bottle near our costal border."

It appeared to be some kind of crude map, depicting various islands in a great body of water.

"And?" I asked.

"Look at the islands near the bottom left," Wyona suggested.

Drawn in an unsteady hand was a small archipelago marked "Terrible Islands of Plague and Strife", in the center of which was a large "X" with the single scrawled word "Treasure."

"Terrible Islands of Plague and Strife?" Etheos asked, raising an eyebrow. "Sounds silly to me."

"It's an archaic pronunciation," Wyona agreed. "Most people now refer to it them as the Tips islands."

Etheos and I both gasped. "The lost Tips?" Etheos cried. "But—but it's just a legend!"

"So was Gorthnak Man Masher," Stryver replied, swinging a silver pocket watch casually in his right hand.

Etheos and I both stared at him incredulously.

Stryver shrugged. "Well, I went and smashed the other one, didn't I? Have to have something to give my own son, like my father gave me."

"A demonized watch?" I demanded.

Stryver shrugged. "It'll make him a man."

Wyona rolled her eyes and turned back to me. "In any case, the Tips may well exist."

"Along with the treasure," Stryver added.

"It would be exceedingly dangerous," Wyona continued.

"But as adventure is nothing new to—"

"No!" Etheos cried. "No! I refuse to get on some rotting old ship in search of some mythical island of death just to find a treasure for you two! No, Sir Humphrey!" he glared at me. "We aren't doing it!"

Stryver and Wyona looked at each other.

"Smashing," Stryver said. "Because you'd just muck things up anyway. No, bird brain and I are going after it."

"What?" I asked incredulously. "But how can you leave your kingdom—"

"In the capable hands of Crispkin and the Earl of Westchester," Wyona finished for me. She shook her head. "Do you know how dreadfully dull and tedious it is to rule a kingdom, Sir Humphrey? It's miserable."

"So you're—you're running away?"

"Not exactly," Stryver said. "We wouldn't get very far. There are too many guards and witnesses. That's where you come in."

Etheos and I exchanged looks. "You want us to kidnap you?" I demanded.

"In a word, yes," Stryver replied with a smile. "You're finally catching on."

And so it was that late that night, Etheos, Lady Orville, and I rode out of Wyona's city in the Forest, the last remaining Changeling royalty smuggled in our packs. It felt rather ludicrous, helping Wyona to escape the very place she had been trying for so long to return to during all the years of her exile. We parted the next day, we back to the city, and Stryver and Wyona back to adventures of their own, just like old times, as Stryver said.

I hope Wyona doesn't die again.